SADJIO

SADJIO

A novel

by

FATOUMATA NABIE FOFANA

BOOKS

Adelaide Books
New York / Lisbon
2020

SADJIO

A novel

By Fatoumata Nabie Fofana

Copyright © by Fatoumata Nabie Fofana

Cover design © 2020 Adelaide Books

Published by Adelaide Books, New York / Lisbon

adelaidebooks.org

Editor-in-Chief

Stevan V. Nikolic

For any information, please address Adelaide Books

at info@adelaidebooks.org

or write to:

Adelaide Books

244 Fifth Ave. Suite D27

New York, NY, 10001

ISBN: 978-1-954351-10-3

Printed in the United States of America

To my rare, sweet, uber cheerful mom, Koné Fanta
Teeyah, for teaching me the joy of living and making
the most of each opportunity that came my way—
and for remaining an emblem of hope in my life.

To my late dad, Amadou Fofana, and Stepdad, N'vasidiki
Fofana, I'm honored to have made you both super proud. You
may be gone today, but your legacy shall forever remain with me.
Thank you for teaching me that nothing is impossible and that
with patience and perseverance, I would never cease to soar.

To my siblings—Salimatou, Maurice, Amadou—
and to my beloved muses —Noura and
Teeyah_B—thank you for believing in me.

Contents

Prologue

IMAGINE THIS: You've just awoken from a deep dream in which you received a substantial sum of cash from a faceless figure. Once awake, to your utmost amazement, you see that your dream has instantly turned into reality: the anonymous character in the dream transforms into a familiar face who places the exact amount of cash donated to you in your dream, in your open, outstretched palm.

Such was the story of Sadjio's life.

Lots of weird things happened to her. Through it all, she persevered, severely blooming like a raging ray. However, certain things would remain unsolved about Sadjio's existence.

Of all the weirdest things about her life, this dream incident stood out as the eeriest. Not a single soul, near or far, could interpret this dream or explain why Sadjio, an unassuming teenager at the time, would be given such a vast sum of cash. The whole saga was as mystifying as it was implausible.

At some point, even Sadjio herself was confused as to who or what she indeed was. Her almost ghost-like ability to thrive effortlessly in the face of unusual odds not only confounded her, but it also scared her. For her and those who knew her well, it was impossible to understand the source of her mystical strength.

In Sadjio's worldly existence, there was a complete absence of darkness. She was fearless in the face of adversity, rising after every fall and soaring like never before. She thrived effortlessly in the face of hardship like an Anacacho Orchid tree.

Of these mysterious abilities of hers, people talked, guessed, and wondered in total confusion, struggling ever so hard to determine the true nature of this slim-build, dark-skinned wunderkind of a girl.

"Something is off about her," neighbors would say, as they warned their children against mingling with Sadjio.

"That girl is mystery personified," one elder concluded. "I think *nasijee* has a hand in all this. Her mother is stuffing her with this rigid concoction for her to look and behave like such a zombie."

While half of the conspiracy theorists of her community believed that her relentless ability to thrive amidst complete darkness was rooted in the power of *nasijee*, others questioned her very existence as a human being.

Chapter ONE

SADJIO AND HER family lived in Djinnadou, a remote settlement that was famous for its dense, inimitable rain forests—making it a tropical paradise. It was densely settled by the Malinké people who lived a relatively peaceful life. They survived primarily on subsistence farming, fishing, and petty trade.

Life in Djinnadou was a routine: residents carried out the same activities every day without getting bored or tired. The majority of the town's men left their homes very early each morning for their respective farms. While some went hunting, others focused on mining the various rivers and creeks for fresh fish to flavor their evening meals, since they only returned home at sunset.

The women were the voices of the fields; they cultivated the land while effectively serving in the role of domestic managers. The town offered a stunning stretch of large golden rice fields; green and red vegetables and lettuce gardens cultivated manually by the town's women farmers. At home, they cooked, fetched water from nearby screams, did manual laundry, and fetched firewood for household use.

Like its neighbors, farming was strictly forbidden on Fridays and Saturdays in Djinnadou. Both days were designated for worship and socialization. Friday was the town's congregational prayer day; it was also its chosen market day. Buying and selling were allowed between the hours of 9:00 AM and 12:00 noon. The market was immediately shut down at noon to allow locals enough time to prepare for the Friday congressional prayer that lasted between the hours of 1:30 PM to 2:15 PM.

Also, on the days of no farming, the town's men gathered at the various *hatai-* a locally brewed drink, tea, and *aucune dose* coffee shops that lined the town's central business district. There, they drank tea or coffee while munching on charcoal roasted fresh bush meat. The meat was seamlessly flavored with juicy seasonings and served with grilled veggie (onions, fresh tomatoes) toppings.

The women, on the other hand, prepared special meals on such days. Nearly every household ate from a single menu on this day: a light, spicy soup, locally known as *Najee*, served with dull brown or white rice. Key ingredients of the soup comprised fresh cow or bush meat, freshly-caught fish, crab meat, shrimps, chicken. Then onions, habanero and bell peppers, tomato paste, a few pieces of chopped cabbage, and some eggplants were added to give the soup a vital punch to ensure that it hit the right spot on the tongue map. Lunchtime was immediately after the Friday congregational prayer. The women would then meet up with friends to chitchat and get updates on happenings across the town.

Most importantly, however, residents of Djinnadou fiercely guarded themselves against beings they assumed were endowed with supernatural powers. Such creatures were considered products of the underworld. As such, isolation was a key weapon used to ward off this evil.

As a child, Sadjio became a victim of this bizarre tradition.

"She must be a jinni," some often remarked. "Her mother probably took an outdoor shower at dusk while pregnant," others claimed, giving the impression that Sadjio was less human and more of a jinni—a supernatural force.

It was firmly believed that djinns that were desperately looking to make their grand entrance into the human world roamed about at dusk in search of soon-to-be or would-be mothers to prey upon. *Why pregnant women?* Because this was the easiest way to cross into the human world. A pregnant woman's body, it was said, was the ideal pathway to experiencing life as a human. All a jinni had to do was simply transform itself into a human-like being and replace the unborn baby in its mother's womb. The unborn human babies were stolen and dispatched into the underworld. So, instead of a human baby, a jinni would be born to the unsuspecting mother.

Such a deeply-entrenched myth had communities strictly forbidding pregnant women from taking a bath outside at dusk and sometimes, at dawn. These periods were considered unsafe and dangerous for unborn babies and their mothers. It was also a taboo for young, unmarried girls to shower outside at dusk for fear that their spirits might be possessed by a male jinni looking to have an affair with a female human.

"On seeing your nudity while in the shower, a male jinni anchors himself in the corner of your house. He will linger your home until he has sex with you; be extremely careful," mothers told their daughters.

As fate would have it, the assumption that Sadjio was probably a jinni was further cemented by a longstanding history that ran in her extended maternal family. A great maternal aunt of hers had previously given birth to a baby that spent sixteen years as a belly crawler.

Phanta, for that, was the baby's name, never walked; she never uttered a word; she never ate anything regular humans could eat. She was always glued to her bed.

Villagers held pockets of gossip sessions with her name heralding each session. The gossips would eventually spill into her home when neighbors began hinting that Phanta was not a human. But her mother's love for her was exceptionally irritating.

Ramata, Phanta's mother, had struggled with childlessness for nearly two decades before having Phanta. As such, no amount of gossip could convince her to take her daughter to the village's renowned fetish priest for evaluation to determine her true nature.

It wasn't until after her sixteenth birthday that Phanta was eventually taken to the Priest for a ritual the entire village had longed for.

That morning, in Djinnadou, it was bright and beautiful. The dazzling blue sky hung enticingly over the town, and across its surrounding tropical forests, tweets of various bird species echoed. The main gathering point for the ceremony was under the lone baobab tree that stood in the heart of the town.

By dawn, the entire area had been demarcated with white chalk, reinforced by reddish kola nut juice spilled across the center of the circle around the tree. Two eagle eggs were resting in a half calabash wrapped in three pieces of red, black, and purple clothes that were bounded together in fishtail braids.

The atmosphere in the town was forceful. Everyone was anxious to know why Phanta had remained a belly crawler for all those years.

"Bring Phanta forward!" the Priest ordered, just as the early morning sun settled directly above the baobab tree.

Chapter TWO

"DON'T YOU think you've overstayed your visit?" the Priest began, on seeing Phanta. "You are missed. Your subjects yearn for you. This wasn't the agreement, Phanta.

"You know they need you back as their leader," he continued, his bulging eyes firmly affixed on the belly slithering little girl on the mat before him.

The crowd was transfixed. Everyone wondered what was afoot between Phanta and the powerful Priest. Soon the gathering exploded into a loud noise.

"Order!!" screamed the Priest, brandishing a long, brown cow tail with which he pushed the air.

Priest Seydou was dressed in a worn-out mud cloth gown with a white line encircling his right eye. This very outgoing young man was a completely different person on this day; he was fearful and forceful. As messenger and task-implementer of *The Sacred Caves*, Seydou was never himself whenever the spirits of the *Caves* descended on him; they took full possession of his mind, body, and soul. The *Caves* were the town's supreme arbiters; they intervened when all else failed. The *Caves* often handpicked the men of Priest Seydou's family as envoys. They were the *chosen ones* and felt honored to serve. Seydou's father had inherited the spirits from *his* father and later transferred them to his teenage son, making Seydou the town's youngest Priest at age 16.

"Order!!" screamed the Priest for a second time. A sudden quiet returned to the gathering.

Turning to Phanta, the Priest continued, "You thought you could stay over here for good, right? Well, that would be selfish of you on two fronts: to your subjects and to the human that calls you *n' den.*"

Now seemingly fuming with anger, Priest Seydou turned to the crowd and announced, "She's a queen!" casting a sudden spell. The once profoundly anxious and noisy gathering was now as quiet as a graveyard.

Seydou allowed everyone to take a deep breath before proceeding: "Yes, she's a queen, a highly respected and extremely powerful and wealthy queen in her jinni world. You may not see it, but her royal highness is currently wearing some of her priceless pieces of ornaments. She has always worn her diamond and pearl covered tiara. Of course, you will never see these because of the darkness covering your eyes."

This disclosure had folks' eyes popping out of their sockets in total astonishment. "What is the Priest talking about?" they murmured, but very quietly.

The Priest could see that a spell had been cast over Djinnadou—exposing happenings within the human world to djinns roaming the area. However, the jinni world remained unseen. The sorcery at work was darker and more profound than anything the Priest had come across; its claws were deeply-rooted, and it appeared impossible to undo.

He paused, briefly bowed, and shook his head before facing the crowd. "She is a mighty queen. She has everything the jinni world could offer. But........!" Then came a second pause, this time, a longer break, leaving his audience on a cruel cliffhanger.

"She was never happy," Seydou finally announced. "Happiness, for her, is visiting the human realm. She longed to experience life in our domain."

Facing Phanta, he screamed: "But...! She doesn't belong here. She's not one of us. Her people need her, not us. She must return to lead them!"

To Ramata, the child's mother, Priest Seydou, asked: "do you know why Phanta never ate throughout her entire time here?"

"Yes, because she's a baby and babies don't eat the foods that we, adults, eat," Ramata, her head bowed, responded.

"Of course, she ate and ate very well. But it was never the food you made for her," Priest Seydou shot back. "Have you ever wondered why she has never walked?"

"No. But what's your point? She's only a baby. It's a process; she will get there someday," Ramata said, gazing at her angry Phanta, sprawled on the mat before the prying eyes of the crowd and the Priest.

Sensing Phanta's rapidly changing mood, Priest Seydou reached into the front, left pocket of his gown, pulled out a bloodshot red kola nut, and began munching on it.

"You can't hurt me," he said, looking directly into Phanta's eyes. "I dare you!"

He turned his gaze back to the crowd, which had now tripled in size and said: "She is a *djinna saa*. Each night, when you all are fast asleep, she transformed into her real self and preyed on mice and other living things in and around your compounds. She spent the nights hunting and transformed at dawn when you all would be waking up."

At this point, he swiftly sprinkled on Phanta, a ritually prepared, potent concoction meant to dispatch her back to the underworld. Before leaving, she transformed into a massive anaconda, made a prolonged hissing sound, and disappeared.

This was the story that lingered in the minds of neighbors and family members in Djinnadou. It was the story that validated the conclusion that Sadjio was a jinni. But unlike Phanta, Sadjio wasn't possessed by any extraterrestrial being. She wasn't a jinni either. She was just a rare human being, a star with rays so bright that even darkness begged for mercy in her presence.

Given that Sadjio was born in a struggling peasant family, that survived on subsistence farming and an on-and-off petty trade, it was no surprise that it took a long time for her parents to have noticed her super abilities, to have appreciated her status as the light of their family. Though both parents loved Sadjio beyond compare, they just hadn't invested enough time into knowing and understanding her strength. They'd been too busy making ends meet.

Sadjio, nonetheless, was destined to travel a delicate path in life, one that was seldom traveled by most of humanity. Defying all odds, she'd make a vast difference. After all, she was the sun. And, as the old folks say, no matter how long the darkness lasts, the sun does eventually shine through. So, it was with Sadjio. Nothing could dim her light, not even a separation from her biological parents—a separation occasioned by her being given to a maternal aunt. This aunt had problems bearing children of her own to the chagrin of her husband and his family. Sadjio was a remedy meant to heal this aunt—a dream that would remain a deep dream forever.

Chapter THREE

IDA LIVED with her husband, Imran, and his family in the distant township of Lanaya. The town was located on the southeastern cape of the Pepper Coast. At the time, Pepper Coast was also known to many as Grain Coast, a tiny state situated along the west coast of the Sub-Sahara.

A relatively wealthy and formidable state, Pepper Coast was famous for its abundance of natural resources, including its signature melegueta pepper, oil, and ore deposits, as well as pure gold dust. The area was surrounded by three strategic neighbors: Ivory Coast, Queens, and *Ville Libre*. It was inhabited by a diverse group of people: Dioula, Mano, Yakouba, Mendé, Gola, and Vai, among others. Pepper Coast's inhabitants lived a relatively peaceful life, surviving primarily on trans-state trade, farming, mining, and fishing.

Ida was Sadjio's maternal aunt. She enjoyed a blissful marriage. In the early days of her marriage, Ida rejoiced in matrimonial peace, *amour*, attention, and affection. To her, she was in a beautiful dream from which she never wanted to be awakened. The more Ida enjoyed her marital harmony, the more she hungered for it. She was in a fairytale of a sort, the happily-ever-after type. But as it is with most things, this fairytale marriage was soon tested.

Imran's family, and to some extent, Imran himself, after several months of marriage, began to grumble over Ida's inability to bring forth a child as quickly as they had hoped.

A short man in stature, light-skinned with a perpetual bushy hair, Imran, to the surprise of many, had won Ida's hand in marriage over several, more affluent rival suitors. He was, she gushed at every opportunity, the love of her life. As a young woman in Sabougnoûma, her town of birth, Ida had stood out for her regal looks.

Her slender physique, smooth as silk and coffee-colored complexion, hair as golden as sunset, and her graceful demeanor were the envy of other girls in the town. Men salivated when she walked past them. It is not a stretch to say her beauty was legendary.

So, when she turned down one suitor after another and settled on scruffy-looking Imran as her husband, she sent a shockwave across the bow of many eligible bachelors in Sabougnoûma and beyond.

Imran and Ida had met through chance. He was a truck driver by trade, regularly hauling marketers and their wares between Sabougnoûma and Lanaya. It was on one such trip that he crossed paths with Ida.

"Who could this earthy angel be?" He had remarked as Ida strolled past.

"Hello, beautiful!" he greeted her on that first day he laid eyes on her.

Ida had smiled at his solicitation, stopped by his truck, and they had a little bit of talk.

For some indiscernible reason which baffled even herself, she felt a special connection to him right there and then. She was smitten. After that initial meeting, Ida frequented the town's lone parking station whenever she could on market days, hoping that Imran would be there. Imran, too, made it a point to make as many trips to Sabougnoûma as was possible.

Given that Ida was notorious for her checklist of qualities a man had to possess to qualify for the race for her heart, it was not a surprise that a whole lot of people were suspicious of her love for Imran.

She had been known among the men of Sabougnoûma as the dagger, for she quickly eliminated unqualified candidates if they fell short of meeting more than two items on her list of preferred criteria. She had been reputed for meticulously evaluating each suitor to determine his suitability.

Strangely, this was not the case with Imran. For him, it was love at first sight, weirdly.

"This short man must have bewitched this beautiful girl. Gosh! I can't believe she turned me down for this shorty," Amidou said to Hassan, both of them former competitors for Ida's heart.

"Wait…... What? You too?" Hassan asked, rather shockingly. "Were you also interested in marrying Ida? I can't believe we were competing for the same girl! Wow, that has never happened to us in the history of our 25-year friendship."

He paused for a breather before continuing: "But, you know what? I don't blame you, my friend. Ida truly *is* a hot cake around here. Too bad, she shunned us, and it hurts badly."

"I agree with you, Amidou. She's under a spell. That grubby man must have charmed her into falling in love with him."

As the townsmen griped, Ida and Imran carried on their love affair without apologies.

So it was, one night, during their courtship, news of Imran's arrival reached Ida as she sat parching salted peanuts in their outdoor kitchen. Instantly, she thought of abandoning everything to see him. But then she realized her mother, who sold parched, salted peanuts in the local market daily to supplement the family's income her father earned from his handicraft work, needed all the help she could get.

Ida did not go to see Imran that night. By early afternoon the following day, however, she was all set to see her man.

The afternoon was cool and breezy, and Sabougnoûma's dusty central business district was overcrowded and buoyant, living up to its reputation as the busiest trading hub in the area. Even the Fula shops, market stalls, and *yanaboys'* trade stations that were usually empty by this time of day were still fully lit. And so was the designated parking station. Scores of travelers scrambled for seats aboard the last departing locomotive—an old, wretched blue bus with visible dents in its frame from front to rear.

Sabougnoûma, like most places in Pepper Coast, was notorious for its transportation crisis. Even though it was situated in the heart of a significant palm concessionaire, the town had no public transportation services. Its ever-growing population, therefore, relied almost entirely on private commercial cabs and raggedy minibuses, which led to commuters always scuffling intensely for seats aboard the few available vehicles. Young *car loaders* would continuously yell: "The strong will survive; the weak will be crushed!" to affirm to sweaty commuters how difficult it was to get a seat on the vehicles.

ONCE AT THE MAIN roundabout in the town's inner city, Ida stood at the curb, waved joyfully at passersby, and exchanged warm greetings with friends and acquaintances. Her large, hypnotizing eyes were attracting more and more bystanders to look her way. It was nearly impossible to ignore

her captivating beauty. Her graceful face lighted up with her
trademark infectious smile as she uttered more greetings in her
native Dioula dialect.

"*Nitélé*," she'd say.

"*Tanamatélé*" folks responded.

A slender five feet and ten inches tall young and elegant
woman, Ida was unapologetically conscious of her astonishing
beauty. In combination with her thin build and height, her
wrinkled neck and large pop eyes garnered the nickname:
Sassilon. Her smooth, light brown skin and her bouncy,
coarse-textured hair shined as if they were rays from the orange
sunset dangling over the town.

On this particular afternoon, she was flawlessly attired in
a colorful, densely patterned wax fabric. The three-piece, deep
blue, and golden suit was known to many within the Dioula
community as *Grotto.* Her outfit was perfectly tailored; the
upper part tightly cuddled her chest and arms. Her *miss* CE-
DEAO-styled skirt softly spooned her hips, perfectly accentu-
ating her Coca-Cola shaped body.

Ida's outfit, her complete look, that afternoon was a perfect display of the Dioula woman in her. The thing is, Dioula
women of Sabougnoûma, in Ida's time, were fussy about the
way they look or appear. They spent a hefty amount of time
and money to look their very best. For them, beauty and good
look were significant indicators of happiness and success, and
they did not have it otherwise.

They spent hugely on most fascinating Hollandais and
glamorous Bazin fabrics to please their obsession with the
latest beauty trends and the desire to maintain a perfectly polished look. These women had an incredible way of blowing
life into their fabrics. They religiously rebranded every textile
that landed on the market: *"Fleurs de Marriage,"* and *"Les Yeux*

de ma rivale" were prominent socially rebranded fabrics, each telling a unique story of its own.

"Fleurs de Marriage" was worn to symbolize the beauty of happiness in marriage. *"Les yeux de ma rivale"* was a provocative social label that made the fabric the favorite of women in polygamous marriages. Rival wives wore it to indirectly say: "Stop giving me such a mean look." It instantly flared up bitter, harsh feelings. Strangely enough, this fabric was one of Ida's favorites.

As soon as there was a break in the flow of traffic, Ida quickly crossed the dusty road into the busy parking station.

THAT EVENING, Ida met and had a heart-to-heart discussion with Imran. Eventually, she would decide he was *'The One.'*

But the sharp contrast between Ida's physique and that of Imran's reinforced people's widely spread chatters that she had been bewitched to love him. Such instances were, in fact, commonplace in Sabougnoûma and surrounding settlements. Girls with promising futures often found themselves matrimonially entrapped with men who stood far below their social status.

There was the mythical story, which most folks in Sabougnoûma held up as the prime example of Taliya, the town's prettiest girl many decades earlier, who had ended up in marriage to a wretched fetish priest.

As the story was told, a young man vying for Taliya's hand in marriage had consulted the fetish priest to assist him in his love pursuit. They agreed that the Priest would fast and pray for seven days. On the seventh day, he would produce a concoction for use by his client to seduce Taliya.

"It's a spray that can *only* be used at dawn, before the sun takes over the sky. The powerful rays of the sun shall reinforce the power of this concoction. Trust me, she will be yours," Priest Kasim had told his client.

In the process of his mid-night rituals, however, the Priest found that Taliya was a star and therefore prepared a concoction meant to entice her to him instead of the young suitor on whose behalf he had initially fasted and prayed.

Taliya, a young and educated woman with a promising future, would end up bearing two adorable babies for the fetish priest. Instead of pursuing her dreams beyond Sabougnoûma as most people had thought she would, she died a sorrowful death during the birth of her third child with the wretched Priest. This was the cautionary tale that had parents on a 24/7 protective guard over their young daughters.

"Never frown or insult any man who approaches you for love. Just smile and say nice things to them to get them off your back. Men these days are bent on *Juju* to entice girls. Remember, *Juju* only works on those who use insult as a way of defending themselves. Don't ever insult any man who says he wants you as his lover. Just be nice to them," most parents advised their daughters, warning them against doing anything that would make them targets of *juju*-brandishing men.

This tale was one more reason why the entire town concluded that Ida had been charmed by Imran. These hearsays did not inhibit Ida, either. She was now officially off the vacancy list. Few months into her relationship with Imran, the pair was ready to tie the knot. Imran and his family were more than prepared to reach out to her family to ask for her hand in marriage.

Chapter FOUR

IDA'S MARRIAGE to Imran was celebrated with significant fanfare. Her dowry comprised: five life cows and jewels made of pure gold. There were two extra-large suitcases fully loaded with some of Sub-Sahara's premium fabrics: seven pieces of Hollandais prints with each costing $100, and three pieces of bloc wax prints – each costing $75.

Also making the list of dowry items were: ten pairs of footwear, four dozen of undies, bedsheets, and blankets, dishes, pots, spoons, among many other assorted things. Moreover, there was clothing donated to Ida's parents, her siblings, uncles, aunties, and even her neighbors. Most importantly, a cash price of $2,500 was given to seal the list of dowry items. All of these items were handed over by Imran and his family as gifts to Ida and her family. Following her marriage, she moved in with Imran to Lanaya but was given the rudest awakening upon arrival – Imran was already a husband and father.

Ida was an add-on wife which was a common practice at the time. In Ida's Dioula culture, polygamy was sanctioned and widely practiced as a matter of tradition and religion.

Religiously, however, men were admonished to ensure fairness in their interactions with their plural wives; to avoid hurting one wife's feelings in the process of pleasing another's as this would be unjust and unreligious. And if, for any reason, this requirement could not be fulfilled, then marrying only one woman was highly recommended. Despite this caveat, polygamous marriage was widespread, with the feelings of rival wives being trampled almost always.

Like most of her peers, Ida did not have a choice. She had to swallow her feelings and deal with such a perfect mess—having to live with the shock of sharing her husband with another woman. And because divorce was an unthinkable cultural taboo, Ida, like most women who found themselves in these polygamous situations, was trapped for a lifetime.

The Dioula culture compelled women in these marriages to be submissive to their husbands' first wives – the *head wife*. Head wives were given enormous power to direct the affairs of the home, including the power of the purse. As a result, they had unlimited access to the joint husband's finances and were empowered to dish out funds—such as food money—to the other wives for the home's upkeep.

WHEN IDA married Imran, she was instructed to address his head wife as "*ngôrô*" which signified seniority. This way, Ida was constantly reminded of her co-wife's power status in the home. It was Imran's way of establishing some sort of harmony between them.

Perceived sisterhood between rival wives was expected to limit the tendency of a frequent clash between them. Unfortunately, rivals could never be real friends because they shared the same man, and even if they tried to pretend, their friendship was easily disrupted because they were often vying to win the attention of the same man.

In rare cases, there existed a very 'slim' mutual understanding and respect between or among them. However, this understanding was easily eroded because a more significant understanding that they were competing for their man's intimacy, attention, his time and his love was always the bottom line.

The friendship between rivals got fragmented when excessive power was vested in the head-wife. With the ability to decide who got what, when, where, and how, the head-wife controlled the home. She was endowed with absolute power to determine what the other wives would cook for the day. Even the husband sought her permission before spending nights with the second, third, or fourth wives.

In Ida's case, despite this sisterhood arrangement or perhaps because of it, she never felt comfortable in the presence of Ramla, Imran's head wife. Like Ida, Ramla was an equally beautiful woman. Fair-skinned with naturally blond hair, she stood about five feet and ten inches tall. Even more striking, Ramla possessed a commanding presence about her that was difficult to ignore. These glaring qualities of hers kept Ida on her toes whenever they came face-to-face in the home.

Ramla had spent 16 years of her life with Imran and had made so many sacrifices to keep their marriage intact, only to be abruptly informed that in a matter of days, her husband would be taking on a second wife. She considered this development as an insult but was very crafty at concealing her disgust for the new development.

"I wonder if I might have been inadequate in some way. I have to stand strong or find myself kicked out. I have first reinforce myself and later do everything to reestablish my worth in Imran's eyes," an extremely bitter Ramla thought, as she began strategizing on how to handle the situation; by so doing, an endless competition for the affection of Imran was set in motion.

WITH THE QUEST for an upper hand, both women found themselves wondering what could be so special about this other woman: what does she think of herself; what makes her tick; what is her mindset; how does she interact with the man we both crave? In polygamous marriages, such as this, many situations were expected to pop up, mainly since Imran had laid down rules that only helped to worsen relations in the home. It started with him preventing the two wives from interacting, though he instructed Ida to treat Ramla with dignity. However, Ida's preference had Ramla doing everything to be and remain the most seductive—therefore, the more desirable—wife in the home.

It was impossible for Imran to love his wives equally. At the moment, it was crystal clear that his love for Ida, his new wife, knew no bounds. He just couldn't get enough of her contagious smile and uber infectious cuddles. He bragged about her everywhere he went.

"My Ida is the most beautiful woman in town," he would say. This declaration is where the head-wife, Ramla —who felt left out—tried to do everything to make sure such a three-way relationship was miserable for Imran and Ida. If it meant finding a way to kill Ida or prevent her from bearing children, Ramla would do just that.

"I must get rid of this problem, no matter what it takes," Ramla announced at a meeting with her best friends, Almatou and Fatim.

"I was wondering how you were handling this new development in your home," Almatou volunteered. "Hmmm ......men are just never to be trusted, you know."

"Are you shocked? This is how Dioula men roll, my dear," Fatim interjected.

"After all the sacrifices you have done to help Imran get to where he is, he still chose to betray you," Almatou continued, refusing to acknowledge Fatim's attempt at cutting her off. Then she inquired, "So, what do you intend to do about all this nonsense? Any plans?" Certain things are best nipped in the bud to hinder their growth. Just imagine the cassava tuber: you only need one hand to plant a stem, but if allowed to sprout, with roots fully extended into the ground, it becomes impossible to uproot it with both sides. You need to act fast."

"Where are you going with this?" Ramla asked.

"Oh, just stop acting like a clueless teenager for a second. Don't tell me you have no idea what I am driving at. For a grown-up woman like yourself, you should have already deduced the point I am driving home. "

"Please stopping beating around the bush and come straight," Ramla ordered, with a slight frown.

"Well, I am just saying......you better shine your eyes, and sharpen your skills in dealing with this issue before it gets out of hand."

"Just stop there!" screamed Fatim. "No. That's not happening."

"What's not happening?" Almatou fired back.

"Almatou, I know exactly where you are going with this. I am not going to sit here and watch you destroy Ramla. I have been there, done that. And I know exactly how it feels."

"Ladies, what's going on here?" a confused Ramla inquired, but no one seemed to care about her expressed confusion. "Almatou? Fatim? Am I missing out on something here? Why are you two fussing when it is *my* problem, *my* battle?"

"Look, Ramla..... Don't even think about putting your hands into witchcraft activities. That's not the only solution to your problem. Almatou is notorious for luring friends into this act, and it has never helped," Fatim finally spilled the beans.

"Almatou, was that the solution you had in mind?" Ramla asked, her eyes locked in with those of Almatou.

"How else can such a desperate problem be solved? Don't you know that desperate problems deserve desperate actions?"

"My dear, Almatou, what are you insinuating?" Ramla asked, looking confused.

"I know a perfect *juju* man," Almatou said. "Let's pay him a visit tomorrow."

Stepping in with a strong caveat, Fatim said, "Ramla, before you decide on falling along, let me share this story with you:

Ten years ago, a fury rivalry occurred in the township of Madiina. A rival wife became insane due to a failed witchcraft attempt at killing the husband's younger wife. In this case, the first wife was unable to produce a child after many years of marriage. The husband became desperate and married a second wife to bear him his much-desired children. And for sure, the younger wife brought forth three kids for him. His love and affection for her became boundless."

"There, she goes again. Fatima, can you please spare us the discourse?" Almatou jumped in, rudely interrupting Fatim.

"Ramla, my dear, please listen to what I am telling you," Fatim noted and continued with her story:

So, as a result, violent clashes erupted between the two women daily. The head wife, who felt she could take it no longer and desired to regain and retain her rightful place in their husband's heart, decided to seek an immediate solution. She confided in a juju man and asked him to kill the other wife by supernatural means. The job was done, and all she needed to do was to go home, bury a bag of concoction under a massive rock in the yard and call her rival's name three times.

"But there was a condition to this: if the younger wife did not respond by the end of the third call, the stuff buried under the rock would disappear, and she (the head wife) would rather go insane. Meanwhile, the younger wife, too, was consulting her own juju man. He had alerted her about the unfolding situation and had told her what to do."

"And you think this clueless, spoiled brat has the time to consult the oracles?" a persistent Almatou said. "Ida is very obsessed with her beauty. She doesn't have the time to go chasing after *juju* men around town. Don't even try to frighten Ramla with that."

"Almatou, could you please allow her to finish her point? You don't have to keep interrupting her for goodness sake. Besides, stories like these are worth sharing. I am very interested in knowing how it ends," Ramla said.

Sighing deeply, Fatim continued:

When the head wife came home, she did as instruct; but there was no answer. She rushed back to where she had buried her juju; it was not there. She immediately started uprooting every stone in the yard, and that exercise extended to neighbors' compounds and eventually the entire city —in search of her missing juju. If the rock is exceptionally vast, she spent days digging around it until she finally got it uprooted. This is just an example of how far extreme cases of rivalry could go.

"Well, that's kind of scary. I don't know what Ida's capable of. But what do you all expect me to do? Sit and watch this good-for-nothing girl take over what I've worked so hard for?" Ramla asked with a trembling voice.

"No! Not at all…..!" Almatou said, defiantly. "That's never going to happen. If Fatim has succeeded in scaring you, that's fine. You don't have to do *juju* or witchcraft to win this battle, anyway. Simply make her as miserable as hell, until she can take it no more.

Eventually, she will leave. You can count on me for support at any time. If you want, we can even ambush her on the way to the Creek and beat her up."

Then Ramla screamed, "Hmmm! I will not allow my hard work to be snatched away by this girl. I mean…. that can only happen when I'm dead and gone, not when I'm here and capable of stopping her."

She paused for a breather and continued, "What?! Over my dead body! I will never allow her to taste or feel peace in this home. Let's all go home, for now, give this a good thought and then regroup to decide on a way forward. This problem needs to be subdued now before it grows out of hands. Like Almatou rightly said, you can easily plant a tree with your one hand. But if nurtured to growth, it becomes impossible to uproot it with both hands."

And with that, the group dispersed.

This was an essential reality of polygamous marriages during those days. Instead of enjoying the uniqueness in marriage, which was widely considered a priceless blessing and opportunity, women in polygamous marriages were forced to compete for the rest of their lives. Sadly, most of these women were products of early or arranged marriages, further compelling them to accept and remain in polygamous marriages with all of the embedded agonies.

Where the first wife did not have children, she was forced to accept the man's desire for a second wife. In some extreme cases, she was bound by fear to have her husband marry her younger cousin with the hope that there would be less jealousy involved. In other cases, it was prestigious to marry more than one wife because it was a testimony to the man's social status. Also, in search of a son, many Sub-Saharan men practiced polygamy. Those with only one wife were considered failures or instead believed to be ruled or controlled by the woman. But with the fear of becoming the loser, these women lived with a deep sense of insecurity. Polygamy stood in the way of the pledge binding husbands and wives. It eroded the natural alliance and sisterhood of women because they had to struggle for the same man endlessly.

FOR SEVERAL months after Ida's marriage to Imran, their home was relatively calm. By their first wedding anniversary, however, she began to notice a change in behavior—from everyone, including her husband. Imran was troubled and displeased by her inability to bring forth a child as early as he had hoped. Ida had failed, in Imran's estimation, to prove her *womanhood* through *motherhood*. Bitter words and emotional torture became constant in Ida's world. This drove her insane, even forcing her, at one point, to entertain suicidal ideations.

Come to think of it, Imran was only playing by the rule. Unbending patriarchy at the time was a mainstay of Pepper Coast. Decades of blending tradition with religious fueled deep-seated misogyny. This sad state of affairs thrived on men convincing women and girls that it was perfectly alright for them to play second fiddle to men. Male chauvinists subdued their female counterparts into not only believing but also totally accepting that women belonged in the shadows of their brothers and husbands. They were groomed to be comfortable with the idea that they lived in a man's world in which women only functioned as silent participants. Everything was done to effectively brand women as a secondary community, expected to remain voiceless, be domestic attendants, and bear children. As such, there existed traditionally-assigned gender roles wherein men were customarily empowered to serve as leaders, decision-makers, and be independent. At the same time, women were expected to be dependent and submissive to decisions reached by the men.

Men, therefore, with all the power vested in them, could instantly alter the future of young women and girls without remorse. Girls were raised to believe that they were never in charge of their very own lives—their male siblings were. Women were expected to accept that their husbands held the keys to their lives. No woman or girl dare question or disobey directives given or decisions made by her brother or husband. This practice effectively stripped women of their right to speak up in almost all circumstances.

Besides, parents, very early on, busied themselves, highlighting this proverbial separation of gender roles in the home. The men or boys were in charge while the women or girls were to remain silent and do as instructed—a perfect way of molding the minds of young girls into believing that such socially-prescribed gender disparity was culturally and religiously ordained. But as though none of that was ever enough, wives were equally under intense pressure to prove their *womanhood through motherhood* or face the wrath of tribal male chauvinists who believed a couple's childlessness was solely the wife's fault.

Ida, of course, became a victim of this belief system. Since her wedding, she ceaselessly longed to bring forth a child to assuage the growing anger of her in-laws—especially her mother-in-law, who had already labeled the young woman wedded to her son: "barren and cursed." But don't be so surprised yet.

In Ida's society, there were some with the conviction that not having children was a taboo. In a typical traditional setting, a woman who couldn't conceive was regarded as having a personal failing—or being under a curse. As a childless woman in a massively competitive polygamous marriage, Ida was discriminated against and isolated. Her inability to bear a child after 12 months of marriage took a nasty toll on her marriage. Her husband, his other wife, his family as well as neighbors, held her liable for the misfortune. Tension firmly rooted in rebuff, ruthlessness, and isolation simmered in their household. Put bluntly, Ida suffered ostracism and stigma.

"You are such a shameless woman, and a *huge* disappointment to this family," her in-laws would say to her, further amplifying her guilt and shame.

Chapter FIVE

IDA'S MARRIAGE was a notable investment. But now, it was considered a colossal waste, and her in-laws were not going to have it otherwise. Six months after her wedding, the countdown began. Her in-laws would daydream and anticipate a baby's gender and possible names to be given the unborn child. Her sister-in-law would intentionally call her "pregnant mama," or her mother-in-law deliberately asked her this: "when should I expect to see my namesake?"

"If it is a girl, she would be named *n' matoma,*" her mother-in-law would say but would be swiftly countered by a rigid father-in-law. "May the lightening of the Sankofa Hills and Caves strike and kill you for uttering such evil words. What makes you think the first offspring of my *only* son will be a girl?" Amadou would say, silencing his wife, Asmawou. "It's a boy, and he will be named *n' vatorma.*"

These were Ida's in-laws' way of reminding her of the need to fulfill this task of hers. Day-in and day-out, they expected to see a bulging belly.

At times, they spoke with their eyes, gazing at Ida's tummy all day.

But one person who could no longer suppress her disgust for Ida's perceived infertility was Alida, an extremely aggressive sister-in-law of hers. Alida was also a staunch ally of Ramla. She was relentless, a thick thorn deeply buried in Ida's flesh. Her mission was to *make Ida miserable* and send her packing.

A CHUBBY, TALL YOUNG woman with fierce cat eyes, Alida consistently confronted Ida. Together with Ramla, Almatou, and a few other women, Alida coined multiple nicknames that mirrored the realities of Ida's life. Prominent among such aggravating names was *mousso dendan*. Being called or referred to this way immediately transmitted chills throughout Ida's body, something Alida and her gang enjoyed witnessing.

"We didn't spend all that money on your marriage to get nothing in return. You must prove your worth by giving us a baby," she would yell at Ida, claiming the attention of bystanders or passersby. "It's a deal: we've done our part by paying hugely for your hand in marriage; now, it's your turn. We need a baby!" she would add, further exposing Ida to public disrepute. "Trust me; I will make sure you go back to where you came from. You don't belong in this family. Barrenness is a disease that has no place here."

One day, while on her way to Jone's Creek to fetch drinking water, Ida heard loud footsteps rapidly advancing toward her. It was 4:30 PM, and the town was unusually quiet. As the sound got closer, she slowed down in hopes to see what this was all about. But the footsteps suddenly ceased.

She thought, "Something's not right. I just heard footsteps but saw no one. What could this be?" Quickly she concealed herself behind a humongous baobab tree and watched the tiny footpath that led directly into the Creek. But no further footsteps were heard, leaving her terrified.

After a brief pause, Ida proceeded with her journey; the footsteps also began. "This doesn't feel right. I better return home, "she thought, running as fast as she could.

As she approached the town square, she observed Alida with her crew of three gossipmongers. They had gathered in their usual meeting spot and were busy discussing, mouth-to-ears. "I've found a suitable solution to our '*madam childless*' problem," Alida announced, setting into motion another juicy gossip roundtable.

"Oh, wait, you mean *Mrs. Childfree*, right?" Raquel retorted, somewhat sarcastically.

"Oh, that's right! Like I always said, that woman is a witch. I had a word with Omar, and he's going to take care of her. This is the only way to liberate us," Alida said. "Honestly, marrying this witch was an immense waste of my family's scarce resources, and I won't have it otherwise."

"Did you just say that you've hired Omar, the brigand, to hurt Ida?" Bijou asked, forehead rumpled.

"I didn't say that. I never told him to hurt her. I only asked him to handle her," Alida clarified, arrogantly.

"And what's the difference? Look, Alida, I understand your frustration, but I don't want to be a part of a death plot," Bijou added.

"I didn't say he should kill her. I only asked him to threaten her to leave at once or get what she deserves."

"Same difference," Bijou said, looking very concerned.

"Ladies, we all thought Ida was a symbol of fertility. But no," Oulimata jumped in. "Your brother married an undercover sorcerer. Yes, that's just who she is—a sorcerer with a pretty female face, silky skin, and nothing else. She's eggless. What a waste! I agree with Alida. Let Omar handle Ida. She's an unwanted burden."

Feeling left out, Bijou softened her tone: "I understand. But I still think we can approach this matter differently. No one needs to get hurt."

"This woman was married with so much fanfare. She can't be parading this place without a child. Let's make this town *hot* for her!" Oulimata said.

The attempt on Ida's life would eventually be aborted, all thanks to the town's elders. Alida and her cliques were severely punished for attempting to take the life of another's. Doing so was considered a crime against the gods of the earth. The elders' decision was only enough to deter the crew from resorting to drastic actions. They remained fervently opposed to Ida.

WITH THIS and everything else in between, Ida's marital woes only deepened as time progressed. It all burst forth when she suffered a miscarriage in her second year of marriage that was condemned as an abominable offense by her husband and her in-laws. Now, full-blown acrimony, squarely directed at her, made Ida helpless and hopeless and pushed her to her emotional limit. She questioned the essence of her very existence and nearly took her own life.

Sitting on her makeshift bed one evening, Ida sobbed quietly, yet profusely. She was lost in her thoughts: "as a young girl, I dreamt of having five kids. But, from the look of things, that doesn't seem to be my path. Today, I am called so many names: *childless woman*, a *wasted effort, eggless woman*, a *good-for-nothing*. I am being insulted, booed, and even physically assaulted at every opportunity. They say I am not a woman because I don't have a child."

With bloodshot, wet eyes, she instantly became suicidal with a plan to cut herself. "But isn't it true?" went her thoughts.

"What kind of woman am I if I can't get what I want the most – a child? How else can I prove my womanhood? With all my beauty and charm, I am nothing more than a worthless woman. As a young girl, I always anticipated having lots of children. I still can't believe that's not happening. Lord knows I am not prepared for this life. I can't take it anymore; it's better to die."

Ida's griefs soared when she crossed paths with herbalist Zara who claimed she had the answers to Ida's childbearing troubles. It all happened so fast. Ida had left home on one sunny afternoon to go to Lanaya's broad street, the main dusty road which divided the town into two halves. She was going to buy some charcoal-roasted plantains as she hadn't had much to eat for the last three days due to mounting stress.

"M' *ma nitélé*," came a voice from behind.

Ida was caught off guard. She had been so buried in her suicidal ideation that she didn't notice that she was being followed.

"M' *ma nitélé*," the voice sounded for a second time, catching Ida's attention.

She turned her head, and her gaze connected with Zara's—a tall, light-skinned, middle-aged woman. Ida was dumbfounded for a split second. She had neither seen nor heard of Zara, a fierce but very reserved herbalist in the area. Zara was famous for carrying on her father's legacy, which was a rare occurrence in those days. Male children were the chosen ones to take after their fathers. But it was different in Zara's case. She was Siaka's only child and designated by her dad to pick up from where he left off.

Zara's father, Siaka, was one of the greatest herbalists of Lanaya. He lived his entire life as a fierce hunter, very notorious for his occasional encounters with djinns. By the time Zara turned twelve, she had become very emotionally attached to her father. She would stage silent protests for days whenever Siaka declined to take her along on his hunting trails.

This had somewhat become a norm until one night when Siaka gave Zara a well-desired chance.

Armed with a blue polythene bag, a machete, a hunting rifle, several rounds of ammunition, and enchanted gunpowder, Siaka led the way into the dense forest. He was followed closely by Zara. The pair trekked for about ninety minutes. Suddenly, Siaka stopped. With his machetes, he cleared the area where they stood and asked Zara to sit down. He reached for the front, left pocket of his shirt, and took out seven enchanted pebbles, which he used to encircle Zara.

"We are here now. It's time for me to begin hunting. You will stay here until I am done. Never, ever leave this circle. The rocks will protect you in my absence," Siaka warned and left.

It was approaching 2:00 AM, and the night was already icy and breezy. For another two hours, Zara sat in the same spot and did as instructed. As sleep crept in, she saw a flash of bright light racing towards her. She thought it was a dream and continued to doze off, hoping that by the time she opened her eyes again, the light would have gone.

That did not happen. Instead, the flashing, shapeshifting light quickly advanced in her direction. But its rapid advancement was crippled upon coming in arm's length of Zara. It stopped and transformed into an extremely tall, bizarre creature, entirely covered in plain white with golden flames blazing at the top of its head.

Zara couldn't resist its supernatural presence. She rubbed her eyes as though driving away sleep. Before her eyes, the creature transformed into multiple shapes and forms, fervently trying to lure Zara into stepping outside of the pebbles, her enchanted protectors. The stones were an equally powerful, supernatural force that countered the jinni's moves. It tried multiple scare tactics, but Zara wouldn't budge. Each time it transformed its physical appearance, Zara responded only with a blink or two. This would go on for the rest of the night. The jinni finally disappeared when it was nearing Siaka's return.

"Let's go home. Tonight was very unproductive. I didn't get anything," Siaka announced.

As they walked away, Zara noticed that there was something off about her dad.

"He seems weird. Should I tell him about what I saw? Zara thought to herself. "Maybe not now."

She looked at her dad, and as she mustered the courage to ask what was going on with him, he interjected. "Did you see something?" asked Siaka, as though he knew what had transpired in his absence.

"Were you reading my mind?" Zara asked, looking confused, but not surprised.

"It was a light that became a tall something," she explained.

"That was a jinni. Its mission was to harm you," Siaka said. "They are very wild in these parts of the forest. I don't understand why they were exceptionally aggressive tonight. But you did great by not moving away from the circle I formed around you with the pebbles. Had you left the circle, the jinni would have harmed you. The pebbles had a force that was as powerful as that of the jinni's."

Like Zara, Siaka had had his fair share of jinni meddling that night. In fact, his hunting mission was fruitless, more shots were fired, but no animal was killed. As the duo continued their walk home, they heard loud footsteps advancing toward them.

"Siaka?! What did you do?!" a pale looking hunter inquired in a frightened voice.

"Nothing," Siaka responded without looking.

The hunter ran past them, went to town, and announced that Siaka had done the unimaginable. He had killed a jinni, instead of an animal. The town's most revered hunters gathered and went to see for themselves. But none of them returned to narrate what they saw. They all perished at the sight of the jinni.

Yes, Siaka had shot and killed a very naughty jinni for being a roadblock, preventing him from hitting his target. Each time he aimed at a wild animal, an enormous creature with a black and white face jumped between him and the target. Siaka would quietly relocate to different parts of the forest only to be disrupted by the same annoying creature each time he took aim at an animal. This went on four times, and by the fifth incident, Siaka took out the ammo and loaded his hunting raffle with enchanted gunpowder meant to shut down the jinni for good. This was, however, an incident Siaka would never admit to.

This is how powerful Zara's father was, making her ascendancy to fame a rather smooth one. Though she kept to herself and only prescribed herbs for those who believed in her herbal prowess to heal, Zara was well known to many as Siaka's lone daughter. She was extremely selective in her practice, and her clients were predominantly women.

Chapter SIX

HOWEVER, despite her claim to fame, Ida knew very little about Zara. Their sudden encounter on that afternoon had Ida imagining Zara to be everything else but human.

"*Nitété...*," she said in response to Zara's greeting.

"It's Zara. My name is Zara. Someone sent me to you."

"Who? And for what?" Ida asked, stunned.

"They told me of your condition, and I thought to help you," Zara added, as Ida slowly backed away.

"This can't be real. Zara looks possessed. There's something supernatural about her," Ida thought. "What do I do now? Run? Stand? Keep talking?"

"It's OK. Don't be afraid. I won't hurt you. I just want you to try my herbs, and let's all pray for a change in your marital crisis over childlessness," Zara said, sensing an expressly odd look on Ida's face.

Without saying another word, Ida took four steps backward before stopping to reevaluate Zara's face. Zooming in on Zara's long, silky black hair, pointed nose, and large round eyes, she shuddered a little.

"I knew it! She's a jinni," Ida concluded, her heart racing, her lips completely dry and a faint sensation rapidly seeping through her pores.

"Who *are* you? What *are* you?" Ida retorted, struggling to stay still. Something kept telling her to dash off as fast as her legs could carry her.

"Come *on*, Ida. I am a *mere* herbalist. All I am asking of you is to try these herbs for three months. By the end of the third month, you should see a change in your search for a child," Zara explained, her right hand stretched forward, tightly wrapped around three small baggies.

"What *are* those?" Ida asked, snobbishly. "Just forget it; I am not drinking anything that will put me in harm's way. No concoction can help me at this moment. I only need divine intervention. I have been told on several occasions that conception, whether naturally or not, is impossible for me. Besides, I believe in medical help, not help from a traditional healer."

"I don't know what these powders and concoction will do to my womb. I am not about to make my problems any worse. Thank you for your offer, but I am not interested."

Zara remained persistent: "pour a half tablespoon of each herb into a glass of warm water. Stir thoroughly and drink. Do this at dawn for four weeks. Skip a week and continue for another four weeks. Remember to conceal yourself when drinking the herbs. You can't be *seen* by a living soul."

Ida would eventually succumb. Two months into the treatment regimen, she began to feel very different about herself. She spotted for four weeks. Yet, nothing signaled to her. Heaviness in her lower abdomen and changes in her body temperature still didn't indicate anything to her.

It wasn't until the first week of the second month that Ida began experiencing intense discomfort throughout her body. She confided in a friend of hers, registering severe concerns about having a minimal monthly period, which she considered very unusual. Her friend responded with an injection intended to trigger Ida's period without performing any test to determine the exact cause of her strange feelings.

Ida would further endure severe pain in her lower back for an additional two weeks before bleeding profusely. She would be rushed to a local clinic where nurses would confirm that she had had a miscarriage—a piece of news that was, for Ida, so harsh to bear, a pill so bitter to swallow.

Back home, Imran and his family were very unhappy. For them, Ida was a curse, an abomination to their family. "She's a complete disgrace to this family," Imran would say.

That night, Ida flooded her bed and drenching her one-piece wraparound with tears: "This marriage is doomed. I get it that conflict in marriage is inevitable, a perfectly normal occurrence, too–an unavoidable part of life. But this one right here is a perfect mess. I need a break.

AT DAWN, Ida hopped on the first van leaving Lanaya to Djinnadou where her sister, Hadjala, resided. The 101 mile trip from Lanaya to Djinnadou lasted approximately 2 hours, 28 minutes. The bus conveying Ida and other domestic travelers pulled up in Djinnadou's central parking station at 9:30 a.m.

Dressed in a two-piece maxi dress made of bubbly wooden fabric, Ida hurriedly grabbed her purse, shoved it under her arm, and headed down the dusty road leading to *Kan'eh Loumaa*, Hadjala's home.

Djinnadou was Joanne County's principal city. The county was ideally situated on the southeastern cape of Pepper Coast. At first sight, Djinnadou seemed a relatively relaxed town. Except for its inner-city area, the town's extensive network of footpaths branching into various directions made vehicle commute rather unimaginable. Along the main street that led to the town's central business district was a mixture of old and new makeshift houses roofed either with new or brownish-looking thatch or zinc. Yet, the city offered an incredible diversity of scenery—tranquil wooded streams and rivers, a thick rain forest.

This was Ida's first visit to Djinnadou, a visit warranted by mounting bullies over her perceived inability to conceive a child. Her husband and his family had concluded she was a witch bent on consuming her very own offspring. Life was a total nightmare that she could no longer condone.

"HEY, look who's here!" screamed Hadjala on seeing her sister.

But Ida had no time for jokes. She flashed a sad smile and asked for some water to drink. Ida tried masking her emotions with sporadic smiles, fervently avoiding direct eye contact with Hadjala. She knew precisely when to spill the tea. She wasn't going to let the pig out of the bag just yet. But Hadjala had a way of getting Ida to talk.

"Why such an impromptu visit? I don't remember receiving any prior notice about this. What's going on?"

Ida asked, "Can I have a tête-a-tête with you, please?"

She had so much to say but felt uncomfortable airing it all out in front of everybody; what she had to say was meant solely for Hadjala's ears.

The duo strolled down the compound's main hallway into Hadjala's bedroom at the far end of the hall. It was a quiet morning in *Kan'eh Loumaa* with the wind combing through mango and lemon tree leaves. Except for roaring tweets from birds nesting on tree branches, there were no other sounds. Hadjala's two-bedroom studio apartment sat on the eastern border of *Kan'eh Loumaa,* a compound comprising five single-family homes.

After several rounds of deep breaths, Ida began: "I have been trying for a while now." She paused as though she needed a rush of fresh air before proceeding. "Still.......nothing seems to be happening. I mean......it's well over 14 months now, still no luck, no babies."

"My closest chance ended with a miscarriage for which I blame myself," Ida said, with bloodshot red eyes and a trembling voice as though she was about to burst into a round of terrible tear shedding.

"I should have known better. Hadjala, I killed my unborn baby," she added, sobbing softly.

"Hmmmm......Go on........." retorted Hadjala. All along, she had been actively listening, allowing Ida to air it out and clear her chest. She was filled with empathy. She felt her sister's pain, fighting so hard to hold back her tears from drenching the beige dress she had on.

"Don't you ever beat yourself over the failed pregnancy. It was never meant to be in the first place," Hadjala said, interrupting Ida. "But did you ever try finding Zara afterward?"

Nodding, Ida continued: "I did but was told that she had moved to Lakota, a remote settlement in Southern Ivory Coast."

"So why didn't I know anything about the pregnancy?" Hadjala asked, still being cautious. With her chin resting in both palms, Hadjala sat quietly on a stool near her bed.

She had an oval, calm face. She was chubby and medium height, with wild afro-textured hair that was brownish. She took excellent care of her hair.

"Hadjala ..... because I am unable to born a child to Imran, I am enduring all forms of marital violence: physical, emotional, and psychological. But guess what?" Ida began, re-fueling the conversation, "Imran has another wife. He has already fathered three: a boy and two girls and jealously protects his children."

Before crossing paths with Ida, Imran was married and lived in Lanaya, a sparsely populated town, together with his family. He was, however, strategic in concealing this aspect of his life from her throughout their courtship. It was an unpleasant surprise that would hit her the hardest, making her marriage to him the case of a happily-never-ever.

"He had the guts to tell me that I may have killed all of my babies through an abortion before getting married to him, which is why I am such a 'useless wife,'" Ida explained, still sobbing. "He beats me, never trusts me with his children, and accuses me of wearing a slight frown on my face to greet his children. He yells, '*can't you bear your own?*' at me as often as he can. I feel humiliated, and out of humiliation grows anger."

"One day, I daringly told him that I never knew he had paid God millions to bless him with his kids. I also told him that maybe I still needed to double my investment to reach that million-dollar mark, so that God could bless me, too, with a child. I couldn't hold it back, it just popped out of my mouth," she explained, tearfully. "First of all, he cares less about me. For him, his investment has gone to waste, because I am yet to satisfy my part of the deal. He says it's all my fault that I am yet to conceive a child. One day, while hitting me, Imran invited his brother, his mother, and sister, Alida, to join in."

"The saddest part about all this is that this act is acceptable in our culture. We suffer spousal violence and are made to think we deserve it all because tradition accepts it," Hadjala said.

Responding, Ida said, "When Imran and his siblings attacked me, I spent three nights at a traditional healer's home.

I was bleeding heavily. They kicked me in my lower abdomen, slammed me against the wall, threw me on the floor, and shoved me down the stairs of our five-bedroom home. They succeeded in uprooting a good portion of my hair, too. Meanwhile, his other wife keeps bluffing and teasing me. And he, too, is adding to my frustration and suffering by taking sides with his family."

This had Hadjala's eyes popping out of their sockets in shock and disgust. The traditional social carpet had, for centuries, been used as a cover for wife battery in many parts of Pepper Coast and elsewhere across the Sub-Sahara. It remained commonplace and seemed to have become almost acceptable to most women since the woman was perceived as her husband's property. In most traditional systems at the time, a woman only had one right, and that was the right to remain silent. In fact, she was a chartered asset and, therefore, not entitled to inheritance since she may herself very well be passed on to someone else as an inheritance. And so, throughout history, women were subjected to the whims and brutality of their husbands – albeit, their societies.

"We are all staying in the same house. The cooking and other household chores are divided between his head wife and me weekly. And so is our husband. But when it is my week to cook, I will have to wait for hours for her to give me the money to go to the market. As a result, I'm always late with my cooking, and that causes Imran to hit me almost every day. Also, whenever it is my turn for our husband to be with me, she will disturb that whole night. Once Imran is in my room, every five minutes, she will come knocking on the door to ask him for something; when that gets addressed, she will come again with a completely different request. And that will go on for the entire night. I am tired of this marriage."

"No woman deserves to be physically engaged. It's wrong, and no one has ever given a decent explanation for brutalizing a woman," Hadjala intoned.

But it wasn't always physical. In addition to the physical abuse, Ida also endured a more severe form of abuse that was silent, psychological. It was subtle and was sometimes overlooked or downplayed by her, but it continued to take an enormous toll on her mental and physical well-being. Its effects enormously outweighed the impact of physical abuse of Ida by Imran. Psychological abuse, as endured by Ida, was even more painful and devastating than the physical abuse. It left intangible scars that hurt far deeper and remained much longer than a bruised skin or a broken bone, in some cases.

At one point, she was compelled to wage a significant hunger strike, eating no more than a slice of bread and a glass of milk in the morning and staying that way until the next day. She denied herself her regular three-square meals per day. And this was because Imran had launched a major emotional abuse campaign.

"He says I am only good at eating. For some reason, I am channeling all my pain through food. He constantly makes fun of my 'out-of-shape' body," she explained with deep emotions. As Ida expounded, tears trickled down Hadjala's face. She could no longer mask her feeling–leaning over to hug her sister tightly. Both sisters cried on each other's shoulders.

Such was Ida's dilemma. Like most women of the Sub-Sahara, she had been served with a socially-prescribed role in her capacity as a wife: to validate her place in the home, she *had* to bear children. Or, face the wrath of her husband, his family, and her co-wives, backed by emotional bullies from members of the entire community.

Children were, for the most part, considered as priceless blessings from above, a source of pride, the absence of which exposed the wife to rebuff, stigmatization, and abuse. A husband further heightened a childless woman's pain by marrying another woman or merely dashing her out of the home. Her in-laws would become primary accomplices to such psychological and physical abuse—tormenting her to unimaginable limits. Again, as dictated by society, such treatments were to be considered as acceptable norms, a part of life. It was perfectly normal for a woman to suffer in silence. After all, she was a woman which made her a member of a socially-secondary class that had just one right "—silence" to do away with repetition. So, from time immemorial, women of the Sub-Sahara endured such ruthlessness that they had to suck up because this was just how life was and would be in their world.

When Ida's search for a child spanned nearly three years, she found herself sinking deeper into a depressive state. She tried mastering the art of handling it all: the physical, mental and psychological bullies. But a very touchy emotional distress would out-power her.

"I HAVE BEEN isolated in the place I call home. No one speaks or interacts with me," Ida continued. "Look, Hadjala," she said, with a straight face, yet refusing to make eye contact with her sister, "each wife takes a weekly turn at cooking and catering to the family's needs."

"The week before last was the other wife's week to cook. She was showered with all the love and help she ever needed or desired. But during my week to cook, no one ate at home. That was so appalling. I mean, I just can't imagine this happening to me," she furthered, this time, with a clear voice.

"*Hmmm*…who would have thought that this was going to be my situation just 26 months into this marriage," Ida asked, somewhat rhetorically, taking a reflective look at how she had met and gotten married to Imran. She was baffled at the fact that the truck driver with whom she fell in love and married just ten months into their relationship was now a different person. It was that fast.

Ida had gotten pregnant out of wedlock by Imran. He took full responsibility and sought her hand in marriage. But, per the Dioula tradition, the wedding *had* to be postponed. The Dioula tradition prohibited the acceptance of kola nuts from suitors of a pregnant bride-to-be. Ida's pregnancy ended prematurely. The baby was lost. Two months later, Imran's family presented Ida's family with three separate knots of 10 kola nuts. The couple was joined in holy matrimony after that.

"I still remember those days, when things were all rosy, when Imran had my back," Ida recalled, making full eye contact with her sister.

"During those days, he would shower me with deep, unfiltered love, and that had me desiring the same experience over and again. But that sweetness has long been replaced with unbending bitterness, and he's very remorseless about it." she ended her recollection with rumpled forehead and temples as though she was about to punch someone in the face.

"Can you imagine that he no longer eats my food? I mean…no one ever does. The meals I prepare are wasted. Last week was my turn to cook. But guess what happened?" she said, pausing briefly. "He prevented me from cooking because he suspects I may poison his family since I've got nothing to lose."

"Yes! That's how bad it has become. I am now being labeled a suspected murderer," Ida concluded with a massive bang on a petit, dusty table next to her.

Refusing to eat meals prepared by their wives was a key strategy used by men of the Pepper Coast to reinforce gender disparity or as a reminder that they were in charge. It was an emotional torture strategy aimed at making the woman feel useless. This is precisely what intensified Ida's desperation for a truce. She knew her days in her home were numbered. Imran, his other wife, and children had taken complete control of the house. Things seemed to be deteriorating at a faster pace than she could ever understand. She had been restricted to a single room and a tiny hallway leading to her bedroom.

"The loneliness is driving me insane! And you know I can't go back to Sabougnoûma. It's a no-go area for me now", Ida noted, flashing a quizzical look at Hadjala.

Ida's rocky marriage was of great concern to Hadjala. Their dad, Papa Moh, frowned at his daughters, hopping from one marital home to another. He raised his girls to be dedicated and committed wives and instilled in them the strict principle of sticking it out or sticking together forever in their marriage, regardless of circumstances, contexts, or conditions that defined such unions. For better, for worse, through thick and thin, was the nature of the deal, as well as the order of the day. He made it crystal clear that there was absolutely no place for divorcees in his home: once sent off into marriage, he was no longer responsible for them. They could only visit, never to stay. He also tasked each of them with the responsibility of keeping his image in tight—a daughter's failed marriage reflected negatively on the parents during those days. It was considered a resultant effect of poor upbringing or parenting.

This worried Hadjala, and she felt personally obligated to do any and everything possible to ensure that Ida remained firmly grounded in her marital home, even if that meant sacrificing her young daughter, **Sadjio**, to ensure Ida's happiness.

57

Chapter SEVEN

UNLIKE IDA'S, Hadjala's marriage was thriving. She had been sent off into marriage in hopes that she would be the *childbearing woman* her husband had always wanted.

Born on June 8, 1959, in Sabougnoûma, Hadjala was the third of 21 children born unto the union of Papa Moh and his three wives—Kadeedjã, Hadjala's mother, (seven children), Ursula (eight children) and Fatima (six children).

She began her early education in Sabougnoûma but was soon pulled out and given into an arranged marriage at age thirteen. She was the second of two wives married to Baaba, who had been living in Djinnadou for over 14 years.

Baaba was not lettered. However, as a young, energetic man, he became a driving apprentice with the dream of becoming a truck driver someday. After a few tedious and stressful years as a trainee, he became a professional, well-known truck driver along with the Cape Palmas, Greenville, and Djinnadou corridors. This effort flourished, prompting him to switch to used car rental and sales. That, too, boomed with him becoming a business mogul in used car deals among members of his Dioula kin.

His business success was rather short-lived, all thanks to delinquent buyers, especially family members bent on carving a dent in his path to success. They took his merchandise and reneged on payments. Baaba, too, was exceedingly soft, and his debtors were very creative in milking this aspect of him. The business was eventually brought to its knees, exposing him to more and more financial difficulties. Soon, he was incapable of sustaining his family, a situation that would ultimately launch him into subsistence farming.

By 1980, Baaba had practically relocated to the Prime Timber Products (PTP) plantation, a leading concession settlement within the county at the time. There, he invested his time and energy into upland and lowland farming. He owned a tiny plot of land on which he cultivated a mixed farm consisting of rice, vegetables, corn, and cassava—all done by hand. He also became a hunter, spending most of his nights in deep forests.

Produce harvested from the farm as well as portions of the meat obtained through hunting were sold and proceeds used to buy items needed by the family. The rest of the produce and meat was consumed at home. Baaba spent most of his days on the farm. He came home at the end of each month for a week or less.

His first or head wife, Saléma, was unable to born a child to him after 14 years of marriage. Hadjala was then given as a child bride to a man she hardly knew in hopes that *she* would be the woman to give her husband the children that he had, for more than a decade, longed for.

After her marriage, Hadjala joined her husband and the rest of his family in Djinnadou. And, as expected, that marriage was blessed with five adorable children: Jamaal #1 (died as an infant), Jamaal #2, Saléma, Sadjio, and Sandjee.

Though she was unable to have a child of her own, Saléma dedicated her time and energy to raising Hadjala's children as though they were her very own. Hadjala's only official duty was to carry the pregnancies. The rest was left for Saléma to handle, and she did so with unrelenting commitment, resolve, and passion.

The children grew up knowing, loving, and calling her *Ma'aa*. They addressed Hadjala, their biological mom, as *Teeyah*. The first girl child of the family, Saléma, was named in *Ma'aa's* honor. That was Baaba's way of demonstrating his love and appreciation to his first love, the woman to whom he said "I do" for the first time in his life.

However, despite such a display of overwhelming love, respect, and appreciation, *Ma'aa* would flee her home to an unknown destination. She had been incited by external forces who considered her commitment to raising her co-wife's children as a display of cowardice.

Her sudden departure came a few months after the birth of Sadjio, an incident that rocked the family beyond measure.

"SALÉMA, Jamaal, I am going to PTP later this afternoon," Hadjala announced one morning. She had had very little sleep the night before and was up very early to get ready for this road trip she had been looking forward to for the past two weeks.

It was a breezy Saturday morning in March of 1984. As the sun rose above the horizon, tweets of birds echoed through the forest. The day promised to be a beautiful, sunny day in Djinnadou.

Hadjala's anxiety tripled with every minute that went by. It was apparent, something was bothering her. And of course, it had everything to do with Baaba skipping a routine visit to Djinnadou the previous weekend.

"Is he OK? Why didn't he come as expected?" Hadjala just couldn't get her mind in one place, and she wasn't about to settle for anything.

"I am going to check on *M'boreen*," she informed *Ma'aa* and the children. "It has been a while since I last visited him on the farm. But look, he, too, didn't come to see us as expected or as he always would. I need to check on him. I hope to be back by tomorrow afternoon."

She proceeded to her room, where she spent most of that morning, making necessary preparation for her upcoming welfare-check mission to PTP, a prominent plantation settlement situated on the outstretch of Djinnadou. PTP was famous for its jaw-dropping natural features that perfectly integrated to provide fantastic scenery. The raw, sublime power of its rainforest, mountains, valleys, swamplands, waterfalls, and lakes allowed for a tropical paradise.

By midday, Hadjala was ready to head out. Armed with a one-piece wraparound clothe, a blouse, a blanket, and some bath accessories neatly organized into an overnight bag, Hadjala was ready to go. A short, dark-skinned, medium build, bubbly woman, Hadjala could not wait to see Baaba. She was in her ninth month of pregnancy and was carrying very low. She carefully swaddled her handbag under her left arm and headed to the parking station, where she would board a minivan to PTP.

As she walked through the compound, a voice came calling on her:

"*Moan,* where are you going?" asked the caller.

"To PTP," Hadjala responded without even turning to put a face to the voice. It was a familiar voice, anyway—it was Sira's voice.

"I think you should stay here today. You are carrying very low. Today is not the best day for a bumpy, rocky road trip," advised Sira, with her forehead crumpled. She was Baaba's eldest and only sister. She was a slender, tall, light-skinned woman with a pointed nose.

As a young man trying to find his bearings in life and get established, Baaba had moved to Djinnadou and stayed with Sira until he was fully ready to take on the responsibilities of being a husband and a dad—a family man. Sira, at the time, was married to one of Djinnadou's renowned and successful Dioula traders, Karamoh Soumahoro—commonly known to many locals as *Oldman Djinna*. He owned a beautiful compound of five family homes, *Kan'eh Loumaa*. The town-home complex was primely situated along the main, dusty street that split Djinnadou into two halves. The buildings were all painted with a unique blend of beige and hot chocolate colors. Baaba and his family inhabited one of the family homes of *Kan'eh Loumaa*.

Though they all lived in the same complex, Sira was taken aback by the news of Hadjala's trip that afternoon. She was expressly concerned about Hadjala's and the unborn baby's welfare. She knew all too well that a rocky ride at nine months of pregnancy was never the smartest thing to do, especially considering the deplorable state of Djinnadou's road networks.

Road trips in that part of Pepper Coast were a total nightmare for commuters. The roads were riddled with potholes and ditches filled with mud and stagnated waters. They were barely passable—gradually becoming death traps. Moreover, a hefty portion of vans plying the roads had almost zero shock absorbers; passengers felt every single bump.

Sira simply couldn't imagine her brother's heavily pregnant wife being bounced around as if she was on a roller coaster ride, certainly not in her 9th month of pregnancy. But Hadjala was unbothered, undeterred, and poised to accomplish this welfare-check mission on this day.

After an approximately 40-minute drive, Hadjala arrived in PTP. She was dropped off at the main road and had to trek her way to their thatch hut in the heart of the forest where Baaba spent most of his days farming, fishing, and hunting. It was half an hour's walk from the main road to Baaba's farm.

THE SUN was blazing hot. Hadjala could feel her skin melting like sheer butter exposed to extreme temperature. Her throat was parched. At some point along the way, she experienced faint feelings. She was later joined by a couple that had also been laid off by another van. Together, the trio walked along the footpath leading into the forest. Halfway in their journey, they were bumped into by a short, chubby, dark-skinned man, also making his way to his farm.

He flashed a cheerful smile, greeted the crew, and moved on ahead of them. He looked very lively and energetic. He was signing a song that was familiar to Hadjala, and that caught her attention for a moment:

> *Everyone has someone they love*
> *If you give a juicy biscuit bone to a dog,*
> *He will forever remain your best friend*
>
> *Everyone has someone they love*
> *If you give a kitty cat some fresh, tasty milk,*
> *She becomes committed to you forever*
>
> *If you love something or someone,*
> *Love them wildly and proudly*
> *Love them intentionally because,*
> *Love and shyness aren't friends*
> *So never mix the two*

Shortly after he had overtaken Hadjala and the others, a loud yell was heard. The sound emerged from the bottom of a steep gravel hill.

"Oooooo, my God! Oooo, my people! Oooo, my God!!!" came the voice, followed by an even louder scuffle and multiple crushing sounds.

The couple walking along with Hadjala pulled her aside, instructing her to be quiet. "Shshshshsh!! This must be a python attack," hinted the husband.

"It sounds like a human has been preyed upon by a hungry, angry python," the wife added.

This news had water oozing down Hadjala's feet. She felt an indescribable sense of fear.

The husband continued: "When a python is hungry, it goes hunting. One of its hunting strategies is to stand on its tail against a tall, huge tree, creatively concealing its visibility behind the tree. On spotting a potential prey, it instantly slams its entire body against the prey and begins wrapping itself around the prey before stretching to smash every bone the prey has. That must have been the smashing we just heard."

"Wait...I think you need help," the wife noted, on realizing that Hadjala had broken her water.

"My husband's farm is not far from here. I need to get there before this baby comes," Hadjala told her new companions.

"We cannot proceed right away. That python is yet to have its dinner," the husband warned. "After killing its prey, a python doesn't immediately start eating. It splashes thick saliva on the victim before inspecting the environment to make sure it is free from enemies, especially ants. Because after swallowing its victim, a python becomes extremely helpless until it has fully digested the food. That could take several weeks, up to a month. And during this period of slow digestion, a defenseless python can be easily killed by an ant."

The trio remained in their spot for another two hours before proceeding, hoping the python was done with dinner. As they approach the scene, Hadjala first spotted the deep blue flipflops of the young man that had just passed them. There was his backpack, his water bottle, and machetes. It was clear— this young man was the sacrificial lamb that day.

Hadjala cried bitterly for the departed, herself, and her unborn baby.

"What if he hadn't gotten ahead of us? What if no one even showed up today, and it had to be just me walking in this forest?" these thoughts further tormented her for the rest of her foot journey. The couple was kind to accompany her to Baaba's farm.

On seeing Hadjala, Baaba sprang onto his feet, rushed over to hug and welcome her. She looked exhausted, could barely walk straight, waddling her way along the bushy foot-path. She also struggled with her words. This situation made Baaba very worried. He knew the roads were terrible and didn't want Hadjala traveling on such roads considering her current condition.

But aside from the rough, very bumpy ride to PTP, Hadjala was engrossed in fear from the python attack. It had a severe toll on her lower back and joints. Though she arrived safely, she felt extremely sored, very uncomfortable, and wouldn't stop crying. Her body ached, the discomfort in her lower back progressed rapidly.

"What's the matter?" Baaba asked, looking very concerned. "You won't stop crying. Is there something that I need to know about?"

"We witnessed a python attack on a young man that was also heading to his farm," the couple informed Baaba. As a hunter, Baaba knew what that entailed. He shook his head, thanked them, and returned to Hadjala, who, moments after her arrival, was already in passive labor with contractions happening intermittently.

"*M'boreen*, I am experiencing mild pain in my lower back. It starts in the back, goes around, and ends in my abdomen", she explained after drinking some water to freshen her throat.

In a little over an hour, the contractions had grown stronger and were happening at close range. It was all so abrupt that Baaba had to walk a few miles to a nearby farm to get some older and experienced women to come and help with the childbirth.

"Hold on, Hadjala. Let me go and seek help. I will call Ali's wife. She might be able to help. Please hold on. I will be right back; I will be fast," a very confused Baaba said to his wife, who was now on the brink of active labor. Her contractions were becoming more durable and more robust. Armed with a 10 1/2" tall flashlight, Baaba dashed out of the hut to go seek help.

This pregnancy was neither Hadjala's first nor second. It was her fourth. The contractions moved on faster and quicker that by the time Baaba and his team of older women arrived, the baby had been born. It was 6 a.m. on Sunday, March 15.

Baaba and his troop of traditional birth attendants met baby Sadjio lying on a bare, hand-woven thatch mat. She was crying uncontrollably from the bits of red, fire ants. Both baby and mom were cleaned and given some time to bond, skin-to-skin. By 8 a.m. the next day, Hadjala and her newborn were rushed back to Djinnadou's main referral hospital, where they both received much needed medical care and were discharged to go home after spending two days in there.

Chapter EIGHT

SIX MONTHS after Sadjio's birth, Hadjala became a sophisticated *mumpreneur,* audaciously crushing a proverbial glass ceiling that had previously barred her from financially contributing to her family's upkeep. She fiercely stepped in and assumed the role of her family's backup or secondary breadwinner at a time when women, especially Dioula women of Pepper Coast, were prohibited from venturing into the public sphere.

Back then, the thought of having a woman perform the role of THE provider or breadwinner in the family was considered a taboo. Women were contained within the home, while their male counterparts had a social existence that extended beyond the domesticated confines. In addition to childbearing and childrearing, women were naturally expected to focus their time and energy on the household—cooking, and cleaning.

At the time, there existed a single type of family across the Sub-Sahara: one in which the man was the sole household financial provider or designated income earner. A family's breadwinner role was the man's. He was responsible for footing all the bills, including the children's school fees. For the wife, she was a stay-at-home mom who functioned as a domestic engineer by default—taking care of the kids, doing the cleaning, washing, dusting, cooking, among many other household chores.

The man could either be employed in the informal or formal sector and doing everything to ensure that the family was well sustained. Either way, he was duty-bound to go out in the morning and return in the evening with something to provide food for the next day. The wife and children would sit outside watching the road, with destitute looks expressed across their faces, waiting to see papa come home.

The men those days took their breadwinner role very seriously and did everything to remain assertive and extremely possessive of this role. Thus, having a woman play the role of primary or secondary income-earner somehow reflected negatively on the man of the house. Socially-induced pressure compelled men to take care of their families ably.

"Only weak men rely on their wives," as Oldman P. T. Morris would say.

Oldman P.T. was a longstanding friend of Baaba's, who would later become a highly respected elder of the family. It was his (and others') belief that having a breadwinner wife put the man in a vulnerable position.

Speaking bluntly to Baaba one night, regarding Hadjala's new role, Oldman P. T. said: "It's both a shame and a source of protracted trouble. The trouble starts as soon as the woman begins to earn more and starts contributing a bit more toward the family's upkeep: meals, school fees, hospital, and other routine expenses."

And how does that translate into "trouble"? Oldman P.T. believed "the woman becomes full of herself, and soon finds it necessary to take her case on the road; that means, announcing to as many in the community interested in other people's affairs, what a great ‹breadwinner› she is." *And the poor husband?* You guess it: he suddenly becomes a "good-for-nothing who no longer brings anything home, as the wife's story would go. The poor fellow soon finds himself a bit less than the man of the house that he used to be. Next thing, his self-confidence begins to dwindle."

Interestingly, however, Baaba saw it differently: "I think insecurity is a greater part of this problem. I see no point in being threatened by a woman stepping into the public sphere. 'Who' brings 'what' home financially should never be an issue. Honestly, I just don't think it is the man's job to assume the income provider role in the home exclusively."

But Oldman P.T. still had a thing or two to add before retiring to bed that night: "You may be right. But I know a few men who dared to experiment this. And trust me, they quickly became frustrated as a result of the wife overstepping her role, courtesy of her newfound position and, wrongly presumed, power. Their 'say' in things related to the home diminished by their wives now asserting themselves perhaps for the first time, obviously helped limit an erstwhile controlling position these men had enjoyed in the past."

One a final note, he said, "and you are fully aware of how such men are ridiculed in our traditional setting, as having lost control." With that, Oldman P.T. carefully folded the thatch mat on which he had been reclining as both men enjoyed a peaceful moonlight night while sipping on freshly brewed *hatai*.

Good thing, Baaba understood that marriage was a remarkable romantic institution, and as such, the behavior of each partner needed to complement the other. Both spouses, he believed, were required or expected to bring to the table a sense of oneness as an added value to this social institution. As such, proclaiming that the family's upkeep was entirely his "duty" was unacceptable. He always wondered, "why not allow the women to help, especially if it is clear that some of us (men) cannot carry the burden alone, in a changing world in which an additional source of income can only generate strength and stability of the family?"

He further understood that women's world of entrepreneurship was large, diverse, and of great economic significance. Thus, empowering and supporting them economically, had the potential to create multiplier effects, especially since their resilience and boundless mental power were a great source of inspiration for others. Enabling them to reach their full potentials by investing in their skills and creating a space for them to use those skills were critical to paving the way for sustained income generation, which automatically translated into societal well-being. Such initiatives promised to make a typical woman more productive.

HADJALA HAD unhindered freedom to contribute to the survival of her family. She immediately launched herself into street vending. As a street vendor, especially one that was compelled by the inevitable need to augment her family's meager income, this ordinary woman would do extraordinary things to secure and jealously protect the peace, security, health, and happiness of her beloved family. She aggressively defied the raining torrents, and scorching sun, wheeling her wares from community to community. She sold wares that were the dietary staples and other bare necessities of her community and beyond. She was fearless, energetic, and relentless. Hadjala was a beautiful mother. She was adorable inside and out, from the tips of her toes to the depths of her soul.

With tightly knotted *lappa* ends around her waist, a pair of striped flipflops that went between her toes and over the top of her feet, Hadjala braved the orders of the day. She ensured that there was food on the table for her little ones by the close of each day.

Though inspired by her unaltered mandate to raise her children, Hadjala's limitless energy had its roots in the story of a paternal aunt of hers, Sophia. This aunt of hers raised ten children as a single mom.

As the story went: Sophia's husband, Sorie, was a tribal warrior. He died during raging guerilla warfare that ravaged the Northern Cape of the Sub-Sahara in the early '70s, leaving his wife to raise their ten children solely. Sophia depended on peanut sales at a local market to make ends meet. The profits she made fed her large family and send at least six of her children to school. Unfortunately, her four grown-up daughters were unable to proceed to college following their completion of senior secondary school or gain any employment in their job scarce country.

It took Sophia years, following the murder of her husband, to stand on her own and be a solid rock for the children. All along, she held the conviction that with divine blessing, she would have been 'lucky' to have met another man who would have helped her with the raising up of her children. After a few years of bitter struggles with this dream buried in her heart, Sophia came to realize that things would not have been as expected.

Hadjala would recall her father, Pa Moh, telling her this about Sohpia:

"Her husband was killed in cold blood during the war.
All of their children were with her; no food, no money.

They were only fighting for survival amid bullets, hunger, and diseases. But she always thought that maybe she would have had another man to help her raise the children. Things were very hard with them. But it never happened that way. By then, when a woman had two or more children, no other man wanted her. And for her, she had ten children (five boys, five girls)! So, men were running away from her, especially after the war."

Sophia was, however, undeterred by her failure to find a supportive partner. She struggled throughout the war. They were living on backyard gardening by then. She would go in search of tomatoes, bitter balls, pepper, and okra for the children to sell wherever those products could be found, at the expense of her safety and protection. The family also sold okra leaves to feed themselves. Some of the vegetables were eaten at home, while they sold some to buy sugar, salt, and soap.

Two years later, a pseudo peace deal signed by leaders of the former tribal warring factions. This deal called for the cessation of all forms of hostilities, and to return peace and serenity to the Northern Cape, Sophia continued with her roadside business. Gradually, her business grew, and she began selling her ware at a local market.

She first started by buying $20 worth of fresh peanuts, which she retailed and made $7 as profits. Six months later, she bought $35 worth and made about $14 as profits. Sophia sold her wares in two rounds. The first round was sold in the morning hours, and the interest from that sale was used for food. The second round was for the next day's food money. Her business soared during the dry season when she was able to generate at least $70 from four rounds of sale daily. Profits generated during this time were invested into *susu clubs*. The money was then used to meet some of her family's basic needs, including education for her children, feeding, among others.

INSPIRED BY this story of perseverance, Hadjala further rolled up her sleeves, remained relentless, brave, and resilient in her struggle for a better life for their children. As early as 8:00 AM each morning, she was already established in her mobile office of wheelbarrow, ready to serve the nearby neighborhoods with all kinds of ingredients needed to nail that sumptuous meal.

From the onset, the prospects of profitability and growth of this gallant economic foot-soldier were very dimmed because her family lived on a hand-to-mouth routine, coupled with a husband that relied exclusively on farming to make ends meet, three children and other dependents. This made the reality of her dual roles as a street vendor and as a critical component of the livelihood of her poor rural household seemingly unbearable.

But Hadjala believed in the power of prayers, backed by unwavering self-confidence. She pushed her boundaries, was always willing and ready to explore new and improved ways to shape and sharpen her ability to provide for her family. She refused to allow roadblocks between her and her goal for a better life for her family. She was poised to do whatever it took to see her family happy and healthy.

Like, Sophia, Hadjala was determined to beat all odds, challenge the status quo, and simply make a living. Hers was the case of a strongminded mother doing astonishing things out of sheer necessity to provide for herself and her family.

Few years into her street selling bustle, Hadjala took a bold step further to become Djinnadou's first Dioula woman to serve as a sales and marketing agent for multiple Dioula, Fula, and Fanti wholesalers. This job allowed her to attract and retain new investors for her clients while building sustained rapport with wholesalers across the county. It also prepared her to launch her very own largescale rice trade two years later.

Already, she had built impactful contacts deeply-rooted in trust and confidence. She also fostered continued relations with varied consumers, wholesalers, as well as industry influencers.

YUM CHEW was officially launched in 1985. It was a sole proprietorship, entirely owned and managed by Hadjala. It served a mixed clientele, including women and men, but was passionate about supporting and empowering fellow *mumpreneurs* - women. Yum Chew specialized in rice, a dietary staple of Pepper Coast, with a business model that was focused on product differentiation. Being a cost leader among rice dealers was never an issue of concern. Hadjala, instead, directed her energy to differentiating her brand through the provision of excellent products and services. She was committed to offering premium quality products at premium prices—something her customers were willing and eager to pay for.

Her years as a sales and marketing agent had taught her that customers would pay premium prices to receive unfiltered satisfaction in return—quality. Her goal was to deliver the highest quality mix of products and services to the delight of her customers. And this earned Yum Chew an unimpeachable reputation.

Housed in an old, castoff shipping container, Yum Chew was focused on elevating consumers' shopping experience through the provision of specialty services, such as free delivery to any and everywhere across Djinnadou; credit, pre-financing, as well as *sell-and-pay* services. The shipping container shop was partitioned into a makeshift office and open-air retail space. In the office, Hadjala kept a thick, yellowish notebook with names of creditors and *sell-and-pay* borrowers. Her team of workers happily wheeled bags of rice to the homes of buyers. They demonstrated active listening in their dealings with customers, as well as the willingness to help.

Yum Chew also offered credit services, while inspiring other women to aspire for fiscal independence through the sale of rice. Hadjala happily allowed women interested in starting a career in retail to take a bag of 50kg rice and experiment with it. The most exciting thing about this was that the women didn't have to worry about any down payments. Such *sell-and-pay* deals were firmly rooted in the agreement that the women would take the products, resell and make periodic payments until they were done repaying what was owed. Profits generated were solely theirs to keep. This strategy kept customers returning for the same experience; it benefitted a multitude of women within and beyond Hadjala's community.

Few years into this, Hadjala expanded her business beyond Djinnadou. She would take several bags of rice and other agricultural produce for sale in Cape Palmas. At the end of each trade, she used income generated to purchase several baskets of both dried and half-dried *bony* (herring fish) and traveled through the southeastern part of the country to Ducor, in the south, for sale. Again, after successfully selling her wares, she purchased bags of onions, clothing, and other non-perishable goods, and headed back to Djinnadou where she sold those and began another round of her tri-county business trip.

For four years, Yum Chew remained committed to strengthening its brand effectiveness, thereby making it the ultimate, effortless choice for consumers, especially the women. It competed on the merits of its services, allowing these services to do the legwork of fostering brand loyalty. This strategy raised the bar higher than ever on the need to offer immense value for enhanced customer experience. Needless to say, Hadjala's business became hugely successful. Her family could finally afford to send the kids to school, beginning with their elder son, Jamaal.

MEANWHILE, *Ma'aa* took care of the children while Hadjala was off on her business trips. Such was the norm until the day of *Ma'aa's* mysterious disappearance, having been crushed by the demeaning powers of hatemongers; her soul destroyed beyond repair.

"Ma'aa is gone," Saléma had announced on the morning of "Ma'aa's" disappearance. This was a major blow to the family. Yet, everyone kept the faith. They remained optimistic that she would be back before or by dusk. Throughout that day, Baaba and his young children hoped and prayed for *Ma'aa's* return. Hadjala had left the day before on a sales trip to Cape Palmas.

Word went out about *Ma'aa's* sudden disappearance, but no one seemed to know her whereabouts. The clock was ticking. It was 6:00 PM, still no signs of *Ma'aa*. It wasn't until 10:00 PM that night when someone informed Baaba that they had spotted *Ma'aa* aboard a passenger bus headed for Toulépleu, a major border town in Ivory Coast, a neighboring state situated on the east coast of Pepper Coast.

"Don't worry. I will find *Ma'aa*," a ten-year-old Saléma had vowed.

With broken hearts, the children wept softly, as did Baaba. That night was one of the saddest nights of their lives. They knew she would be missed. The children already missed eating together with or being fed by *Ma'aa*. They missed being pampered by her; her early morning and bedtime hot baths were missed. *Ma'aa* gave them daily doses of a relaxing, full-body massage. This mini-spa moment had become a tradition.

With a bucket filled with warm water, she would soak a small towel in it and begin to massage their entire bodies, letting the steam from the towel absorb into their tiny bodies. She would then use the *black country soap* to scrub their bodies with her bare hands. This would go on for seconds, minutes. That bath would be followed by a thorough full-body massage with soothing body ointments.

Ma'aa also dressed them up in their favorite clothes, which cheered their hearts. Words could not express how much they loved, adored, and cherished *Ma'aa*.

Most importantly, *Ma'aa* tucked them in bed with traditional folktales every night. One of their favorites was the story of the King who banned the birth of girls throughout his kingdom out of fear that a woman might succeed him. This fairy story was entitled: *She Shall Rule* and *Ma'aa* religiously told this story, night after night:

> *Once upon a time in an isolated land. There lived a powerful king called Amédi. He was one of the most revered sons of Sababoü Empire, who later became the empire's greatest ruler in the early 12 century. A massively wealthy empire, Sababoü was settled by the N'Gö people who lived a relatively peaceful life. They survived primarily on trade and farming. Sababoü was famous for its abundance of natural resources, especially gold dust, as well as its varying landscape.*
>
> *Amédi Kamissokho, the empire's leader, was a warrior king extraordinaire. He launched successful warfare on neighboring kingdoms, expanding Sababoü and making it one of the largest, most influential empires*

in the history of humankind. In addition to the power of his sword, King Amédi's rule was firmly strengthened by a ridiculously powerful, all-men Assembly. The 13-men Assembly played a critical role in the empire's daily operations.

King Amédi was also reliant on an authoritative, super-natural being for guidance. Nantènè, a light-skinned female jinni, was his right-hand woman. He inherited her, together with the throne, from his father. Nantènè was handed down from one generation of the royal family to the other. Amédi and his predecessors looked up to her for spiritual guidance. She was a formidable force.

Life across the land was relatively calm, until one night when a mysterious dream occurred to King Amédi. In this dream, the King found himself sitting at the foot of a humongous pyramid made of solid gold. He was wearing a white robe that was nearly covered in blood. At one point in the dream, Amédi could see his subjects bowing to a faceless figure that appeared to have feminine characteristics. He tried to speak up but sounded very rough and raspy. He sought acknowledgment from his people, but they remained unbothered. This shocked him beyond measure; it angered him.

Then came a soft voice from behind:

"Amédi, Amédi."

He turned but saw no one. "What's going on? What's happening to me?" he wondered.

"A girl shall be born! A girl shall rule Sababoü!" added the mysterious voice.

Amédi looked up again, and this time, he saw a shape-shifting flame that quickly transformed into Nanténè, his jinni advisor. Such was Nanténè's first time revealing her natural self to Amédi. She always appeared to him in human form. But in this dream, she came as her true self—an intimidating jinni of wind, sea, and fire.

"Nan.....ténè " Amédi attempted to speak but was quickly shut down by Nanténè.

"Yes, Amédi.... It's me, Nanténè. Today, I am showing you who I am, and the reason is straightforward: your days as King are numbered. A female shall lead Sababoü after you."

"Why a female successor? Have you forgotten about my family's tradition?

I only have sons, and they are my designated successors," the King said, forehead severely wrinkled in a frown.

Amédi was husband to four wives and father to two sons by his first and third wives. His second and fourth wives were yet to born a child to him.

"It has been decreed. Sababoü shall have a female leader after your reign," Nanténè responded.

"That's very unusual. It is abominable. You must stop this, Nanténè. You protected my great grandfather; you did so for my grandfather and my father. Now, I, too, need

your help. Please protect me and my family's honor," the King furthered, visibly upset.

"Amédi, this has been decreed by the Great Oracles. Nothing can stop it: she shall rule," Nanténè continued.

"But.... I can sacrifice 1000 cows if that's what will please the Oracles.

I can sacrifice 10,000 cows, camels. I am willing to do anything just to please them, as I have always done. Why are they punishing my people with a woman leader?

Where did I go wrong?" Amédi asked, angrily.

The Great Oracles of Sababoü empire comprised 10,000 shrines grouped in a single cave, dubbed as the "god of the winds." They were the most powerful of all other shrines tucked away in the forests, and caves dispersed across Sababoü. Traditional chiefs and kings, herbalists, cultural authorities, including fetish priests and tribal warriors, consulted with the "god of the winds" in their search for power, wisdom, stability, prosperity, and security in life. And every visit was kicked off with the offering of blood: white chickens, sheep, cows, and camels were sacrificed. The spirits in the "god of the winds" were believed to feed off the life-blood of these animals. Goats were forbidden by the "god of the winds" due to their stubborn smell.

Amédi routinely offered cows and camels in his endless search for power, wisdom, and courage to lead Sababoü in his capacity as a warrior king. He never went to war without first offering blood to the Oracles. He believed *strongly in the power of blood and remained faithful to this belief throughout his rule. No wonder he instantly thought to offer blood to reverse the prophecy being revealed to him. But Nanténè had a surprise for him this time.*

"You can do nothing about this prophecy; not even a human sacrifice can help you this time," she concluded and disappeared, ending the dream.

The next morning, King Amédi convened an urgent Assembly meeting to discuss his dream and decide on a counteraction. For him, the thought of a female successor was just unacceptable.

"It will be a nasty blow to the royal family's tradition of having male successors," he thought for a moment. "A female successor is a curse, an unwanted disruption. I will fight it with every ounce of my being."

After an entire day of deliberation, the Assembly agreed on the following: (a) establish a law banning the birth of girls throughout the empire, (b) every newborn baby girl must die, regardless of societal status.

"Girls must take care of our homes, not an entire empire," Vasco, the Assembly's majority leader, intoned.

"I agree. Women are too soft to make tough decisions," retorted Almãme, the Assembly's longest-serving member.

With this, the recommendations were compiled and presented to King Amédi, who swiftly established a task force responsible for implementing, monitoring, and enforcing every aspect of the new law.

As the law went into full swing, the King's second wife became pregnant and had a bouncing baby boy. Then came a second boy by the third wife, further exposing the childlessness of his fourth wife, Nayoüma.

This situation reduced her to unimaginable treatments, including isolation, from her co-wives, with a sturdy backing of the King. It threatened her social interaction, marital stability, and mental health. She was reduced to a maid, barred from sleeping in the King's royal palace. In addition to unending household chores, Nayoüma dutifully fetched firewood from nearby bushes and deep forests for household use.

As a tradition, King Amédi's wives took weekly turns at spending nights with him. But he barely fulfilled this part of his marital obligation to Nayoüma over her perceived inability to bring forth a child. This went on until one night when he suddenly ordered the guards to go and fetch her. It wasn't even her designated turn to be with him.

That one-night encounter would, however, result in what the entire empire had been longing for – a baby was finally onboard.

THOUGH PREGNANT, *the King still rejected Nayoüma. Nothing angered him so quickly as to see her. He hated the sight of her so much. One day, he ordered the guards to move her into a coop-styled hut, situated in the far east of the royal complex. There, she had minimal access to food and water. Yet, she regularly fetched*

firewood and did intensive chores. Even in her 9th month of pregnancy, she did as instructed; her co-wives controlled her life; they treated her as they wished; she was answerable to them.

One day, while roaming the forest in search of firewood, Nayoüma was knocked down by an aggressive, rapidly advancing labor pain. She crawled over to what looked like a sparkling blue lake in the heart of the forest. There, she sat, resting against the trunk of a huge mahogany tree, in hopes that the pain would eventually subside. But that was far from happening. Before she knew it, the urge to push had become more robust than ever. She cried for help, but none was around. So, she began to pray and made a wish for a helper.

Then suddenly, an old lady appeared from nowhere and offered to assist with the delivery. Nayoüma was in such excruciating pain that she didn't even bother to probe the woman's identity and intent.

"Child, you are in so much pain. And, it looks like this baby is ready to come right now, right here," the old woman said. "Letme gather a few leaves. You need something to relax on and be comfortable."

Within a twinkle of an eye, the leaves were woven into a beautiful, smooth mat. She carefully stationed Nayoüma on there and instructed her to push.

"It's almost here. Just keep pushing," the woman ordered.

After a few pushes, the baby was born.

"It's here!" shouted the mysterious birth attendant.

"Is it a boy?" a curious Nayoüma asked.

"It's a beautiful baby with sparkling blue, almond-shaped eyes, and caramel-colored skin," answered the birth attendant.

"Oh, great. But is it a boy?" Nayoüma reiterated.

"It's a bouncing baby girl," the woman responded.

On hearing this, Nayoüma cried bitterly. She knew this meant the end for her. She knew the baby was doomed to die. She sobbed softly.

"Are you alright? You should be happy, instead of crying," the old woman said, refusing to look Nayoüma into the eyes.

Nayoüma said nothing but continued to sob while hugging her newborn tightly.

"I can't take you home," she said, staring at her newborn. "You can't come home with mama. I don't want them to hurt you."

"What do you mean?" asked the old woman. "Are you afraid that she would be killed?"

With popped eyes, Nayoüma asked, "who are you, and how did you know about this?"

Ignoring Nayoüma's inquiry, the old woman said, "don't worry. I can keep the baby for you until the time is ripe for her to go home. She is the child referenced by the prophecy. She will be a great leader."

"You are a jinni. I can tell. But how can you take care of my baby? She's human, not jinni? What do I tell the King? What do I tell everyone hungry to know?" Nayoüma wondered.

"Don't worry. Just tell them you had a stillbirth in the forest and buried the child."

"What if I am asked to point out the grave?" Nayoüma shot back.

"Just get over it, woman! No one cares or loves you to want to probe you any further! You are a maid, and that's all you are and will be to them. Go home and tell the King that you had a stillbirth," the woman ordered.

She cleaned and got Nayoüma ready for her journey back home, leaving behind her baby. The deal was that Nayoüma would come and feed her baby daily, at a specific time, and she did so with unwavering commitment until one day when a snoopy hunter spotted her. By then, her baby, Aïdaa, had grown into a stunning young woman.

During each visit, Nayoüma announced her presence with a song. Her daughter would then appear from the sparkling blue, but a very stagnant lake, adorned with precious gems of unimaginable proportions, from head to toe.

Having discovered the unthinkable, the hunter went to town and asked to see King Amédi. After several attempts, he was granted an audience.

"King Amédi, I have one question for you," he began but was interrupted by the King.

"You went through all the struggle to see me just to ask a single question?

Are my people this less busy now?" the King asked, sarcastically.

"What happened to the pregnancy of your wife, Nayoüma?" asked the hunter.

"She's nothing more than a speck of dirt," the King retorted, without giving it a second thought. *"Why, you ask?"*

"With all due respect, Your Highness, we all are dirt. If I were you, I would ask my wife what became of a pregnancy that lasted nine months but no child to prove," the hunter fired back, and excused himself.

This had Amédi thinking hard. A few days later, he summoned Nayoüma, but she insisted on having had a stillbirth. The King then cited the hunter and demanded details.

"I don't believe in talking; I will let you see for yourself," he told the King. *"I want you to come with me on my routine hunting trail next Friday. There's no need for guards, just you and me."*

As planned, the pair headed into the deep forest on that Friday afternoon with the King having no idea what this was all about. Once at the blue lake, the hunter tied up King Amédi to a tree.

"Look straight ahead and tell what do you see," he ordered.

"I see a lake," the King responded.

"Awesome," said the hunter, fastening a piece of cloth across the King's mouth to prevent him from doing anything that will alert Nayoüma.

Shortly after that, Nayoüma appeared and began singing. Aïdaa then came forth, this time, signing along with her mom. On seeing his daughter, King Amédi defecated on himself. He eagerly leaned over to catch a clear first sight of the exceptionally charming princess.

At home that night, King Amédi summoned Nanténè, his jinni advisor: "Forgive me for trying to suppress the prophecy. It has come to pass. She has been born, bred, and is ready to claim her rightful place in the royal palace. I have seen her—our new Queen, my successor. She is as charming as a precious gem, as bright as a star. She is a light, one that will illuminate Sababoü for good."

Nanténè smiled and said, "I have been her guardian all these years. You can never contest a prophecy by the Great Oracles. Aïdaa, my fair princess and daughter of the great King Amédi of Sababoü empire, shall rule."

"I should have listened to your advice. I was consumed by greed and the fear of failure," the King said, admittedly. "How can I undo my mistake?"

"Convene a meeting of the Assembly and announce your decision to repeal that evil law and issue a public apology to the people of Sababoü, to Nayoüma. Then gather your people at the lake by next Friday for a turning over ceremony."

*The King did as he was instructed. He was later re-
united with his daughter, Aïdaa–the chosen leader of
Sababoü. She did wondrous things as a female leader.
And they all lived happily ever after.*

THE END

Another traditionally told tale that cheered the kids' hearts was
the *Crushed Dream*. A story, *Ma'aa* told with exceeding passion:

*There lived a young woman who always dreamed of
nailing a perfectly-polished look, and by that, I mean a
glamorously fresh, pretty and manicured look, someday.
Every girl in this faraway kingdom was obsessed with
rocking a touch-up look nearly every day. They assembled at the various beauty salons around the country
in search of a designer's look—spending real cash to
obtain that polished look. This meant styling their hair
in ways that stay put, looking after their nails, their
brows, and their lashes; and not forgetting to buy some
of those vaunted cosmetics that work well with their
skin. If these activities seemed to require little physical
exertion, you had better think again since, in reality,
they did not. The truth is, it was a time and cash consuming affair that took loads of effort—and plenty of
money as well. And so, in keeping with this 'tradition,'
this young woman longed and prayed for her day at a
beauty parlor.*

*One day while sitting under the lone mango tree that
stood tall and firm in their compound, she made a silent*

wish. Fortunately, the kingdom's fairy godmother happened to be flying through the area and overheard the desire. She quickly ascended to make this wish a once-in-a-lifetime reality. The young woman arrived at a salon, and one could tell from the look on her face, that she was indeed expecting to be 'put to town' —nothing too complicated, just a simple redo of her nails, her brows and lashes.

When she first entered the salon, the young woman headed straight for the salon owner to explain what she wanted to be done that day: hair trimmed; permed ends clipped to allow the new growth a chance to flourish, while she rocked that natural look. But that day was a sad one for the salon owner who had just lost his girlfriend in childbirth. He tasked his assistant to take care of the young woman. But the young female did not feel pleased about having a fellow woman do her a favor.

"I've never had a woman cut my hair before. I don't trust the skills of a woman. I prefer a man," she said, finding herself a chair and sitting.

That didn't come as a surprise, not at all. Sometimes, women, those days, tended to underestimate other women's potentials. And so, after a short while, a newly-hired male apprentice decided to respond to the female's preference for a male hairdresser. He managed to ask her to come so that he could do the job. Without any hesitation, she moved towards the guy.

But....., instead of grabbing a pair of scissors for the trimming or cutting, this young man reached up for a shaving machine, turned it on, and gradually began chopping off the woman's hair.

Soon, the back of her head was shining in all four giant mirrors in the parlor. Now, she was officially sporting a near-bald hairdo she had not dreamed she'd be caught wearing. She had not noticed what was going on—in fact, no one had, as everyone had been busy weaving, braiding or styling other customers' hair. But by the time the guy reached the front of her hair, she took a glance at the mirror and became furious.

"Oh! So, you decided to give me an old man's hairdo?!" she yelled at the top of her voice.

And suddenly, everyone noticed what had happened to her dream of acquiring a 'knockout' look.

"I can't go home looking like this. My family may think I'm insane. I have never shaved my head before. What is this that you've done to me," she asked, with tears streaming down her cheeks.

Besides being worried about what everyone might think of her, she was equally concerned about what her neighbors, her siblings, and parents might think of her new look. With all these in her mind, she cried. She soon noticed that the front of her head had not been touched. So, she demanded that what was shaved off be replanted. Of course, the salon lacked the material and instruments to attempt such a procedure.

The female's screaming alerted the salon owner, who came out to find out what was the source of the ruckus.

After being told what had happened, the supervisor told his staff to apologize to the woman. For the next couple of months, the young lady had no choice but to scarf her head, to keep from moving about with a near-bald hair condition. She left the salon that day with her head wrapped in a purple silk scarf. And that too did little to satisfy her. She complained that it usually took five to six trials before having her scarf beautifully wrapped in a way that suited her face. She termed scarf sheathing the most tedious aspect of her morning formalities before leaving home for work. It was tough, but she had no choice but to deal with her crushed dream.

THE END

THESE WERE REAL life lessons delivered in the form of tales. And the stories told by *Ma'aa* further cemented the bond between her and the children. Without a tip from an insider, most community dwellers considered the kids as *Ma'aa's* biological children. They were inseparable. She showered them with limitless love, and they faithfully reciprocated.

As fate would have it, the children were all light-skinned, skinny, and tall, as was *Ma'aa*. Though they got these physical features from Baaba, who was light-skinned, slim-built, and tall-height, *Ma'aa* also possessed all these physical characteristics, which made it difficult for third parties to draw the line. Hadjala, their biological mom, was dark-skinned.

Ma'aa also did a fantastic job of teaching the children how to fearlessly take on the world because this world was never a just place. She showed them responsibility and their ability to do whatever it took to be successful. She made them believe that they could do anything imaginable. She taught them to be forgiving, made them feel beautiful on the outside in addition to feeling beautiful on the inside. *Ma'aa* uniquely shaped Saléma and Sadjio into strong, fearless, and independent women. With such a robust foundation, the girls went on to do wondrous things while fearlessly following their dreams. Thanks to *Ma'aa,* the children were happy and adventurous in their individual lives. She was strong, dedicated, committed, and unwavering. She raised the children without ever showing them her struggle—the inner battle for a child of her own, a battle she fought so hard over the years.

She taught Saléma, her namesake, the art of cuisine. *Ma'aa* felt a personal connection to cooking. She was a firm believer that cooking was an art, and the more a man's belly was capably taken care of by his woman, the more attached he became to her. "You see," she would say, "the stomach is not something to joke with, in any case. In a typical Sub-Saharan context, no matter how smart, pretty or attractive a woman is, if she cannot cook a hearty meal, she has a problem. The quality of food she cooks at home attracts her man to her the most; it encourages him to stay at home."

One day, as the pair got set to prepare deep-fried potato greens stew, *Ma'aa* sat Saléma down for a brief lecture.

Ma'aa said, "N' *dorma*, I want to tell you something before we start cooking."

"Oh, lord. There we go again. Another lecture?"

"Nothing too long. I promise."

"Ok. What is this time? What dos and don'ts do I have to be aware of this time?"

"*N' dorma*, as a woman in this world of ours, you can rest assured that your cooking will define your womanhood.

Note these few tips to prepare you for that day—*Taste:* always remember that what makes the food tasty is the seasoning and preparation. It doesn't matter how many ingredients —ranging from the different kinds of fish, meat, shrimps to crabs, and other exotic elements a woman might have in there, if that food is not seasoned correctly, the taste will not hit the right spot. Here's why: with all the flesh and bones that made up the body of the dish, it goes nowhere without the soul—the seasoning. Note that it is not only about adding salt, cubes, and curry to the concoction. It is about knowing what goes with what."

"For many young women these days, cooking is simply another household chore that might require the usual haste that most mundane tasks require. The risk of arriving at an insipid creation is high. Rember to do *it with lots of love in your heart*, and the inevitable flavorful dish striven for will prove gratifying," she said, smiling. "Anything short of this would be a tasteless, watery and salty cassava leaf dish, prepared and served with over-cooked butter rice. Just imagine that. Or a spicy and equally watery 'pepper soup' that, if you positioned yourself at the right angle, you could even see yourself in the soup. Come to think of it; there are others whose soups often are taken off the fire prematurely, be it cassava leaf, fried potato-greens, fried eggplants, palm butter, to mention a few. In that case, you will always find more water than needed in there, which dilutes the taste, kills the presentation, and causes the dish to go bad sooner than it should."

Then she motioned to Saléma to start cutting the fresh greens and veggies.

"You know what's funny?"

"No," Saléma said.

"An experienced cook simply needs a few elements to nail that sumptuous meal for her man. This category of women effortlessly prepares simple meals like dry rice that has gotten their men longing for home-cooked meals."

"Now, you got me yearning for dry rice. Why are we cooking greens today anyway?"

"*N' dorma,* greens are a bit sophisticated. I thought to show you the processes involved with its preparation."

"Can we cook dry rice tomorrow?"

"And you think it's that easy to cook? It may sound simple, but its preparation can be complicated. We often see couples hopping between restaurants, cookshops, or even the food booths around here. Why? Because the wife has no idea about, nor time, to cook. Such couples commit their bellies to the various food courts with no attempt by the woman at a home-cooked meal. Half of their monthly budgetary allotment is set aside for eating out. This lifestyle can be costly and unhealthy. Eating at home is less expensive and sufficient. There are yet others who also become the regular visiting type, especially around lunch or dinner time, to other relatives. They can't cook at home. But their situation has less to do with cooking and more to do with self-sustainability."

Releasing a hearty laugh, Saléma asked, "Why are you so obsessed with this whole cooking business?"

"Traditionally, during the very first encounter between a woman and the parents of her man, the first thing they do is assess her ability to cook. They can hardly wait until they have tested her cooking ability. *So, when will you come and cook for us?* They ask at the first opportunity. Do not underestimate this question. They mean it, and she can never escape it. Usually, they will want her to cook the meal in their presence to erase every doubt that someone might have assisted her in the preparation. So, she must try to prove herself capable of doing it."

"Moreover, some die-hard traditionalists continue to hold that a woman is incomplete, once she cannot cook well. Many marriages these days are easily broken because either the husband or the husband's people realize that his wife cannot cook well. She is often sent to her parents to learn cooking and may return later—or never. A woman must cook mouth-watering meals, not just an excellent meal, or a simple, delicious meal, or probably a hearty dish; I mean a culinary work of art that, if her man could, he would frame it and put it on a wall. Being good at catering, not at cuisine, will hurt your relationships. It's important to love the kitchen and cook with love."

Cooking moments were priceless chances for *Ma'aa* to offer several pieces of advice to the girls, all referencing the need to be a great culinary artist.

Sadly, *Ma'aa* would eventually fall prey to the voices of hate that echoed in her mind, inciting her to leave her home. External family members, who always reminded her of her childlessness, bullied her into fleeing.

"Don't hide your uselessness behind the children of your mate," they would say to her. "Stop pretending to be a mom when, in fact, you are incapable of being one."

Ma'aa would flee in 1987.

Fourteen years later, in 2001, her namesake, Saléma, located her in Anyama. Ma'aa's new home, Anyama, was situated at about 20 kilometers north of Simaya. After fleeing her home in Djinnadou, *Ma'aa* settled in Anyama, a large city in southeastern Ivory Coast, not far from that country's central city, Simaya. Most dwellers in this area considered it to be a suburb of the nation's capital, Simaya.

In a conversation with Saléma, *Ma'aa* recalled the following: "I felt humiliated each day. It was too disgraceful for me. They mocked, gossiped, teased, and even insulted me for not being able to bear children."

Ma'aa never remarried until her demise in the mid-2000s.

Chapter NINE

BY THE EARLY 1980s, life had changed for the better for Baaba and his family. Hadjala's tri-county trade, backed by her shipping container store, was booming, and Baaba's farming activities were thriving. From a subsistence farmer, Baaba was now farming commercially. He sold the majority of his harvests at local farmers' markets across Djinnadou.

Baaba grew mainly vegetables using compost hauled in from various localities across the city. He also raised chickens and ducks. He still spent most of his days on the farm, in a mud hut tent adjacent to his crop to keep a close watch on his produce. He would spend an entire night awake, trying to prevent deer from mashing his vegetables and raccoons from destroying the baby chickens and ducks.

Incomes earned from his farm and Hadjala's business were enough to make the family's budget whole. The couple had all the business they could handle, growing and selling fresh food to diverse households while managing a fast-growing rice trade dubbed *Yum Chew*. They lived a rather peaceful, undisrupted life until Ida's marital crisis spilled into their home.

ON THE NIGHT of Ida's arrival in Djinnadou, Hadjala, being the people pleaser, she always was, assured her sister of doing everything possible to remedy her situation.

"I will talk to my husband in the morning," she told Ida as they sat in her bedroom.

"With his approval, I will let you adopt one of our daughters to keep your company."

But Ida greeted her sister's suggestion with a frown instead of a smiley face. It came off as an annoying proposal, leaving her to wonder where was Hadjala headed with such a dumb idea. Then she began hearing mean, critical voices inside her head: "Is she out of her mind?" she wondered, with frowning brows. "Is she serious? Maybe she's bluffing. I thought she would offer to take me in. That way, I don't' have to worry ever about Imran and his mean family."

Hadjala sat patiently, waiting for a response, but got nothing. The voices in Ida's head had morphed into nocturnal demons as Hadjala spoke:

"But why are you surprised? Didn't you expect a ridiculous reaction in the first place?" went the competing views in Ida's mind.

Of course, Hadjala was notorious for putting everyone's (especially her siblings') happiness first. She went above and beyond to please them. For her, their satisfaction mattered the most. Generally, it almost seemed like life in her world revolved around the happiness of others. She did everything to see others smile, even if that meant going a day or two without food just to put a smile on someone else's face. She cared less about the fact that there was more to life than being a people pleaser at your very own detriment.

Granted, it felt great to help others. In fact, in some contexts, it could be a morally, spiritually, and emotionally fulfilling act. But it was never always a win-win situation. Most often than not, the person you put before yourself got what they wanted while you were left unfulfilled and drained. Not even this life lesson could deter Hadjala from fulfilling her mission to serve humanity selflessly. She was knee-deep in the vicious cycle of wanting to make everyone, including Ida, happy before herself.

"Ida, did you hear what I just said?" Hadjala said, reclaiming Ida's attention. "I want you to adopt one of our daughters."

As she attempted to reecho her offer, Ida looked directly into her eyes, with beads of sweat rolling down her forehead, and began bombarding: "....... but what has *that* got to with my marital troubles? I said my husband and everyone hate me over my inability to born, and then, you choose to throw your daughter at me? What for?"

"Wait......are you trying to bluff me, like everyone else is doing?! What has adoption got to do with it, Hadjala? Have you lost it? I thought I could come to you for solace. But I guess that was a silly mistake. Do you think I won't ever be able to have a child of my *very* own? What really will giving me your child do to my soaring issues?"

Hadjala was baffled at her sister's sudden rage. Ida's stone-cold gaze made Hadjala very uncomfortable.

"Look, Hadjala, I came to you expecting to stay here. I don't ever want to go back. So, that offer of yours isn't pleasing to my ears."

"What a rage?" Hadjala managed to say.

"I don't need that negative energy from you and certainly won't allow it in my house! This anger is unwanted. And don't be mad that I am making this proposal instead of telling you to flee or abandon your marital home. You know very well that I won't do that. Get yourself together! Hadjala blasted, with an index finger pointed at Ida's forehead."

"You just told me that isolation and loneliness were killing you. I thought to let you have one of our daughters as a remedy to that problem."

"Did I tell you that I came all the way here to borrow a child?" Ida interrupted, with gritted teeth. Her scrunched face had suddenly turned dark red, with a sizeable throbbing vein in the middle of her forehead.

"Well, it will be a good distraction for you; it will take your mind off the emotional bullies, to some extent," Hadjala explained.

Feeling her sister's pain, Hadjala relaxed her tone, "Ida, calm down. I know you are hurt, but don't take it out on me. You know very well that you cannot leave your marriage, no matter what. Besides, giving you my child in no way validates your husband's or his family's perception of you. I am positive that you will be a great mom someday. It's only a matter of time."

This revelation suddenly birthed a compelling twist in Ida's mood: "Hadjala, I am sorry I came off that way. I am just furious. I apologize for being harsh. You know, though this may seem a lesser remedy to my worsening woes, I still think that having a niece around will be great. It will help to reduce the soaring feeling of neglect I have been nursing in my own home. With this arrangement, I will always have someone by my side—someone I can talk to, play, and laugh with."

With that, the sisters called it a night.

Hadjala's response to this steamy marital crisis was focused primarily on addressing Ida's growing sense of loneliness. She settled on convincing Baaba to approve the adoption of one of their young daughters.

Sadjio, their youngest daughter at the time, was the *chosen one* for this deal. She was barely three years old, but Hadjala was determined to let her go, hoping that such an in-family adoption, though informal, would be nurtured with some *TLC*—tender loving care. It was also a perfect opportunity for Ida to practice parenting while awaiting her turn.

Chapter TEN

NEWS OF SADJIO's adoption was greeted with mixed feelings by residents of *Kan'eh Loumaa*. Hadjala's initial attempt at concealing the development in her family was fruitless. The news blew across the area like a wild bush fire during the harmattan, with most neighbors frowning at her for what they termed as "broad day human donation."

Sadjio was barely three years old, and *that* irritated neighbors and other relatives.

Some relatives of Baaba's wondered if Hadjala truly cared about her daughter. Others quickly concluded that she was a reckless, and most ridiculous mom to ever walk the earth.

"Do you think Hadjala is in her right mind?" murmured Jolie.

Mimi shook her head hard. She was equally upset at Hadjala. As both women trekked to the Crystal Caldera Creek on that sunny afternoon, they discussed the ridiculousness of Hadjala's move to *give a human away*.

"I think she's insane. Who donates an entire human being?" Jolie continued.

"Granted, Ida, maybe her blood sister. But that still doesn't justify such a radical action."

Zedia, a close friend of Jolie's, then joined the crew. She, too, was headed to the Creek to fetch drinking water. On hearing the topic under review, Zedia wasted no time in offering the following, "Such an arrangement could go bad; the consequences could be horrible. Who knows, Ida could hurt the little girl."

"I agree!" Jolie jumped right back in. "She could be a wolf wearing sheep clothing. I just don't trust her; there's just something evil about her. Her smiles are never genuine. They don't sink in; they are mere flashes. I hate people like that; they are dishonest."

Another woman carrying a large pot on her head joined the trio about halfway down the tiny footpath. All four women headed to the Crystal Caldera Creek. This Creek was where most of the town's women would converge nearly every morning to fetch fresh water for daily household use, wash dishes and perform manual laundry, or simply take a cold morning bath in the clean water.

The Crystal Caldera Creek sat in one of the town's most wooded parts. It was notorious among inhabitants for its noisy, clear water and slightly chilly feel. But most importantly, the Creek was famous for its human-size catfish that locals were forbidden to eat. Photographing the fish was also considered a spiritual offense and offenders lived in profound fear for the rest of their lives. Throw a few breadcrumbs in the Creek, and a band of catfish would instantly respond to the invite. If you were lucky, their queen, a gigantic silver-colored catfish sporting a white beaded tiara on her head, would also grace the occasion. The usual catfight that marred such meal periods was immediately halted whenever the queen made her grand royal appearance. Every catfish stood at attention, allowing her to enjoy a smooth sail to pieces of breadcrumbs floating in the Creek. The scuffle for food would only resume when the queen was done and gone.

Despite this mysteriousness of the Crystal Caldera Creek, locals would visit it in search of inner peace, self-cleansing, and a chance to catch brand new waves and rays in their lives. And the beautiful clear water of the Creek effectively served that purpose. It presented residents with a priceless opportunity to re-connect with nature and with themselves.

Women struggling with marital issues, among other social matters, would trek in pairs to the Creek, carrying large pots, dishpans, or buckets on their heads. They would make themselves comfortable under one of the gigantic trees bordering the river and hold hours of hearty conversations about those problems.

"Ladies, honestly, I have never liked Ida. She's got such an evil demeanor. Those large eyes of hers speak evil; she looks mean to me. There's just something.... something's not right about her," Sheri interjected.

"She looks like an emotionally abusive person; she could cause that poor baby severe mental injury."

"What? No. That's too harsh," Mimi said.

"Don't give me that look," Sheri said, pausing and taking a long, hard look at Mimi. "I just have a feeling that her heart is stained."

Then Jolie said, "Ah! Should that be the case, Hadjala will be so miserable about her decision. I can imagine her asking herself this question someday: 'why would my sister treat my child like a stranger?'"

As Jolie spoke, Sheri focused her gaze on Mimi after sensing a sudden change in Mimi's demeanor.

"You don't have to be mad, Mimi. We are all just worried about that poor, innocent baby," Sheri said, with a quizzical look that compelled Mimi to expand.

"She will regret this big time. I find this ridiculous. I don't understand why a mother that supposed to raise her children would decide to throw away her youngest baby. For me, this is first-degree emotional abuse and child neglect."

Of the four women, Mimi was the one who felt a personal connection to the topic under review. Her upbringing was-outsourced after her mother died while giving birth to her younger sister, Lumière. A member of her extended paternal family had agreed to take care of the kids but subjected them to unimaginable treatments.

"Look," Mimi began, commanding the attention of the crew, "No amount of money, gifts, or whatsoever, can pay our mothers for boring us. A mother's love is so invaluable. Look, just imagine how our lives would be without a mother to cheer our hearts. Our mothers guide our first steps. They open our eyes to the wonders of this world and support all of our caprices."

She paused for a breather. "Think about your development in your mom's womb to the day she bore you. That way, you will realize that, for her part, your mom has never failed in letting you know how important and precious you are to her life. Indeed, our mothers do love us naturally. Out of love, some mothers would go the extra mile to challenge their daughters to accomplish everything that they (mothers) didn't have a chance to accomplish during their young age."

She paused again, searched her compatriots' faces, inviting them to join in the conversation.

"That reminds me of a semi-lettered mother who has done everything possible to see her daughters climb higher on the educational ladder," Jolie responded. "This mother has worked as a house-help in different homes in their neighborhood only to see her daughters move from one level to the other, academically. And she always does something special for her girls whenever they come top of their classes. At one point, the youngest daughter dux the entire school, and this mother did laundry for people in the community to raise money to throw a party for her daughter."

"But then again, there are mothers like Hadjala who are so selfish that they even desire to live an extended life through their children. How can you love your daughter if you want to live her life and not yours? Believe it or not, Hadjala's forcing that little girl to do what she (Hadjala) wants. That little girl may never live a life of her own but that of Hadjala's. I feel so sad for Sadjio. Baaba should quash Hadjala's plans to interfere with Sadjio's life. Exposing this baby to potential mental, verbal, and physical abuse is a complete violation of her human rights."

"Are you trying to make this look like a modern-day slavery trade?" Sheri asked, laughing uncontrollably. "Since when you became a human rights advocate?"

"Since today," Mimi responded, launching the entire crew into a round of laughter.

"This is not funny, my people," Mimi continued, regaining everyone's attention. "I am assuming that Hadjala hates Sadjio. We all know very well how some mothers discriminate when it comes to the love they give to their children. They pick among their children which one to love the most and which one to bully at all times. In most families, the distinction is clear: the oldest child is the one who bears the brunt of insults, shouting, and (sometimes) humiliation, with the youngest, especially the last born, always showered with praises and boundless love. In some families, the line is so clearly drawn that you may wonder if that child belongs there biologically. But, in some families, you hardly notice such division; the love flowing from the mother to the children is pure. Interestingly, Sadjio's is a complete opposite of this."

"That reminds me of the story told of a girl who mercilessly beat her mom in the market simply because she could no longer condone her mother's aggravating attitude," Jolie said. Such was Jolie's usual way of ushering herself back into a conversation.

"The girl was the oldest of the children. She was responsible for making sure that the family survives. In the end, the girl had no other way out but to roam the streets as a woman with easy virtue to fulfill that assignment given her by her mother. Unfortunately, it was this same mother who would go out into her gossip corners to tell others in the neighborhood that her daughter was doing nothing in life but prostituting herself. Is that part of a mother's love?" Jolie asked, searching everyone's face for a response, but there was none.

"After their gossip sessions, the very people she told would use that to humiliate the girl in public, and then tell her that 'your mom told us.' When she felt she could no longer take it, she grabbed her mom and beat her."

The group then busted into another round of juicy laughter.

Then, Mimi came in, "My dear; there are some mothers who compete with their daughter over fashions, relationships, or men. Such mothers are sick but don't know it. But that's a different topic by itself. Hadjala has a major problem, and I don't think she understands the damage she's about to cause, to her relationship with her daughter, and by the time she realizes it, it might be too late to repair."

Despite the multitude of small talks ongoing across town, Hadjala stood firm by her decision. For her, it was a matter of must, a desperate situation that demanded a harsh response. All she wanted was to see Ida back and grounded in her home.

"I won't mind the small talks by small-minded people. They are all self-centered people," she would say to console herself.

Chapter ELEVEN

BAABA was due in town by that weekend, for his routine visit from PTP. The family was excited. Hadjala cooked his favorite meal – fufu, chased down with light, juicy pepper soup. Primary ingredients of the soup included: habanero pepper, onions, cilantro, some cabbage, baby eggplants, fresh tomatoes, assorted seasoning, dry and raw fish, lamb chops, crabs, shrimps, and chicken. The fufu, a cassava-based dough, was boiled, smashed, rolled up into smaller balls, and served with the hot pepper soup. It was such a fulfilling meal, and Baaba hardly had enough of it. Fufu was mostly eaten with bare, right hand. Eating with the left-hand was considered disrespectful.

On this day, in addition to this hearty meal, Hadjala made enough warm water for him to have a hot bath upon arrival. As expected, by 5:00 PM on that Friday, Baaba arrived from PTP, carrying loads of assorted produce harvested from his farm. He, too, was overjoyed on seeing his family but felt a little uneasy with the presence of Ida.

That night, Hadjala engaged Baaba on the subject.

"*M'boreen*, my sister needs our help. She is lonely in her home. She needs company—someone to joke, play with, someone to speak with."

Baaba listened as she spoke: "*M'boreen*, they are bullying her for not having a child of her own. But the pressing issue right now is this feeling of neglect, hopelessness, worthlessness, and isolation that she's nursing. I am just concerned that she might turn to suicide if we do nothing to help her. I think we should give Sadjio to her. That way, she will always have someone by her side."

That final portion of her speech caught Babaa's attention; he almost immediately pounced onto his feet from his reclining position.

"What? Hadjala, what has gotten into you?"

"Calm down. Let's take it easy," Hadjala responded.

"No. I am not calming down. We are talking about a human being here, my daughter. I need you to explain to me why I must agree with you on giving my youngest child to your sister—just because she's having issues in her home."

"What sense does that make to you? Besides, you know how much I adore being with all of my children. I love them extremely," Baaba said, foaming with bitterness. "I waited for nearly 20 years to have a child of my own, and now you want to snatch a critical portion of my happiness from me. Don't snatch my happiness and dash it to your sister."

"*M'boreen*, that's my sister," Hadjala insisted. "She will not treat our child anyhow. She will be a loving mom to our daughter."

It would take an entire week to finally convince Baaba to settle with the idea of letting Ida adopt Sadjio. Deep down, Baaba loved to have his family together. Yet, he obliged, refusing to hurt his wife's feelings. But he was never pleased with the arrangement. He felt that something about Ida wasn't right. He just couldn't figure it out at that very moment.

At barely three years old Sadjio was separated from her parents, her siblings. She would never cease to long for

Hadjala's tightly enclosed embrace, Saléma's gentle touch, Baaba's cheerful laughter when he played with them, and Jamaal's smile when he returned from school.

ON THE MORNING of their departure, Hadjala dressed Sadjio up in a navy-blue dress with two large pockets on both hips and a little belt making the round, just above her hips. Sadjio's clothes were piled in a simple, white plastic envelope. Her right hand cuddled a brown teddy bear, her sleeping buddy.

She looked terrified, but Hadjala refused to acknowledge her (Sadjio's) facial expression.

"Imran's home is yours until he throws you out," Hadjala reminded Ida. "Go back and continue to be the wife you are. Wandering off is not an option. Divorce is certainly not going to happen from our end. Let's leave that to Imran; if he's serious, he will initiate the process. Until then, you are and will remain his wife. Take Sadjio and go back home."

For Hadjala, gifting her daughter to Ida would have distracted her from everything else that was going on as it related to her fruitless trials to bring forth a child. Throughout the last years, Ida had endured much heartache and stigmatism because, as a woman, she was viewed as a child bearer. The fact that she *had* to produce a child to be valued in her marital home, especially by her in-laws, which she couldn't accomplish as early as expected, made her suffer in silence.

Six months after her return, Ida introduced Sadjio to doing the dishes as a taste of manual household chores.

"This will be your job for now. And don't always expect a reminder from me. Because if I do, it won't be so gentle. Don't expect praise from me either. Do you hear me?"

"Yes," said little Sadjio, looking very troubled. She drew her lips tightly together and won't talk. Suddenly, her heart gave one hard punch.

The look on Ida's face was everything but friendly. Watching a four-year-old struggle to carry a dishpan was the funniest thing ever, for Ida.

At age seven, Sadjio had effectively assumed the post of *a chief maid* in the home: regularly fetching water for household use, taking out the garbage, washing the dishes, and keeping their home tidy and organized, always.

At age eight, her tasks doubled. She was now doing severe chores instead of going to school. While most of her peers attended St. Michaels' Elementary School, Sadjio fetched water, cleaned up, and cooked plain rice and rice porridge as directed by Ida.

She was often sent off to fetch water from the Blue Lake, which was a 20-minute walk from home. The part of the Lake where she lived with her aunt had reduced currents and flowed at a lesser pace. The cold breeze combing through tree leaves made the Lake an exceedingly cozy place to be for most people, except for Sadjio.

By sunrise each morning, this tiny little girl totting a 15-pound pot of water would trek for 20 minutes to get back home before the sun entirely took over the sky. Walking nearly 40 minutes, to and from, per roundtrip, this dark-skinned girl with large brown eyes and bouncy black hair would make multiple rounds to the Blue Lake before the day came to a final close. Her day began as early as 6:00 AM and ended as late as 11:00 PM. She suffered the brunt of all the chores as well as other hard and manual labor (at most times).

Exhausted from continuous chores, Sadjio would cry, not screaming tantrums because if she did, she would be whipped.

Instead, she unleashed quiet, deep sobs whenever she took the dishes to the backyard to wash, making sure that she wasn't overheard. She would sob softly and continuously until she was done with the dishes.

Without a friend to play with or talk to, or an adult to confide in, crying was the only way she discovered her inner peace. Those incoherent crying moments were self-cleansing moments, a chance for her to air out deeply buried agony; they were priceless opportunities to offload the pain in her heart. Silent sobs were Sadjio's natural painkillers for years.

At age nine, her life was a living hell. Ida applied a range of torture techniques against Sadjio: beatings, starvation, and consuming fermented leftovers. It was a relentless around-the-clock campaign of terror waged against this minor. She was starved, growled at, like a dog, whipped with electric cords, belt knob, high heels, wooden spoons, and rattans. She was forbidden to cry or make noise while being tortured. Each day, she received two merciless floggings by sundown.

When it came to down to torturing Sadjio, Ida's energy was remarkable. She was relentless, had an inexhaustible supply of hatred, used daily, yet burning fiercely year after year. She had a designated torture spot in town—the infamous Ants' Hill. Here, she had the pleasure of exposing Sadjio's bare body to fire ants' stings.

The Ants' Hill sat along the bushy footpath that led from the heart of the town to the Blue Lake. It was a vast, brownish hill renowned for being a constant hub of fire ants. It had been in existence since the founding of Lanaya Township. The Ants' Hill, as most residents referred to it, was always avoided by locals in fear of the fire ants that inhabited it. They were terrified by the rage of the ants. And so, they did everything possible to avoid any encounter with a colony of ants residing in this Hill.

This was one of Ida's favorite places in town since the arrival of Sadjio. She visited the Hill every Friday morning to perform a heartfelt ritual: *feeding Sadjio to fire ants.*

She would wake Sadjio up as early as 5:00 AM and have her take the dishes outside to wash while she (Ida) remained in bed for another hour. By 6:00 AM, she would get up and begin pulling the young lad by her hair until they got to the Ants' Hill.

"Climb up and sit down! I will deal with you if you dare touch one of those ants. Don't you dare remove them from your body! Am I clear?" she would say, flashing a sinister smile. "I am feeding you to them. Sit still and let them enjoy their breakfast."

Atop the Hill, a terrified Sadjio would do as instructed, provoking a colony of ants into fighting back. The ants aggressively swarmed her body, stinging her repeatedly. She sustained countless firing stings her tiny body riddled with hundreds of red bites.

Watching an army of ants climb all over Sadjio and bite her everywhere tickled Ida to no limits. She would discharge a burst of loud laughter that would suddenly cease, again, rumbling her forehead.

"Don't you dare make a sound," she would say, reasserting herself.

"She's insane. Her childlessness has made her crazy," angry passersby would murmur.

They would watch in disgust but never dared to question or interfere with Ida's activities. The iceberg tip of Ida's hate was visible to locals of the area, but everyone chose to ignore it. Neighbors and friends were powerless. They occasionally showed disapproval but were very afraid of Ida's rage and ability to keep speech from them for protracted periods. Ida was very skilled at excluding folks that were too bold to show their disgust, leaving Sadjio isolated. Ida wielded absolute power and control.

Sadjio hugged herself convulsively, heartsore. She was forbidden to cry or make any noise from the ants' bites. She was equally forbidden to defend herself from the ants' attack. She had only one right, and that was the right to sit still for an hour or more, fighting back her tears. And by the time she was out of there, her entire body (face, hands, etc.) were inundated with groups of swollen red spots that developed blisters on the top. For up to a week, she would deal with painful, yet, very itchy ants' stings.

Sadjio was also compelled to eat every disgusting, fermented meal, especially plain brown rice.

"I hate to see food go to waste," Ida would say, brandishing electric wires.

Without saying a word, Sadjio would bury her face in the ceramic bowl and eat every grain in there. It didn't matter whether she threw up while eating the fermented meal. The goal was to ensure that by the end of the encounter, every drop would have made it into Sadjio's tiny belly somehow, even if they didn't stay in there. To top it off, she had very minimal access to food, which made her a notorious beggar in the area. She would sneak into neighbors' homes to beg for food. She ran errands for neighbors in exchange for a snack to munch. She was always smelly, wore filthy clothes; she barely had clothes to cover her body. Whenever she fell sick, it was the neighbors taking her to a home-based quack doctor next door for treatment. And, whenever Ida decided to braid corn-rows on Sadjio's head, she yanked out her hair with the brush, braiding tight braids that damaged her scalp, destroyed her edges.

With Sadjio, Ida was rough, filled with eternal, unbending rage, verging on violence. It was the reinvention of the fairy tales, Cinderella, or Snow White, either of which paints an evil picture of step-parents, foster parents, and in this con-text, guardians. Ida was violent, grabbing Sadjio by the hair and slapping her face, banging her head against concrete walls. She even instigated the beating and mistreatment of Sadjio by other community dwellers. She inflicted pain, meted out severe punishment, or assign challenging tasks to Sadjio. And did it quite cleverly—pretending to love Sadjio whenever there was a guest present. Sadjio was safe until they were alone. Ida did her worst in silence, treating Sadjio with much cruelty.

She was never interested or willing to be as generous and loving as Hadjala had been. She put on her powerful preten-tious act of love while in Djinnadou. And it worked, she se-cured Hadjala's trust. Once back in Lanaya with Sadjio, she cared less, not even a drop of empathy for Hadjala.

Such was Sadjio's life until one morning when a strange occurrence ceased the spotlight from her, at least for a moment.

UNKNOWN men stomped their thatch-roofed home with an eviction notice. That morning, Ida was glued to her hand-crafted rice straw mattress, locally know as *qui m' a piqué*. She rolled painfully from end-to-end. She had been nursing a ter-rible headache, accompanied by sharp ear and eye pain, and toothaches for weeks. To many, the gods were making her taste

114

the fruits of her labor. They laughed, guessed, and gossiped about her instead of empathizing with her.

Visibly paralyzed by her condition, Ida remained in bed until 7:00 AM that morning when she and the rest of the family, including Sadjio, were rudely awakened by violent knocks on the front gate of their two-level home. A gang of scruffy-bearded men had assembled there, ready to kick them out of the house they had inhabited for years.

Claiming to have been legally empowered by the Chief Council, these red-eyed men, charged with violence, would leave no stone unturned in enforcing an eviction order approved by the land's Supreme Leader.

Every tenant of the building had only a couple of hours left of their tenancy. The men were adamant, vehemently quashing any suggestion for negotiation put forth by tenants.

"Move! Or be removed!" was their mission on that wet Saturday morning.

From the onset, Ida had no idea what this was all about.

"They are kicking us out!" screamed a first-floor neighbor.

"But why?" inquired Ida.

"Biggie is no longer in charge of the building. It now has a new lessor. The money we paid to Biggie has gone in vain. What kind of trouble is this?" retorted another neighbor in distress.

It was now clear that Biggie, the man with whom the families had entered a new 12-month lease agreement and had made a full cash payment of rent for lease-year 1986, had been booted out of power through legal means. The once bubbly residence was suddenly a sad, distressed house.

Standing tall in the heart of Lanaya's city center, the McCarthy Residence-In building was now under the command of a new leaseholder. The building was adored by its inhabitants, predominantly merchants, because of its prime location, very ideal for business transactions. Some tenants had been dwelling there for more than 20 years. They had skillfully transformed the building's basement into retail stores, beauty parlors, boutiques, phone booths, and restaurants.

Both Biggie and the new lessor of the property were Ajarmsville's nationals residing and running large businesses in central Lanaya.

"It turns out that Biggie and the new lessor had been fighting in court for years," LeaYah, a next-door neighbor, whispered.

"Wow! And we knew nothing about this?" Ida inquired, but silently.

"Yup! This battle had been going on for the last two years, unknown to us, the tenants. Now, it is all over. The Council found Biggie's lease agreement to be a bogus one. He's currently occupying a cell at Lanaya's Central Prison," added Sha'Ronda.

Overwhelmed by what was unfolding, Ida fished in her purse for her 3310 Nokia phone; she needed to call for support. Her friend, Cali, a Chocolate City resident, was the first to respond, then came her best friend, Lolita. By then, the 1st floor had been cleared by those ruthless men. They trespassed and invaded tenants' privacy under cover of a writ. They entered tenants' apartments, dispersed tenants' personal belongings into the streets and nearby alleys, damaging scores of tenants' properties. Not even the stores, boutiques, beauty parlors, and phone booths located in the basement were spared during that eviction exercise. These men cared less; they even assaulted tenants who stood their grounds, saying they were unlawfully evicted because no prior notice served to this effect. Most interestingly, the abrupt eviction happened when the majority of the tenants had left the country on various business trips across the Sub-Sahara—Gold Coast, Ajarmsville, and Sankarala. Even Imran was out of town when this happened. But their absence was insufficient to stop those brutes from kicking them out of the building. They insensitively did self-help eviction: locking those tenants out by changing the locks on their doors.

This scene further intimidated Ida and the rest of the families. Little Sadjio was horrified; she was visibly trembling.

Generally, the entire family felt battered by this intentional infliction of emotional distress.

Convinced that the family wouldn't be spared the disgrace, Cali made a quick trip down Waterside, where she grabbed a couple of *"Must-Go"* bags and dashed right back to the house. Meanwhile, Ida made several fruitless attempts at striking a deal with the guys, painfully pleading to be allowed at least a two-week grace period for her family to find another place to move in.

"Our family head is out of town. Please have mercy. We will be homeless if you insist on throwing us out today," she cried, but no one care.

Lolita and Cali packed everything in the house in five *"Must-Go"* bags, four large suitcases, and other smaller containers. The *qui m' a piqué* mattress had been rolled up and neatly tied into separate knots. The wooden bedframe was dismantled and piled up in one corner. While this was going on, Ida's corner of the house had been visited more than ten times by the men, itching to throw her belongings out in the streets and have the lock on her door changed.

"Surprised?" Cali asked, kicking off chitchat with Ida, but Ida only shook her head.

"Well, I'm not. It is only in Pepper Coast that you can see lessors violating the rights of lessees with impunity. Sadly, the very law that should have protected you and co-lessees against such abuse is the same law being used by the lessor to his advantage. This, too, is Pepper Coast," Cali added, searching Ida's face for a reaction. But there was none. The entire event had rocked Ida's world beyond measure. All she did was stare. Soon, arrangements were made to have her properties transferred to Cali's house in Chocolate City. It was decided that Ida and Sadjio would move in (temporarily) with some relatives across the street while waiting for Imran's return. But that was only wishful thinking.

Neighbors and relatives refused to accept Ida in their homes; they blatantly communicated their disgust for her. Unfortunately, Sadjio had to suffer along with her. Both Cali and Lolita had guests over and so couldn't take them in. Meanwhile, the rest of the family had moved in with Imran's family, leaving the two of them to roam the area in search of a place to call home. They hopped from one relative's outdoor kitchen to the other, in search of a space to sleep. It was a stern struggle that lasted two weeks.

UPON HIS RETURN, Imran managed to retrieve $375 of his $900 paid to the lessor as rent for that year. Not every tenant was this fortunate. No one received any reimbursement though the lease agreement was grossly breached.

It turned out that that Saturday eviction was only the tip of the iceberg.

Two months later, Imran's truck driving trade suffered a huge fiscal blow, eventually shutting down his business. And being that he wasn't the type that would return to the soil in the event of hardship, Imran resorted to relocating his family.

He hated farming, so moving his family to the nation's leading city was a positive step in his search for greener pastures. He organized and held multiple yard sales to raise enough money to transport them to Ducor.

Once settled in Jacob's Town, a key suburb of Ducor, Imran kicked off an intense word-of-mouth campaign for a driver position. He spent most of his days visiting the various homes of well-off Dioula families in search of an employment opportunity, eventually landing a driving job with Mr. Corneh, earning meagerly, and barely sustaining his family.

All along, Ida's search for a child lingered, as was Sadjio's agony. Their new neighbors held pockets of gossip sessions on Ida's maltreatment of her little niece. Like their neighborhood back in Lanaya, the word in Jacob's Town had it that she was insane, judging from soaring brutalities meted out to Sadjio.

In addition to food, Sadjio was starved of love and affection as a child. It felt like Ida was repaying what she had endured at the hands of her husband and her in-laws. Her insatiable fury was mentally exhausting; she showed no mercy.

Chapter TWELVE

APRIL 8, 1987, marked Ida's 4th wedding anniversary. She still didn't have a child of her own. At this point, everyone concluded that she was unfit to be a mother.

"The gods are angry at her," neighbors said of her at gossip roundtables.

"She's a curse. Growing up, we are often reminded that in the hereafter, we *will* be held accountable for the sins we commit today. But in Ida's life the case is different: the sins she's committing are very impatient. They would rather be repaid right here," one neighbor said. "See how she treats that little girl. No wonder she's barren."

Back in Djinnadou, Hadjala's emotional hunger for Sadjio was rapidly compounding. She felt haunted by guilt. "I miss my baby," she would say. But she dare not let neighbors, and even Baaba, in on her emotional distress.

It was her little secret told only to her pillow at bedtime. She drenched her bed with tears every night. Hadjala knew better than to appear weak in the eyes of the people who denounced her action in the very beginning. She buried her tears under pillow every morning and pretended all was well in her world.

One night as she laid in her makeshift bamboo bed, she felt a strange feeling rapidly tearing through her soul; it was a brainwave about Sadjio starting school. That night, she dreamt of her daughter wearing a plain white robe with a color pad, a pack of color pencils, and two markers in her left hand. There was something else in her right hand, but Hadjala could barely identify it.

In the dream, Sadjio said to her, "*Teeyah*, I have learned to write my name.

Do you want to see it? Wait…... I will show you."

Puzzled by what she had been told, Hadjala asked, "But, Sadjio, how can that be possible? You are yet to start school."

Sadjio responded, "I have been practicing all along. I love school. I want to wear a pair of uniforms, carry a backpack and a lunch bag. I want to be dropped off at school and be picked up after school by my mom. But since it's taking you so long to understand this aspect of me, I decided to get a step ahead – I am homeschooling myself."

Then suddenly, Sadjio began to cry. Hadjala attempted at calming and cheering her up to no avail. She cried so hard that Hadjala felt the need to jump in. Both mother and child wept bitterly.

That morning, Hadjala woke up with puffy eyes and quaking feel.

She proceeded to N' vakarmoh, a highly respected religious leader in the area, and explained her dream:

"I don't see any harm in this dream. The tears of your daughter are good. You don't need to offer any sacrifices or perform any rituals. Just check on your daughter and see if she's in school. And if she's not, make sure she is," advised N' vakarmoh.

That night, Hadjala penned a handwritten letter to Ida:

Hello Ida,

I hope this letter will find you and Sadjio doing great. For us, there's no bad news here. We are all doing fine. If you haven't already done so, Sadjio needs to be in school. Please do not keep her at home instead of being in school at this age. She was wondrously made and is destined for greatness. Keeping her out of school will be such a devastating roadblock to her reaching her dreams. I will support you financially; just try to get her in school as soon as possible. I will be visiting you to check on her progress in school.

Sincerely,
Hadjala, Your Sister

Two weeks later, Hadjala got a response from Ida:

Hadjala,

Sadjio is already in school. But things have been difficult here. Imran's driving job can merely feed us. So, if you can send some money to help me with Sadjio's schooling, that will be awesome. If not, she risks being kicked out of school due to tuition nonpayment. Please send some money now.

Thanks,
Ida

The thought of Sadjio starting school had Hadjala blushing; it cheered her heart. It was an indescribable feeling.

As a semi-literate mother, Hadjala never took the education of her children, especially her girls, for granted. She always hoped and prayed for her daughters to be academically enlightened, no matter what. She was a staunch believer that educated women and girls could educate entire generations. Besides, Hadjala's love for her children was beautifully irrational. Granted, she dispatched Sadjio to go live with Ida. But that decision was rooted in good faith.

And with Sadjio now lingering on her mind, Hadjala did everything to remain actively involved in her little girl's life. She frequented Djinnadou's truck parking station on the first Thursday of each month to dispatch money and goodies to Ida for Sadjio's upkeep.

"Hey, Hadjala! What brings you here again?

Oh, wait....is today Thursday?" inquired Maurice, a prominent bus driver along the Djinnadou – Ducor corridor.

"Of course, it is" retorted Hadjala, who had come to ship some money and provisions to Ida.

"Ah! I see why you are here this early, trying to get those on the first bus, right?" Maurice further inquired, pointing at the bundle of provisions Hadjala held.

"You are so right, Maurice. I have saved up some money for Ida to use for Sadjio's needs. Sadjio has started going to school, and that entails lots of expenses. I feel compelled to contribute," she explained, her face beaming with smiles.

OF COURSE, the realities on the ground in Ducor were far from what Hadjala was being told. Distressed by her marital woes, Ida couldn't control herself from assaulting Sadjio. She became excessively abusive. If she had no reason to, she would invent one. Whether it was deliberately hiding something and asking Sadjio to find it or claiming that Sadjio had authored abominable things—Ida had a way of justifying her assaults.

Every money or provision sent by Hadjala in support of Sadjio's schooling never got to her. Ida sold the items and spent the money on her own needs. Sadjio was never going to be in school, at least not anytime soon.

Reports of Ida's maltreatment of Sadjio would eventually reach Hadjala. But she shrugged it off as mere gossip.

"I refuse to heed gossips. Gossips are peace spoilers, home-wreckers, hatemongers, and relationship breakers. They want to create problems between my blood sister and me. I won't allow it. Besides, I don't think Ida is capable of mistreating my child," she would say, reassuring herself that Sadjio was in good hands.

Ida also knew how to cover her tracks. When Hadjala finally visited the family in Ducor, she barely noticed any signs of abuse. Ida skillfully dressed Sadjio to conceal bruises, lacerations, and swellings. She was also coached against doing or saying anything that would make Hadjala suspicious.

On one occasion, Ida nearly squeezed the life out of Sadjio on claims that she heard Sadjio telling her mom that she missed home and wanted to leave with her. Hadjala had come over on her second visit but was rushed out by Ida, who was afraid that Hadjala might notice the cuts on Sadjio's belly, which were concealed under a long dark-brown dress.

ONE DAY, she asked Sadjio to get a kitchen knife from the room. Sadjio fruitlessly searched everywhere—among the dishes, where the blade was typically kept. After an unproductive search, she gave up. Facing Ida's wrath at this point was the only way out. Besides, Sadjio by then was nothing less than a robot. She desensitized herself to being hit. But inside, she was very defiant.

Of course, she would have never found the knife; Ida had concealed it into a bag hanging behind the doorframe of her bedroom. That day's beating was characterized by repeat head slamming against the concrete wall of the room, resulting in Sadjio losing a new tooth. Scars from that encounter remained indelibly etched on Sadjio's right thigh.

A day later, Ida claimed she heard Sadjio telling her peers in the backyard that when she grows up, she would love to go to school and have children. That, for Ida, was abominable and a justifiable cause to further terrorize her little niece.

Sadjio was again whipped for hours, with Ida taking intermittent breaks. She bled profusely from her mouth; a new tooth was broken, all thanks to Ida for banging her (Sadjio's) head against the concrete wall. Sadjio sustained multiple lacerations on her upper and lower lips. Her entire head and neck were swollen with bruises and cuts all over her body.

This was enough to stir up anger among neighbors, who ganged up against Ida. "Are you trying to kill this girl?" inquired the next-door neighbor.

"You are incapable of bearing a child of your own. So, killing someone else' really means nothing......., right?" came a follow-up question from another neighbor.

Ida immediately interjected, "this is my family matter, not anyone's business."

Usually, this would work, shutting down everyone and keeping them in their place. But on this day, the reactions she received were shocking. The exchanges between Ida and neighbors drew in a dozen others who soon became active participants in the brawl.

"Let's take her to a police depot," a member of the crowd suggested.

"No, this is no police matter. Ida is a devil and must be treated as such; devils are flogged," added another.

"So, why are we waiting? Why not beat the devil out of her?" another inquired while advancing towards Ida. Sensing the fury in the eyes of her neighbors, Ida retreated to her room and shut the door behind her.

IN SEPTEMBER 1988, Ida was finally blessed with a baby girl—the long-awaited miracle child had finally arrived. It's interesting how Ida never got a convincing response as to why every gynecologist, traditional herbalist, believed she had zero chance of having a child of her own. She dreaded hearing that conception was impossible for her. It broke her heart, shattered ALL her dreams. She yearned to experience motherhood, but always received a brutal blow whenever she saw a GYN or herbalist.

On September 27, 1988, Ida went on to defy the odds and, she did so big time. She had a cute baby girl, entirely naturally. When Ida found out that conceiving a baby would be highly unlikely for her, she was destroyed. When she eventually fell pregnant, she thought it was a miracle. She had no idea she would go on to have the cutest baby girl ever.

Of course, this was an excruciatingly painful experience for Ida. She grew impatient and eventually stopped praying for a change in her condition. Her patience ran out, and her attitude changed for the worse. She spent her night entertaining such thoughts:

"Why is this happening to me? Am I not good enough?" The birth of baby Mabatou also birthed additional responsibilities for Sadjio. Washing diapers was an added task. Ida would wake Sadjio up as early as 5:00 AM to go wash diapers, sometimes under raining torrents, while she marinated in bed with her newborn.

On one morning, Sadjio was awakened with whips for misplacing her underwear. She was sent into untrimmed, thick bushes in the back of the house to search for the missing panties. Ida never allowed Sadjio to take a shower in the indoor bathroom–she had to do so outside in the thick bush behind the house. Ida cared less if the girl got bitten by a snake or so.

It was raining heavily that morning. Everyone was in-doors except for this 10-year-old who had to find a missing underwear or never return indoors. But that undergarment was never going to be recovered, anyway. It had been washed away by a torrential downpour the night before.

"*Teeyah, Teeyah nangô*" Sadjio cried in her native Dioula dialect, calling on her mother to come and get her.

As fate would have it, Hadjala had arrived in Ducor the night before but slept at her aunt's house in Logantown. Early that morning, she decided to stop by Ida's, to see Sadjio before proceeding with the business aspect of her trip. She had packed a plastic bag of toys and clothing for Sadjio, and another for Ida's baby girl.

As Sadjio roamed through the bush, she yearned for so-lace, love, and affection.

Meanwhile, Hadjala had been dropped off by a yellow taxicab on the main road and had walked into the yard, but instantly became speechless and motionless on seeing Sadjio.

Dressed in a three-piece wax print with a spare garb wrap-ping around her hips and enormous pink and white art décor earrings, Hadjala stood and watched her daughter with cuts all over her face, swollen eyes, bloody nose, and mouth. She also noticed that Sadjio was busy searching for something in the bush under the torrential rain accompanied by thunderstorms and lightning.

After searching in vain, Sadjio decided to return to the house and face another round of flogging. As she turned, her eyes locked in with those of her mom. But Hadjala was still very motionless. With a red, stripy umbrella in one hand and two heavily stuffed plastic bags in the other, Hadjala stood, tears racing down her cheeks.

"*Teeyah! Teeyah!*" Sadjio screamed, running towards her mom.

But Hadjala could barely hear a thing. Saijo's voice was completely hoarse.

Then a voice immediately began calling Ida to alert her of the situation outside.

"Ida! Ida!"

"Yes...!"

"Check outside," the voice instructed. Ida looked through her bedroom window and saw Sadjio deeply buried in her mother's bosom.

"Sadjio, is this you? Let's go," Hadjala said, grabbing her daughter's hands and off they went. She didn't even bother to enter the house; she didn't also want to see Ida.

It would take Ida and Imran two days to show up for a meeting with Hadjala. "Sadjio was being punished for mis-placing a brand-new pantie," said Imran. But Hadjala had no interest in dialoguing with her child's abusers. She said, "I've had enough. What I saw was enough. Let's put a full stop to this madness."

"I now have my child. Thank you. But I've forgiven you."

This was in late 1989. After Hadjala completed her trans-actions, the mother and daughter returned to Djinnadou to the rest of the family where they lived.

Barely after three months, rebels, led by a famous brigand known to locals only as C.T. and his bloodthirsty thugs, launched an assault on Pepper Coast. The attack forced thousands into exile, including Sadjio's little family. For 14 years, their beloved homeland was engulfed in one of Sub-Sahara's bloodiest civil wars.

Chapter THIRTEEN

PEPPER COAST was Sadjio's native land. It was built as a haven for free *jhöns* who had secured their freedom and had been dispatched to the Sub-Sahara from the Northern Cape through the intervention of several powerful traditional rulers. They settled in Pepper Coast, declared themselves *Hôrô*, and immediately created a settler-colonial state that maintained a tenuous relationship with the larger indigenous population. The new government mirrored that of their slave masters in the North. It was centralized, and its services did not extend to the country's interior where the indigenous, the majority, resided.

The *Hôrô* monopolized politics and the economy while restricting the voting rights of the indigenous population. They dominated all sectors of the country for a century and a half when the government was overthrown by members of the *fasso* tribe, the original inhabitants of Pepper Coast.

Once in power, the *fasso* ethnic group began expanding the gap between and among the people by placing only members of their kin in critical positions of government and the security forces. Moreover, the founding Constitution was designed to suit the settler population's needs, with little consideration for and involvement of the indigenous people. In the early days, for instance, land and property rights of the larger indigenous population were placed under a system of customary governance. In contrast, the land under statutory governance was owned by settlers. And for a member of the *fasso* ethnic group to own land under the statutory regime and get a deed, he/she needed to be 'civilized' enough according to the hinterland regulations of 1905/1949 and the aborigine law of 1956.

The country's urban-based policies of successive administrations would perpetuate marginalization. Political power would remain concentrated in Ducor, the capital, and mainly in the Presidency. Most infrastructure and essential services were concentrated in Ducor and a few other cities. The marginalization of the youth and women and the mismanagement of national resources were widespread—contributing to stark inequalities in distributing benefits. As a result, the over-concentration of power bred corruption, restricted access to the decision-making process, and limited the space for civil society participation in governance processes.

The consequence was a high level of resentment toward the ruling *Hôrôs*. This raised ethnic tension and stirred antagonism between the politically and militarily dominant *fasso* tribe and other ethnic groups. The situation became violent after an abortive coup birthed a group of warriors on a mission to overthrow the *fasso* government regardless. This shockingly exposed how deeply wounded Sadjio's motherland had been politically, socially, and culturally. Soon, a small band of rebels, calling themselves the *Jarsar*, led by C.T., invaded Pepper Coast, fighting a series of tribal wars that ravaged the country beyond imagination.

The country would experience one of the Sub-Sahara's bloodiest tribal wars ensued, claiming the lives of more than thousands and dispatching a million others to refugee camps in neighboring countries. Sadjio's family fled the country into neighboring Ivory Coast, where a completely new life awaited them.

FOR NEARLY THREE decades, the land bled profusely and was inhabitable. The gods of the earth were enraged by the ongoing tribal cleansing that marred the war. The land was cursed; every crop, cattle, and source of water was destroyed. As though that wasn't enough, the gods withheld the rains throughout this period, unleashing severe famine and drought on the land. But none of that was enough to deter some tribal rulers who were endowed with economic, social, and political means to fuel the conflict. Such rulers favored the escalation of the war at any given opportunity as a way to continue business-as-usual for self-enrichment by abusing resources through illegal extraction and export of Pepper Coast's natural resources, particularly timber, rubber, diamonds, and gold. Both tribal warlords and government warriors exploited the country's natural resources to their advantage.

Warlords and their associates and even external chiefs from neighboring lands were heavily reliant on their control over valuable resources to fund arms purchases and patronage. To pay their war-related expenses, warlords, government troops, and their foreign allies exploited the country's natural resources. Simultaneously, frontline warriors, due to their ability to loot, conceal, and sell these resources, further exploited Pepper Coast's diamonds and gold.

As the war raged, several factional groups formed along tribal lines to protect themselves against their real and perceived enemies. Among them was ULIMO, which emerged

in 1991. The group eventually split into two separate militias—ULIMO-K, a Dioula-based faction, and ULIMO-J, a
Guéré-based rebel group—due to internal power struggles. In
late 1993, the PPC surfaced. Its' mission was to defend and
protect members of the Guéré ethnic group. In that same year,
the LDF popped up with the sole mission to preserve their
Loma kin and villages from attack and looting bands of ethnic
Dioula fighters.

C.T.'s *Jarsar* initiated the war when it took up arms
against the government of ruler Pitte and soon became a
powerful rebel group. Soon, internal wrangling kicked in and
birthed a breakaway faction — the Independent *Jarsar*, which
equally became a significant force in the early stages of the war,
controlling several strategic points within the nation's capital,
Ducor. This new group operated under the command of warlord Yommie. Both factions played vital roles in the country's
first tribal war that spanned eight years (1989 – 1997).

Chapter FOURTEEN

AND WHILE AN UNSPECIFIC number of tribal women were themselves active perpetrators of violence, during the country's protracted war, a relatively significant number of them dared to stand face-to-face with factional leaders for the cause of peace. This group of peace-brokering women's sole mission was to have peace, security, and stability restored to their homeland.

During the war, some women were preyed upon and victimized in every unimaginable way. They were forced to participate in the conflict right from its onset. The truth is, most citizens of Pepper Coast, *especially the women*, fell into this category of victims.

At a certain point during the heat of the war, when it was extraordinarily unsafe or dangerous for men to be seen in public, these wives, mothers, and sisters had to risk their lives and virtues for the survival of their families. And as victims of endemic sexual violence, some were mutilated with guns and other weapons during the war, exposing them to diseases, including *Sida*.

In most cases, the brutality with which these inhumane acts were carried out led to complete damage to some women's reproductive organs. After the war, such women were abandoned by their husbands because they could no longer have a child. Others were excluded from the public scene because they had a fistula, making the issue of reintegration/acceptability by their communities of origin a challenging experience. This also made their condition's psychological effect even more draining; it further subjected them to secondary victimization.

Meanwhile, some women survived the war by allowing themselves to be recruited by fighting forces, serve as sex-slaves, cooks, or wives-in-captivity. For these women, they did so for survival. After the war, this category of women continued to face discrimination by their kinsfolk because they had intimate or other relationships with fighting forces.

They found themselves shouldering compounding blames by their fellow women and men for aiding and abetting atrocities perpetrated against their communities, by siding with the fighters. In some extreme cases, such women were denied access to their communities of origin.

It got even more complicated for those women who 'volunteered' to join the fighting forces during the second conflict (1999 – 2003) to either protect themselves from sexual violence or to avenge an abuse or the death of family members.

Women in rebel militias played numerous roles; some served as fighters and wives of soldiers, while others served as recruiters and spies. Others were manipulated or forced into various functions, such as forced sexual slavery and domestic servants for fighting groups.

However, for material gain, women who had the power, political influence, or financial backing supported military activities at various points during the conflict. For the protection of particular interests, during the first (1989 – 1997) and second conflicts (1999 – 2003), some voluntarily and openly supported the armed rebellion, and others did so more latently. Key among women's multiple roles during the early stages of the war was to facilitate warlord C.T.'s contacts with influential individuals in the Sub-Sahara who could support his war ambition.

Jarsar's thirst for blood was financially nurtured by a group of influential women that believed in C.T.'s cause. Dissatisfied with Pitte's autocratic rule, this group of women played significant roles in seeing an end to his tyrannical rule. However, they would abandon C.T. and his thugs after realizing, especially after Pitte's gruesome murder in September 1990, that C.T. was harboring an agenda that was against the original purpose of the struggle.

IN JUNE 2003, a peace deal aimed at putting an immediate end to hostilities in Pepper Coast was signed in Gold Coast, setting the stage for the return of peace to the war-torn country. This compromise, dubbed as 'negative peace,' meaning the return of relative calm to the nation through a cease-fire deal, despite serious psychological, ideological, economic, and political effects that lingered, was necessary at the time.

Chapter FIFTEEN

IT WAS BARELY six months after the signing of the peace deal in August 2003, when Sadjio arrived in Ducor, the capital city of Pepper Coast, accompanied by Hadjala. This Accord led to the restoration of relative peace to Pepper Coast after nearly three decades of bloody tribal war.

She had previously spent a year in Ducor in the late 1990s. By then, the war was raging, and she had to flee the country again.

However, when she returned in February 2004, notwithstanding the tenuous environment of peace that obtained at the time, she was deeply motivated to stay, remain steadfast and contribute in whatever way she could to the restoration of peace to Pepper Coast.

As a country just emerging from years of brutal civil conflict, life in this post-war context was not easy. It was especially challenging for the survivors who had endured unimaginable brutalities during the battle.

Sadjio's return was decided during a peace deal brokered between Hadjala and Ida.

Ida had sought forgiveness and promised to be a changed person, especially since she was now a mother and was fully abreast of the ordeals of childbearing and childrearing. Thus, Hadjala accompanied Sadjio to Ducor.

They left Man, the western capital of Ivory Coast, on a cold, breezy Monday morning but never made it to Ducor until Friday afternoon of that week.

The roads were deplorable, and the vehicle conveying them was a hazardous, dilapidated motor. It broke down at nearly every mile. Besides, it was the peak of the rainy season, and driving through the super muddy, sticky, and sometimes slippery roads were a nightmare for motorists and passengers.

Sadjio, Hadjala, and other passengers spent hours pushing their car through the mud to access Ducor. They couldn't wait for this one-day journey (under normal circumstances) turned five-day nightmare in the dirt, to be over.

Upon arrival in Ducor, Hadjala officially handed Sadjio to Ida and Imran. Among their luggage was an enormous bag of textbooks Sadjio had compiled from her secondary school in the Gold Coast and brought along.

Textbook fees were infused into the tuition, and the books were given to students as theirs to keep. And, because Pepper Coast was freshly emerging from war with limited infrastructure, Sadjio thought why not take her books along and share with local students. Fifty percent of the book was donated to needy students while the other fifty percent was sold to facilitate Hadjala's return to Ivory Coast.

Thirty-five United Stated dollars was generated from the book sale and was used to pay Hadjala's way back home. She left the country a week later to join the rest of the family in Man, western Ivory Coast, their new home.

Few months after Hadjala's departure, Sadjio landed a job at a bi-weekly newspaper, *Le Quotidien* newspaper, making barely $30 per month. She also had a 3310 Nokia given to her by the media agency for work-related purposes only.

Sadjio made it a duty to focus her reportage on the various internally displaced camps, with a keen focus on documenting and telling the stories of women war survivors. At the time, she as a young and aspiring female journalist, affiliated with a tiny newspaper company that published and circulated only in Ducor.

She felt the urge to tell, sell, and share the stories of these women because she had had her share of brutal experiences during the war.

It was a matter of compelling empathy.

HER PARENTS lived in Djinnadou before the onset of the decade-long tribal war. They lived a relatively undisruptive life until 1989 when C.T. and his gang of thugs launched an assault on Pepper Coast.

Predominantly of the Yakouba and Mano tribes, members of *Jarsar* rebel faction unrelentingly waged arbitrary reprisals against members of the Guéré tribe of Djinnadou in vengeance of atrocities experienced by Yakoubas and Manos of Nimba during a crushed 1985 coup.

Hundreds of citizens of Pepper Coast, most of them Yakoubas and Manos, were massacred by loyalist troops of King Pitte. Such arbitrary reprisals inflamed existing simmering ethnic tensions between these indigenous tribes, something C.T. exploited to his advantage during his warfare.

During the early days of the war, Hadjala suggested to Baaba that they move the family to Ducor, which was, by then, considered by many, the safest haven.

"*M'boreen*, let's take the family to Ducor. It's safer there because it's the capital," she suggested. But, Ducor would prove to be not much of a haven after all.

The main highway connecting Djinnadou to Ducor, through Nileville, had been cut off because C.T. and his men made their grand entrance into the country through Nileville.

The only other way to access the country's central city—Ducor—from Djinnadou was through Pike County. Baaba had a used Nissan, which he gassed up and drove the family to Pike County.

Upon arrival, they found that driving on the main road was increasingly dangerous because C.T.'s *jarsar* rebels had erected limitless roadblocks and were specifically targeting members of the Guéré and Dioula ethnic groups. Sadjio and her family belonged to one of those groups; they were Dioulas.

This was when it occurred to her parents that the 357.7 kilometer or 6 hours 35 minutes travel to Ducor from Pike County wouldn't have been as easy as it appeared.

WHILE IN PIKE COUNTY, the family hid in the home of a Fante family with whom Hadjala traded for several years as she bought and sold *bonnie* (dry herring fish) between Djinnadou and Pike County.

This Fante family belonged to one of Sub-Sahara's largest ethnic groups found in the coastal areas of southern Gold Coast and southeastern Ivory Coast—the Akans. Fante men were primarily engaged in fishing while the women possessed considerable economic power mainly as fish dealers, which was why Hadjala was familiar with this family. For four days, they were boxed into a single room without a chance of sighting the sunlight; food and water were quickly and quietly served.

On the night of February 16, 1990, they heard a soft knock on the door:

"Hadjala! Hadjala!" a voice came through the makeshift doorknob.

"Yes….." Hadjala responded softly.

It was their host, Fifi. She informed Hadjala that there was a canoe available to take them to Cess City, but for a hefty price. They paid the fare almost instantly.

At about 2:00 AM., they set sail, leaving behind their vehicle and all other belongings. It was more about their lives now, nothing else mattered.

The night was clear and moony. Unforgiving waves practically controlled the tiny canoe conveying Sadjio and her family. At the one point, the engine went off and had to be manually paddled against giant waves, nearly capsizing. The waves looked large, and the possibility of this canoe being knocked down or rolled over by a stream was high.

As they travelled that night, Hadjala kept the kids' heads buried in her bosom, preventing them from looking around since they were sailing a long way from land. But Sadjio won't stay still. She sneaked her head out and watched the mighty body of water that surrounded them. Halfway through, the canoe operator announced that they were approaching a danger done, an area frequented by djinns of the wind and sea, an area with super-strong waves. This got Sadjio even more curious to keep peeping at the ocean.

As they entered the danger zone, Sadjio saw a humongous creature with a head as round like a soccer ball, two little hands that looked more like those of a Tyrannosaurus rex. It was tall, shooting directly for the stars. It was as dark as night, yet, dazzled in the moonlight.

Sadjio fought to get her gaze off the creature, with each attempt yielding no results. She was too curious, always desirous of exploring.

Upon arrival in Cess City, they boarded a vehicle for Ducor.

The city seemed calm for the first few weeks until they began noticing family heads, especially those belonging to the Dioula ethnic group, loading their families and trucking them to neighboring countries: Queens, Sierra Leone and Ivory Coast.

Sadjio and her family would come out and bid them goodbye, hoping that Ducor remained untouchable. But that reverie was short-lived. Ducor was a hard hit.

Chapter SIXTEEN

AS THE WAR flared up and spread to every corner of Ducor, Baaba and Hadjala sought refuge at Queens Embassy. This facility housed more than 5000 people predominantly of the Dioula tribe seeking safety from the rebels who had killed thousands of Dioulaes because members of this ethnic group were accused of backing Pitte's government.

Queens Embassy was a stone throw from their home in central Ducor. It was believed that embassies, as diplomatic grounds, were the safest places to seek refuge from the raging violence.

Unfortunately, for those in the Embassy, that would soon prove to be a costly mistake. For no sooner had Sadjio's parents thanked their lucky stars when a gang of C.T.'s marauding beasts launched a broad-day assault on the Embassy, killing hundreds of unarmed civilians.

As bullets whisked helter-skelter, her parents struggled to escape the Embassy along with their four young children: Jamaal, Saléma, Sadjio, and Sandjee.

It was a sunny, hot Saturday afternoon. Most families, including Sadjio's, had just finished having their afternoon meals that mainly consisted of plain palm cabbage boiled along with grass, identified in Pepper Coast as "five-finger leaves."

Suddenly, a group of young men appeared on the main street overlooking the Embassy compound. That seemed very unusual because, at the time, all of Ducor's streets were usually de-peopled; the roads were considered battlegrounds. No one dared walk up or down the streets without getting hit by stray bullets.

However, on this Saturday afternoon in August 1990, the street right across from Queens Embassy had a band of young men dressed up in blue jeans and red blouses with rainbow wigs on. Some had black-painted lips and eyebrows. There were at least a dozen men, and each had an AK47 gun hugging his chest. This scene was enough to put everyone on high alert. But it was too late, at least another dozens of rebels had already infiltrated the Embassy.

Those in the street were only a distraction.

While everyone focused on those, the batch that made its way into the compound was busy setting the stage for the attack. They erected vast piles of tires, ready to set ablaze, and when the time was ripe, they took three Embassy guards hostage and began setting the piles of tires erected, ablaze.

Thick fumes emanating from the burning plastics made any attempt to escape the compound a tough thing to do, especially since one could barely see beyond one's nose. The entire atmosphere was dark and smoky. The blazing fire that looked like a fire-breathing dragon, puffing away vicariously, was also used to burn women, children, and the elderly.

Meanwhile, the gang standing in the street had climbed the compound's walls where they stood and opened fire on the population.

The only accessible exit point was a tiny entrance at the rear of the Embassy's compound. Miraculously, that door, inundated with sharp objects, including nails, was left untouched by the rebels. They had sealed all other entrances, leaving no safe passage for unarmed civilians. The battle for survival at *that* tiny exit was even more deadly.

As hundreds of civilians rushed to pass through the door, Sadjio could see the elderly, young children, the sick, and women dropping to the floor. They were subsequently crushed to death by the hurrying crowd. Moreover, the nails on the doorframes tore out human flesh as people rushed through the doors. Only the strong were lucky to escape Queens Embassy on that hot, sunny afternoon.

Those who managed to escape were forced into the street where fierce battles raged.

Sadjio's parents were among those who made it out, together with their children. Sadly, though, Hadjala's youngest sister, Aimee, had to pay the price — she was kidnapped and subsequently forced into becoming a wife-in-captivity by the commander (identified as Marcus) of that band of C.T.'s *Jarsar* rebels that attacked the Embassy on that day.

At the time, Aimee was a tall, dark-skinned girl with pop eyes and a charming smile. Growing up, Aimee was a soft-hearted and soft-spoken person. She was hardworking, always willing to lend a helping hand, and never said "no" to a request to play with kids, including Sadjio and her siblings. She always cheered their hearts with her bedtime folktales and was sure to spoil them with their favorite snacks.

BY THE TIME SADJIO again laid eyes on Aimee in 1999, she had given birth to two beautiful daughters for this brutal frontline commander and was no longer the Aimee she used to be. The once quiet and shy young woman was now a very wild woman who resorted to violence in dealing with every situation.

She had become extraordinarily hot-tempered and very abusive in her approach to matters. It turned out that she was silently struggling with memories of her own wartime experiences. She was battling some deep-seated rage she had within herself.

When Sadjio finally met Marcus, he laughed and said you have grown up. He then told her that it took his band of rebels two weeks to study the environment while planning the attack on the Embassy. Across the street from the Embassy was a tiny stream where Aimee took Saléma and Sadjio to fetch water.

The stream was surrounded by tiny bushes, which Marcus said housed his thugs as they planned their assault. He told Sadjio that on the Thursday before the attack, the girls had again gone to fetch water when some members of his troop suggested that the girls be killed:

"My boys had the feeling that you all had seen us and were afraid that you would expose our plan, but I was the commander. So, I ordered my men not to shoot you girls because I was beginning to really love Aimee," Marcus recalled.

Thus, during the day of the attack, he said, his first target was to locate the family and capture Aimee. Fortunately for him, they were easily found. He immediately kicked Aimee with his massive army boots, knocked her to the floor and stepped on her head. That was the last time Sadjio saw her once sweet, cheerful, and caring aunty. There was blood oozing out of her ears and mouth. She only stared at the family as they ran for their lives.

"My men were going to take your brother and train him to become one of us. The plan was to shoot the rest of the family. But when I got Aimee, we couldn't find the rest of you. We thought you all had been killed already," narrated Marcus during a 1999 conversation with Sadjio.

"Were you actually going to shoot us if you were to find us?" Sadjio asked Marcus looking straight into his eye.

"Let's forget the past. Right now, my goal is to seek Aimee's hand in marriage officially. So let's not bring up things that will turn the family against me," he responded, flashing a fading smile.

Marcus's bid to marry Aimee was unsuccessful because nearly everyone in the family was uncomfortable with him. Everyone wished Marcus and his thugs would face justice for their acts during the war.

Chapter SEVENTEEN

MEANWHILE, on the Saturday of the attack on the Embassy, Hadjala nearly passed out. She couldn't bear the thought of being torn apart from her sibling, Aimee. The guilt was just too much for her to handle. For her, it didn't have to be her sister; she preferred to die than to lose her sibling in such a gruesome manner.

"Aimee was my responsibility just as the rest of my family, but I failed her," Hadjala always said, tearfully.

Escaping the embassy on that Saturday afternoon was a matter of life and death.

Once the family made it outside the embassy's fence, Sadjio's parents realized that her brother Jamaal also was missing. Baaba had to defy the bullets to go back to search for his son. He found Jamaal hidden under a broken table in one of the rooms upstairs.

As they struggle to escape the Embassy of Queens on that afternoon intensified, the next possible target destination to stand out was the Barclay Training Center (BTC) at South Beach, Ducor, which soon became a prime target for C.T.'s *Jarsar* thugs. The BTC was the stronghold of the-then King Pitte's troops.

Once again, to escape the fighting at BTC, Sadjio's parents had to endure a life and death scuffle to board the handful of vans provided by ECOMOG, the regional peace-keepers who had arrived in the country to help broker peace among the warring parties and stop the bloodshed.

ECOMOG was an intervention by regional countries in the Pepper Coast civil war. The troops were responsible for imposing a cease-fire and helping to form an interim government, while ensuring that elections were held within 12 months of their arrival in Ducor. Sadly, with the war raging across the country, there was certainly no peace to keep. And soon, the troops found themselves rather involved in the combat. They had to take on C.T.'s *Jarsar* in an attempt to push those goons from making any further advances on the nation's capital, Ducor.

So, the only way out of the BTC Military Barracks was a handful of ECOMOG vans that headed for the Freeport of Ducor, where civilians could board the various rescue ships for other Sub-Sahara countries to escape the escalating turmoil in Pepper Coast.

The harbor at the time fell within the zone controlled by Independent *Jarsar*, a warring faction that was a significant force in the early stages of the war.

The struggle to escape the BTC Barracks heightened as no one wanted to be left behind, making it a matter of life and death with the strongest trampling the weak. Sadjio was ten years old by then, and my little sister, Sandjee, was six. But the memories of that life and death struggle remain indelibly etched in her mind.

Amid the chaos, somehow, her short and chubby mom, Hadjala, managed to squeeze Sandjee and Sadjio into one of the vans. Off they went, not knowing where or when they would again set their eyes on their parents and other siblings.

THE FREEPORT of Ducor was littered with dead bodies in all manner of states—freshly killed, bloated as decaying set in, while others were in the latter stages of decomposition. People were summarily executed based on all kinds of flimsy accusations at checkpoints erected byYommie's Independent *Jarsar* fighters. Some of these control points were decorated with human entrails.

At this point, Sadjio was no longer afraid of seeing dead bodies. She had seen enough already. However, after seeing these new bodies around, her mind went to her parents and other siblings.

"Will Sandjee and me ever see Hadjala and Baaba? How about Ngôrô Saléma and Ngôrô Jamaal?" she thought, as her mind wandered off.

She then rushed over and held Sandjee so tight, never wanting to let her go. Sandjee was her only family at that moment.

At the Freeport, without their parents or any other surrogate adult care and guidance, Sandjee and Sadjio were helpless. Some of those who had made it to the Freeport, with them, managed to claw their way onboard the rescue ships and had already left the country. But, at their tender ages, they did not have the physical wherewithal to engage in the crab-like scuffle to fight their way onboard the rescue ships.

So, while they waited for the opportunity to board one of the rescue ships, Sadjio, and her sister were made to sleep in empty containers at the Freeport. There were new batches of civilians arriving at the Port daily, and they prayed that their parents and other siblings would come with one of the groups.

Chapter EIGHTEEN

THE SANITARY conditions in the containers, with so many people, were deplorable. But what made it even worse was that they sometimes had to sleep alongside dead bodies, some of which as they decayed, oozed out a greyish fluid, which contaminated the entire area.

As a result, a cholera epidemic began to spread among the civilians. Sadjio's five-year-old sister, Sandjee, was one such civilian who fell prey to this disease.

When Sandjee fell sick, Sadjio tried to do all she could with her ten-year-old powers to nurse her sister back to health. She realized that Sandjee was dead one morning, a few weeks after they arrived at the Port when a fresh batch of civilians arrived.

Some of them were sent to their container to stay until the next ship was ready for boarding. So, the old inhabitants had to make space for the newcomers.

She had just finished bathing Sandjee and wrapped her in a blanket provided to them by some ECOMOG soldiers. That was when she heard their neighbors shouting for them to scoot over to make space for the newcomers. She tried to wake her sister so she could move and make space for the newcomers, but Sandjee was not responding.

Sadjio began calling out to her:

"SANDJEE! SANDJEE! SANDJEE!"

Still, she did not respond. Sadjio then decided to shake her.

"Sandjee, we need to move to make space. The man is shouting at me that we should move. Please move," she said to her little sister in their native Dioula dialect.

But Sandjee would never scoot over. Sandjee was gone.

Her eyes were closed as though she was fast asleep; her skin looked smooth and silky. She was glowing. Sadjio was too young to understand what was unfolding. She continued to shake Sandjee, talking to her and hoping that there would be a response.

Meanwhile, an ECOMOG commander, who had been listening and watching keenly, realized what Sadjio still had not grasped in her ten-year-old mind – her dear, brown-skinned little sister, her only family at the time, was never going to respond to her calls.

"Get that girl from her sister," Bangoura ordered a few of his solider. He spoke Mandinka, a language Sadjio also spoke.

He also ordered that Sadjio be taken to his apartment. It was the part that rang a bell in Sadjio's ears. *Why are they coming to take me? How about Sandjee?* She wondered as the men, perfectly attired in their brown camouflage suits, approach her. Sadjio could tell that something was off; she could feel her temperature rising at a faster pace.

She resisted every attempt by the men to pull her away from her dead sister. For her, it was the battle of life and death. She wasn't going to let go of her dear Sandjee.

"Where are you taking me? And why are you trying to take Sandjee from me? Don't you see that she is sleeping?"

"Why are you trying to disturb her sleep? Don't you see that she is sick?" she cried while resisting the men.

"I will not leave Sandjee here. Sandjee must come with me," she said, gradually elevating the pitch of her voice.

"Hadjala and Baaba are not here. I must take care of Sandjee. She has a running stomach. Please let her sleep, or I will tell Hadjala that you want to take me away from Sandjee," she added, crying and screaming tantrums.

A roughly 15 – 20 minutes struggle ensued between the soldiers and Sadjio. She would not let go of her sister, and the soldiers were gentle with her. It would take Bangura, himself, to separate Sadjio from the corpse of her baby sister.

Sadjio was taken to Bangura's apartment but would not go in. She stood on the stairs and watched Bangoura and his soldiers wrap Sandjee's corpse in a piece of black plastic bag. They dug a vertical hole in the ground, placed the body near it, and performed critical Islamic rituals over the corpse before burying it.

This scene aggravated Sadjio's pain. She wondered what just happened. The fact that Sandjee was gone for good was yet to settle in fully.

"Where is Hadjala?! Where is Baaba?!" she cried bitterly. But they were nowhere around.

"Why put Sandjee in a hole?! What did she do to deserve such a treatment? Bring Sandjee back or put me in the hole along with her," Sadjio cried, tussling with the ECOMOG soldiers.

Bangoura took her to his apartment, gave her a warm bath, dressed her in clean clothes, and got rid of the filthy ones she had been wearing all along. For the first time in six months, she had a decent meal to eat, clean water to drink, and slept in a room, on a mattress.

Civilians at the Port had to share some of the containers with dead bodies, especially victims of cholera, and no one bothered to take them out for burial. There was no such time.

People were struggling to survive the bullets and board the rescue ships and cared less about spending a couple of days in transit alongside dead bodies in a container.

Two weeks after the death of Sandjee in September, Hadjala showed up at the Port, and instead of her two children whom she had dispatched ahead to safety, she only found Sadjio. Her youngest child was no more.

SADJIO was seated in the exact spot she had seen Bangoura and his men burry Sandjee.

The spot had been her favorite area from the day of Sandjee's burial. She would sit there and cry, hoping and praying fervently, that Hadjala would show up one day and see where Sandjee had been laid to rest.

"I will tell *Teeyah* that Sandjee is here," she would say, pointing at the spot.

"Sadjio, where is Sandjee?" Hadjala asked, looking all suspicious, seeing Sadjio with bloodshot eyes.

And as she had always prayed and planned, her response was very concise.

"Sandjee is gone."

"Where?" Hadjala screamed, with eyes popping out of their frames.

Sadjio pointed to where Bangoura and his soldiers had buried Sandjee.

Hadjala stood in silence for a while with eyes fixed on the grave, then scooped Sadjio from the spot and gave her a tight hug—*one that says stay with me; I will never you go.* It was too much for her to handle. She could not cry. She just couldn't. She was in deep shock, too much pain to cry. All she wanted at that very moment was to have Sadjio in her arms and never to be left alone.

The emotions expressed by her action was enough to have tears racing down the cheeks of Queens ECOMOG soldiers on scene, including their commander, Bangoura.

"This man gives me food. I sleep in his house," Sadjio explained, pointing at Bangoura.

Hadjala thanked Bangoura and asked if she could take her daughter along with her because Baaba and the other siblings were staying at a warehouse in Logan Town. They couldn't access the Port.

It was easier for women than for men. The rebels were looking to forcibly recruit Jamaal, who was a teenager at the time, to fight. They brutally flogged Baaba the first time the family attempted to enter the Port.

Bangoura agreed. Hadjala and Sadjio joined the rest of the family in Logan Town.

Everyone was happy to see Sadjio but had too many questions to ask about Sandjee's whereabouts, and just when they learned the truth and began to cry that she was no longer with them, they saw someone spying through the window.

There was an instant silence in the house, and judging from their ethnic background, it was clear that the only safe place for them was the Port. They immediately made our way there.

Hadjala, Saléma, and Sadjio miraculously made it back to the Port without Baaba and Jamaal. Once in, Hadjala informed Bangoura about the situation.

Bangoura took it from that point. By nighttime, the two men were brought to their container by Bangoura and his men.

Chapter NINETEEN

BOARDING THE rescue ships heading to neighboring countries was again a life and death struggle. Hadjala nearly got killed as she fought to secure a space for her family on one of the ships. C.T.'s *Jarsar* continually bombed the Port.

On that hot afternoon, as Hadjala headed to the harbor, a rocket dropped and exploded right ahead of her. Her face was severely hit as tiny particles from the projectile made their way through her jaws and cheeks.

It would take the family nearly two months to finally get onboard one of the rescue ships that was headed for Freetown, Sierra Leone. The vessel was initially headed for Nigeria. But it was hit by a rocket and was taking in water as it sailed off.

It was in Freetown that Hadjala underwent surgical procedures to remove the rocket particles from her face. The scars remained visible in her smiles forever.

Baaba did not make that journey along with the family. With both arms spread around his family, he elbowed his way to the entrance of the ship and made sure they boarded safely. When it was his time to get on board, he declined. In a soft tone, he asked Hadjala to take the children to safety.

Hadjala pleaded with him to no avail. He would not board the ship. As though he knew his days were numbered.

They all cried. The children pleaded with him, but he insisted that he would be fine, adding that he was happy seeing them escape the escalating violence.

Few months after their departure, they learned of his death. He, too, succumbed to cholera. He had gone back to the warehouse that housed them in Logan Town and stayed there. His bloated body was discovered by a family friend, who was also making his way to the Port, to escape to safety. It is this friend that broke the news of Baaba's death to the family.

HADJALA, along with her three young children, spent nearly eight months navigating their way across Sierra Leone and Queens before finally arriving and settling down in Bloléquin, in the west of Ivory Coast. They spent nearly three months in the Sierra Leonean town of Mile 91, a major trade center in Sierra Leone, situated along the Freetown – Bo highway.

She had to work as a servant—doing all sorts of domestic chores, including laundry and cooking—for Sierra Leonean families to raise money to feed and enable them to continue their journey. It took them another month to finally arrive at the Koindou – Nongowa crossing point.

Koindou was a Sierra Leonean town bordering neighboring Queens, while Nongowa was Queens side of the border, separated by the Makona River. They arrived at the Koindou – Nongowa crossing point with enough money to get them through to Guéguédou, a major trading city in Queens from the border town. Unfortunately, the canoe operator charged huge crossing fees, which rendered them penniless, crippling their journey once again.

Upon arrival in Nongowa, Hadjala took her children to the mosque. The Islamic Thuhr prayer was ongoing. They quickly joined in. After the prayer, she approached the imam about our situation. The imam responded with an announcement, urging the congregation to reach out to Hadjala and her children. That impromptu rally raised enough money to get them to Guéguédou, where they spent nearly two months trying to raise bus fares to go to Belleville.

Here again, Hadjala did intensive laundry on a daily basis to raise money to feed and enable them to continue their journey.

They arrived in Guéguédou by 7 PM. The town's principal streets were all de-peopled by a torrential downpour. As usual, they knew no one and nowhere to head. They sat under a thatch-roofed hut at a roundabout in the heart of the town.

Hadjala wrapped a piece of torn cloth around the children to keep them warm. Soon, they were approached by a man of the Fulani tribe, who had been observing the family all along from the windows of his brick-house provision store.

Convinced that they were helpless and homeless, he approached them and offered to host them. Hadjala instantly accepted his offer, thanking the Almighty for sending an "angel" to their rescue.

In his compound was an empty warehouse to which he instructed the family to stay. Unfortunately, the warehouse had a price tag—the desire to exploit a helpless single mother battling all odds to take her children to a place they can call home.

There were no locks on the warehouse's door, which happened to be at the advantage of this husband of four wives and 13 children. Each night, while they slept, he would try forcing his way in on them.

What Hadjala did in response was to line the door with cooking utensils during bedtime, so that whenever he tried to force his way through, the sounds from the utensils would wake them up.

"He has come! He has come!" they would scream for help, loud enough to send him running back to his room.

Jamaal had to stay up some nights to protect the door and watch over the girls.

This continued until one of Baaba's friends, Boulayee, spotted Jamaal in downtown Guéguédou on one beautiful day.

Boulayee at the time was a bus driver along the Guéguédou – Simaya corridor. He immediately identified his friend's son and asked the boy to take him to see the rest of the family. After a brief interaction with the family, Boulayee offered to take them free of all charges and paid their way from Simaya to Bloléquin, a small town in western Ivory Coast where they settled.

Bloléquin was their home from 1992 until 2002 when Ivory Coast plunged into its brutal civil war. That war went full-blown in September 2002, forcing the family, save Sadjio, to seek refuge in Simaya, a bustling city of Queens.

They stayed in Queens as dual refugees—having been uprooted from their community of origin in Pepper Coast, they were, again, fleeing the outbreak of a raging conflict in their newfound, safe haven, Ivory Coast.

Chapter TWENTY

THEREFORE, Sadjio's experience of the wanton devastation by the Pepper Coast tribal carnage paralleled that of hundreds of citizens of Pepper Coast. But as a woman, she was especially interested in the *experiences of Pepper Coast women during the country's civil war.*

This was why *women* became the primary subject of her reportage back in 2004 and after that. She felt obliged to amplify the voice of women war survivors, like herself. As such, her reporting became an avenue through which other women could voice out their agonies and set into motion a healing process for them.

She felt an unwavering personal passion for telling the stories of women war survivors. Throughout her career in the media, Sadjio focused on how women coped with trauma–specifically war trauma. For her, effectively capturing and telling these women's war experiences, their stories of healing, of restoration, of inspiration, of moving forward was a cause worth pursuing throughout her life as a journalist.

"It is healthy for our emotional and spiritual well-being," she thought.

As a reporter, the stories Sadjio gathered from women over the years told a narrative that could be likened to a double-sided coin. Though they disproportionately bore the brunt as victims of Pepper Coast's atrocious civil war, which was characterized by widespread sexual and gender-based violence, the women were also instrumental in ending the brutality in the country and bringing peace to its people.

The period between 1994 - 2011 was when the women of Pepper Coast finally rose and took those first tentative steps beyond relief work—distributing food, beddings, and clothing to thousands of internally displaced persons (IDPs). The women began directing their time, energy, and resources at the source of Pepper Coast's turmoil. The aim was to attack and cut off that source and, in-so-doing, end the fighting.

The war was raging throughout the countryside. Fighters on all sides of the conflict (government and warring factions) looted and burned down villages, raped women, and recruited young children to fight. In search of safety, hundreds of thousands of unarmed civilians fled their homes. They made their way to the nation's capital, Ducor, where they resided in internally displaced camps without much food, clothes, or drinking water.

The more forceful of these outstanding women peace brokers began intervening in the conflict as individuals during the early 1990s. They reached out to the needy, IDPs found in camps for the displaced and those spread around the country. In 1994, the women began coming together to face and pressure the warlords to focus on a plan for peace. An anomic interest group, the women were.

At that time, they were spontaneous groups with a collective response to a particular frustration; often, they would disintegrate after the issues they opposed were addressed. Throughout the early 90s, and up until 2003, these women did not relent in their cause for peace in their country.

WERE AN unspecified number of Pepper Coast's women themselves perpetrators of violence during their country's brutal civil war? Of course, they indeed were. Some had the power, political influence, or financial backing to support military activities at various points during the conflict. However, the inordinate number of women and girls who were victimized—in unimaginable ways—over this same period, dwarfs that group of women.

Women were subjected to torture and sexual assault, including rape. Collectively, they endured systemic abuse, witnessed unspeakable cruelty resulting in the brutal trampling down of whatever cultural virtues they enjoyed as pillars of the typical Pepper Coast family. Rape, sex bartering, insertion of objects in female genitals, and molestation were among weapons of fear used during the war, mainly perpetrated to reinforce inequalities between men and women.

So ubiquitous had the sexual abuse of Pepper Coast women become—as a result of their designation as the fighters' new 'sex slaves'—that they no longer could contain the passion that beat beneath their breasts. Breaking away from their passive approach to the conflict—the distribution of relief items to thousands of internally displaced persons—to launch a non-violent movement that would restore peace to their motherland.

It was time for women to venture into peacekeeping, a culturally forbidden territory. Rather than playing second fiddle to men as was expected of them, they pushed themselves right into the middle of the conflict and began attacking the war at its source in hopes of bringing the turmoil to an end.

As was true of women in other parts of the world at the time, the women of Pepper Coast made daily sacrifices for peace, often making the ultimate sacrifice by giving their lives in the quid pro quo exchange that characterized the conflict. They challenged governments, militias, and juntas, urging reconciliation over retribution.

The women contributed to peacebuilding as activists and as survivors of the most catastrophic and horrific effects of a most atrocious war, which was characterized by widespread crimes against humanity for nearly three decades. Yet, these patriots were able to transform and influence the various peace processes in their country by organizing across political, religious, and ethnic affiliations locally.

Through her reportage, Sadjio uncovered and further revealed that women's role in Pepper's Coast war was proof that they were indispensable to peace. They were more than just victims in conflict—they were agents of change, representing the untapped potential for creating more peaceful, secure, and just societies.

The truth is, Pepper Coast's peace-brokering women made it their duty to connect the relevant dots along the way, instead of warmongering as did others. They ensured that the parties were brought together to the dialogue table in hopes of transforming one of Sub-Sahara's deadliest conflicts. And, here, the pivotal role played by these women came into focus.

Traditionally, Pepper Coast women were not active in public positions. Men dealt with matters outside the home, and the women were confined to the domestic sphere. They resided in the shadows of their husbands. Typically, a girl was often sent to live with another family [in marriage], which deprived her of the right to say very much. The only 'right' she was allowed was to remain silent, but this did not deter the women's resolve to break away from that situation when Pepper Coast's war reached its peak. Thousands of them had been subjected to gang-rape and other violent crimes during the war. Hundreds of them were used either as 'sex slaves,' or cooks for marauding armed gangs, or were tortured.

Hearing of these atrocities moved women leaders into forming pressure groups to advocate respect, protection, and the rights of women. These pressure groups of revolutionary women searched for and brokered the peace by bringing both warlords and heads of state to the table to negotiate their way to lasting peace.

It was because of the fearless and relentless roles they played in bringing peace to their society that they were later recognized among other credible peace advocates in Pepper Coast and other parts of the Sub-Sahara. Though physically drained from traveling from one displaced camp to the other, Sadjio felt excited and fulfilled by her discoveries and the opportunity to amply the voices of these women war survivors.

Chapter TWENTY-ONE

AFTER FLEEING the raging civil war in Pepper Coast, Sadjio and her family settled in Fortesville. The town was a couple of hours drive from Ivory Coast's border with Pepper Coast, through Toulépleu and Toe's Town.

Fortesville was a remote town with a population of less than 150,000. It had limited electricity and running water. It was situated on flat and featureless land and was predominantly inhabited by members of the Guéré ethnic group who shared blood relations and social ties, through intermarriages, with Pepper Coast's Guérés, binding them together. Its locals survived mainly on cash crop farming – cocoa, coffee, cashew, and palm – and petty trading.

A few *attiéké* stalls lined the main dusty motor road that split the town into two. There were also a few makeshift coffee, tea, and *hattai* shops lining Fortesville's chief business district, along with a lone video club and a makeshift superstore. These coffee shops' hours of operation ranged between 21:00hours and 2:00 AM – Fortesville slept at 2:00 AM.

The shops also functioned as mini restaurants, serving quick meals such as spaghetti and fried meat with freshly baked French bread, *du pain*. They served a wide selection of unique teas. Night commuters and residents hopped into these shops for a quick cup of hot tea, coffee, or *hattai*. A single, makeshift nightclub, backed by a few bar and *maquis*, ran Fortesville's nightlife.

The town distinguished itself as a major trading hub, especially on Thursdays, its designated primary market day. On this day, Fortesville was exceptionally noisy, colorful, crowded, and vibrant. Scores of cocoa, cashew, palm and coffee farmers, from Diboké, Doké, Tinhou, Toulépleu, Tai, and Zéaglo, among many other surrounding towns and villages, converged on Fortesville's central market to vend their wares. Petty traders, drug smugglers, as well as fresh produce dealers also sold their products on this day.

Apart from Thursday, the town was quiet and nearly empty for the rest of the week. This is because a bulk of its inhabitants worked the cocoa, coffee, palm, rice, and vegetable fields.

In addition to the exchange of goods and services that characterized Fortesville's market day, the day was also a critical meeting and debt collection day. Creditors went from stall to stall, shop to shop, table to table to collect their money. Most creditors designated Thursday as debt or due payment day because that was when debtors' businesses boomed, all thanks to the influx of buyers from nearby remote villages.

DURING THEIR early days in Fortesville, Saléma suffered much headache. *Why?* Because of her skin color – light skin. People were obsessed with fair skin and couldn't but automatically refer to her as "*jolie femme, sans produits Gold Coastian,*" "*la blanche*" or "*femme clair.*" *Her response?* Tears! She cried whenever she was addressed by her color, not by her name. It was an uncomfortable feeling. She felt harassed and, at some point, discriminated against for her complexion. But to locals of the area, this teenager was very blessed to be called that way: it was an obsessive admiration and blatant acknowledgment of her light or fair skin.

The family would later realize that socially, Fortesville's, or perhaps the entire Ivory Coast's signature skin color at the time was fair skin. This was a blunt eye-opener for Saléma, a clueless girl that had no business whatsoever knowing or talking about skin bleaching.

It was a rude awakening to the reality that indeed, others would do any and everything to gain Saléma's skin color even if she looked brownish at times from not taking proper baths consecutively for three days. She felt beleaguered and would come running to Hadjala for safety and comfort whenever men randomly referred to her as *"teint clair"* – light-skinned. She would eventually get accustomed to being called that way because that was just how everyone would address her.

The sad fact was that chasing fair skin wasn't a trend at all; it didn't look like something that would be going out of style. Bleaching blackness was there to stay.

The town's women were obsessed with toxic whiteness. Prominent among whitening products that made the hit in the mid-90s was *Top Gel*, a pink-colored squeezable tube stuffed with white, boiling cream. It did a quick job of peeling off blackness and was a favorite of young women. The cream cost 500 francs (roughly $1) and was the go-to for users. Saléma would later learn that the number of users of these products swelled in a flash, making toxic whitening a booming activity across the country.

At one point, the government outlawed the products because they contained harmful ingredients that exposed users to chronic diseases such as kidney failure. But bleaching blackness would still go on, regardless. *Why?* Because widespread cosmetic lighting across the country was less clinical but more economical and social.

Saléma's childhood friend, Banawatt, was a committed skin bleacher and was very proud to admit that she didn't bleach her skin in vain: "It gives me a certain level of social and economic advantage. Don't you see that dark complexion is less attractive?"

This made bleaching her naturally silky, shiny blackness a rational, well-calculated decision on her part. Remember, if you were light-skinned, you were automatically admired and distinguished as *"jolie femme"* – pretty or beautiful woman. Brown or dark girls like Banawatt received little to no attention at all, thereby reinforcing the urge to chase toxic whiteness.

Besides, a woman's fiscal or social status was, for the most part, defined by the color of her skin. If a light-skinned woman started to appear darker in complexion, she was immediately accused of being broke. This put many users under intense socially induced pressure to keep up with the trend, even if that meant starving for a day or two to save up for *Top Gel, Carol White, Mekako, Clinic Clear,* or *Maxi White* lightening products. They must continue to look "beautiful," and that was all that mattered.

"For faster results, I love to apply a combination of lotion, facial cream, soap, and oil—all at once. I don't care if they burn my skin. All I want is to be, feel, and look beautiful among my friends," Banawatt would say whenever she was confronted on the subject by Saléma.

In the mid-2000s, the Ivorian government would outlaw the sale and importation of bleaching pills, injectables, lotions, among many others, declaring them as public hazards. Violators were fined heavily and charged with a criminal offense. But users' addiction to bleaching creams, injectables, soap, or lotion further increased the demand for these products amidst the ban.

Thus, the enforceability of the ban was an uphill battle. Without the necessary resources and data, tackling the issue remained a huge problem. Users' willingness to do or pay anything for "fairer skin" dimmed the prospects of any piece of legislation.

Generally, Ivory Coast had a long way to go in its fight against colorism because bleaching blackness was more sociological and psychological. There was consistent, high demand for toxic whiteners, despite health concerns.

And this high demand meant the products would continue to be mass-produced and sold, even if they were illegal.

It also meant that an embargo was only a drop in the ocean—bleaching would continue as long as "fair skin" remained the preferred skin color, and the sale of lighteners remained profitable.

Thankfully, there was still hope for change. Like the Natural Hair Movement that made considerable strides in encouraging black women to appreciate their natural afro-textured hair, there was an equal need for a *Natural Skin Movement* to support women of color to love the skin that they were in.

The natural hair movement discouraged the use of straightening chemicals on black hair. It also advocated against the use of wig-tensions as black hair concealers—simply encouraging black women to embrace and be comfortable with their unaltered/afro-textured hair.

"Embargoes won't work. We need a natural skin movement to encourage black women to embrace their blackness," Saléma would say whenever the topic popped up.

ONCE ESTABLISHED in Fortesville, Hadjala had first to honor a traditionally and culturally prescribed widowhood rite.

She had to go through a period of confinement that lasted four months and ten days. In this period, she was not allowed to leave her room, and her hair was completely covered. She was fully adorned in a navy-blue outfit with marching feet wears and head wrap and remained indoors.

Per tradition, she was not allowed to change her clothes; she wore blue throughout the four months and 10 days. On the last day of this rite, she received religious cleansing and was once more a free woman.

In honor of her promise to Baaba, Hadjala surrendered the children to their paternal uncle's (Sidique's) custody before leaving for Tiassalé, a bustling town along the expressway leading into Simaya, in southern Ivory Coast. Her older sister, Massia, lived there. She needed a change of space to help her bridge the gap between her and her inner peace. But her time away was very brief.

In less than two months, Hadjala was back and had come to stay. She had heard of the mistreatment of the children by their uncle's wife and was not about to let a repeat of history, not if she could do something to protect them from being harmed.

She agreed to marry Sidique, Baaba's little brother, in line with religious and traditional guidelines. What moved her into settling with her brother-in-law? It was her only access to gaining full custody of her children. That's just how life in such a heavily patriarchal society was; she had no choice but to accept this traditionally-prescribed role. After all, as a woman, she was the *property* of her husband and his family. Had she married into a different family, she would have lost sight of her children, would have been denied the right to have a say in the design and implementation of decisions that affected their lives. She would have been a complete outsider in their lives.

Besides, Hadjala also deemed it necessary to shield her children from harm. They had had enough pain at this point in their lives, especially considering their war experiences and struggles across the Sub-Sahara to reach where they were. She felt obligated and entirely responsible for their happiness and solace. By then, they were already wrestling with hunger and pain. She sacrificed her happiness to restore their hope — their *Teeyah* was back to absorb it all for them.

Once fully settled in, Hadjala launched herself into petty trading to make ends meet for her family.

Chapter TWENTY-TWO

LIFE IN FORTESVILLE was initially an absolute nightmare for the family, considering their status as refugees. It felt like an eternal horror movie. Their desperate search for inner peace and healing made it even difficult. It also became harder with the illness of Sadjio.

Sadjio had suddenly fallen ill. She had a puffy face, hands, and feet. People quickly assumed she had gained extra weight. *But from what?* Certainly not from the few slices of boiled bush yam, with salt sprinkled upon and a dash of vegetable oil splashed across, on which the family survived at the time.

The swelling in Sadjio's face, hands, feet, arms, legs, and ankles spoke volumes. Yet, no one noticed the danger at hand until one day when a passerby observed Sadjio and asked to see her parents.

"Who are your parents, and where are they?" asked the stranger.

"My mom is at home," answered Sadjio.

"Where's home?"

"There…" Sadjio responded, with an index finger pointing in the direction of their brown bricks one-bedroom home.

"Take me to your mom. I need to speak with her about your swelling condition." The pair walked across the dusty footpath into the yard.

"Knock, knock."

"Who's there?" responded Hadjala.

"Hello, *m' maa*. Is this girl your child?"

"Yes…..she is. Is she in trouble?"

"No. But is this child receiving any treatment for her swollen face, hands, and feet?"

"No. There's nothing wrong with my daughter," Hadjala said.

"Of course, …. she needs immediate treatment.

The swelling may have occurred because of excess fluid in her tissues. I am not a medical doctor. I am a herbalist, and this is my diagnosis."

"Sir, thank you. But, I am too poor to afford your payments. We can barely afford to eat," Hadjala said, kneeling before the stranger, with both hands outstretched on the bare floor.

"You don't have to pay me. All you need are a few branches and leaves of the evergreen bamboo plants. Boil the plant thoroughly in a large pot made of pure silver. When ready, take it down and separate the liquid from the leaves and branches. Let the liquid get cold before bathing the girl with it. Meanwhile, bury the girl and the pot with the steaming leaves under a thick blanket. Directly absorbing the steam will make her sweat profusely. Don't panic; it is the excess fluids coming out. Repeat this for three days, morning and evening, and that will be it."

With this, the stranger excused himself and left. The next morning, a machete-brandishing Hadjala headed for the deep tropical forest that surrounded the town. About an hour later, she emerged, heavily loaded with bamboo and bamboo products.

At home that evening, she did as instructed by the herbalist, and as anticipated, Sadjio was well after three days of treatment.

DURING THE early days of their stay in Fortesville, Hadjala attempted to work as a maid in various homes. She spent an entire year searching for employment but never got one. She then settled on putting her hands to work the way she knew since her childhood.

But her initial attempts at petty trading crumbled down just a few weeks from the start date. Yet, she held on tight, knowing that her family's survival rested on her shoulders. She kept pushing her boundaries and would eventually discover that most sought-after snacks were being made the traditional way and sold only by road-side vendors. She got creative with them, and her trade flourished into a full-blown business.

First, she noticed that Ivorians had only one way of eating coconuts – they ate it with uncooked cassava. She transformed the raw coconuts into chips and sweets. She also produced coconut oil. With only cinq cents cinquante francs (roughly $1.5), Hadjala bought a cup of sugar, four coconuts, and a knife to begin her business.

She used recycled water bottles to package her products. Her primary customers were ordinary people. The coconuts were: cracked and peeled, with salt, sugar, lemon, and ginger added before they were toasted into crunchy, sweet chips. The chips were preserved for up to three months.

In Ivory Coast at the time, a country with a struggling economy, for many women entrepreneurs, starting your own business was never a choice but a necessity. Hundreds of them worked in what was considered just above the lowest ebb of the economy, vending wares that were the basic dietary staples. There were scores of them – predominantly single moms – who dared to establish and operate a full-time, home-based enterprise.

However, they soon found themselves unconsciously allotting more time and even affection to their business than their families. Balancing work and life became a real sticky issue for these *mumpreneurs* – women who were organized, enterprising, in charge, determined to succeed, full of faith, often scarred and overworked. Their sole motivation was to give their families a fighting chance beyond mere survival. But there was also one strict rule: when it was time for business, family members – or family matters for that matter – better not interfere, or else everyone would feel the pinch.

Hadjala, an audacious *mumpreneur*, operated her home-based snack business on these very principles. She dealt in popular Ivorian snack, *aloko sec* made of plantain. The plantains were: peeled and sliced, with a tiny bit of salt added and fried into crunchy chips. They were preserved for up to a month. And because she went the extra mile to add value to these food products, she was able to establish herself among a niche clientele who regularly purchased those products.

It followed that, with such clientele, there was a high demand for product quality, especially in food production, which required meticulous supervision and zero-margin for error. And then there were the kids who expressed an equally high demand for attention from her. Besides, some of her kids, especially Sadjio, even wanted to participate in what Hadjala was doing. But like every responsible parent, Hadjala believed that children must have their place.

This mother of four began her business at the lowest ebb of the snack business, selling the *cinq cents francs* (roughly $1 at the time) chips and *aloko*. For her, it was the most straightforward business to do as a startup because it never required much investment. With as little as *trois mille* (roughly $6 at the time), Hadjala was able to set up her chips enterprise. That fund enabled her to get the needed ingredients: vegetable oil, table salt, and green plantains.

Gradually, she became a road-side vendor at the corner of a dusty road that led into her Kéibli community. Though she added very little value to her product at the time, her craft still caught the attention of an influential neighbor who initiated a partnership with Hadjala. This neighbor enjoyed both influence and contacts with the town's lone *supermarché*—the supermarket.

The deal was that Hadjala would be paid US$50 at the end of each month, but the chips get produced for her business partner. Unfortunately, after a year and a half with no success, Hadjala negotiated her way out of the deal and began her own value-added chips production. This time, she managed to secure a US$100 loan from a local business entity to infuse capital into hers.

However, as her business grew, Hadjala realized that she was investing more time in her home-based enterprise than in her family. There was an imbalance – work-life got more time, attention, and even affection than her family-life. Her initial strategy was to make sure her kids had something to eat to get their attention off her while she produced her wares. She sent them away, to play on the other side of the yard, well out of the way of her production space.

The dichotomy of satisfying her kids' desires for affection at the crucial time of production compelled this *mumpreneu*r to, sometimes, numb herself in favor of the latter. Unfortunately, the production process was an entire day affair, and that ran throughout the week. And by the time she was done – either by 7:00 PM or 12:00 AM – her kids were already fast asleep, and she was slightly too exhausted to entertain any child.

Few years into this, Hadjala's business suffered a significant blow: an entire consignment of plantains and coconuts was smashed when a runaway truck with failed brakes rammed their home. After that, every effort by Hadjala at a startup crumbled. So, Sadjio willingly assumed the sole breadwinner role.

BY NATURE, Sadjio loved to be the rock for others. She was kindhearted, thoroughly enjoyed being helpful and impactful in the lives of others. She hated seeing human sufferings and did everything to help wherever and whenever she could. She was an emblem of hope to many within her community, always offering to help, still volunteering her time, energy, and resources to see others smile. To her family, she was their last hope.

If all else failed, they knew they could turn to Sadjio for solace. Personally, Sadjio found the act of helping, restoring the hope and faith of others gratifying, very fulfilling. On the one hand, her days at Ida's molded her into a strong, phenomenal woman, one that was ever ready to take on any odds thrown her way. But then again, this is a girl whose very existence remained a mystery to many, right from her birth. Her mental prowess, physical strength, and daring spirit left many to wonder if Sadjio was one of them or one of the others – the djinns.

As Hadjala continued to grapple with mending her business, Sadjio did street vending to feed her family of six. She was in her early teens, and each day, she was sent out with a massive bowl of deep-fried fish balls, nicely decorated with delicious vegetable stew. She began her journey by visiting the various homes in their Kéibli neighborhood before heading to multiple video clubs and ending up in the market where a niche clientele awaited her. She made more than three rounds daily, making enough money to feed five mouths.

The first round of fish balls sale kicked off early in the morning, and by 10:00 AM, she was back home for a refill. By 2:00 PM, the second round was finished. Sadjio's owl was again refilled for the final round, which would be done by 4:30 PM. Hadjala sumptuously made the fish balls. She effortlessly transformed those tilapia fish into mouthwatering doughs that were rolled up, fried, and served with tasty vegetable gravy; they spared no taste bud, ensuring consumers' taste buds were fired up at every bite.

Hadjala was super creative, inventive, and passionate about food. She loved to cook and took great pride in her culinary skills. Hadjala would cook just about any type of food. Her philosophy was that providing sustenance was sharing the love—she didn't need or have a cookbook. Hers was natural. Each bowl of fish balls sold by Sadjio was made with tilapia, peanut butter, assorted seasonings, a dash of vegetable oil, spices, an assortment of vegetables, and some tomato paste.

The resultant effect was that Sadjio had less difficulty finding customers. She had pretty much a niche clientele that remained loyal to her. In addition to providing the highest quality of fish balls, Sadjio actively listened to customers' suggestions and ensured that Hadjala used them for improved results. Being responsive to customers' needs, wants, and expectations helped her to establish and maintain strategic rapport with every customer. It also ensured, enhanced customer experience with her fish balls.

The truth is, Sadjio's wildly tasty fish balls had customers returning for the same experience, thereby differentiating her products from the competition. Besides, she was exceptionally patient with her customers, especially delinquent buyers.

From early 1994 through 1995, Sadjio's entire family depended on her for food. At the time, Hadjala was penniless, and so was Sadjio's stepfather. Sadjio's paternal aunt (Sira) sold snuff and kola nuts in tiny quantities, and income generated from that was only enough to buy kerosene for the few lanterns that keep their unfinished brownish bricks home lit at night. The house they lived in at the time was but a naked frame with un-plastered walls and the floor not laid–everything in the house was dust-coated.

ONE MORNING, she went to the market to buy the required ingredients for the fish balls. Hadjala would typically do so but was overwhelmed with other chores that morning. She felt obliged to have Sadjio do her a favor.

Sadjio sped off to Fortesville's central market to shop. After buying everything else, she realized that she was still left with the spicy aspect of the dish – she needed some hot peppers to give her fishball a much-desired heat or *spicy punch*. She turned left and spotted a middle-aged woman carefully displaying her green and red-colored peppers on a table at the edge of the sidewalk. This selling location was ideal for grabbing the attention of potential patrons. Sadjio moved quickly towards the woman, so attractive was the mixture of hot red, green and light-yellow peppers.

Sadjio asked, "*combien?*"

"C'est *cinquante francs,*" she responded without lifting her head to look Sadjio in the eye.

"*Je n'ai pas besoin de tout ça,*" Sadjio retorted.

"*Je peux avoir pour 25 francs?*"

"*Bein sûr,*" she said, adding that Sadjio was her first customer, and so, she would do anything for Sadjio.

Sadjio began fishing in her purse for the 25 francs coin she had placed in there a few minutes earlier. Luckily, she found it and handed it to the woman. It was then that she lifted her head, catching Sadjio's eye. But she would not take the money from Sadjio directly. Sadjio placed it on the peppers arranged in tiny mountains on a piece of cloth spread across the table, as instructed by the seller.

Sadjio would later ask why. Without mincing her words, the woman said:

"You are my first customer. I need more luck so that my goods can finish soon today. Receiving the money directly from your hand could reduce my luck today. I don't want that. That's why I declined."

Sadjio was intrigued, but only for a second, recalling that this was the Sub-Sahara, and one could expect local customs to intervene at any point in one's dealings with people. This incident helped her to admire the beauty of diversity further. They were a mixture of different people with a variety of cultural practices to prompt their actions at any time.

In some quarters, if you were the first customer and a female, the seller would instead you channel the money through a male than directly accepting it from your hand. If no grown-up male, were around, they would do everything to fetch a young male to do the honors. They believed that a female's luck was less than a male's. So, they preferred men to make the first purchase, rather than women—talk about gender bias against women by women.

In the Gold Coast, if you were the first customer and for some reason, you don't agree with the seller—probably because the bargaining process failed to produce results—the seller would not allow you to leave without purchasing that particular item. The Gold Coast was a bubbly, beautiful country of the Sub-Sahara.

In this case, they preferred giving it to you at the lowest price—sacrificing their profit—rather than let you take off without dropping some cash in their hands. And if you insist on not buying the item at all, they would follow you to wherever you would go for that day! Strange! Sellers believed that if you allow your first luck to slip through your hands, you might as well pack up and go home as you have ruined your entire day of business.

In Spencertown, a wealthy and formidable state of the Sub-Sahara, a trader would be delighted if a light-skinned customer showed up as his/her first buyer. For them, the brightness of that skin would translate into their luck, and their fate would shine for the day – this takes no consideration of gender—only complexion.

Be that as it may, such practices were subtle forms of discrimination swept under the traditional or cultural carpet of different societies. Worst of all, in some die-hard Sub-Saharan traditional settings, [and sometimes, even in urban areas] left-handed people, especially women, were discriminated against, consciously or not. Women who were left hand dominant were not allowed to prepare meals because the left hand was perceived as an "unclean" hand. Interestingly, such advocacies had etiquette as an underlying motivation in most cultural settings.

Many old folks believed that to preserve cleanliness when sanitation was an issue, the right hand, as the dominant hand of most individuals, was used for eating, handling food, and social interactions. The left hand would then be used for personal hygiene, specifically after during a trip to the restroom.

Left-handed girls were always shunned and forced from childhood to convert to using their right hands.

The story was told of a bride who was nearly chased out of her marital home by her mother-in-law. The mother-in-law had spotted her sipping coffee with the cup held in her left hand. For this mother-in-law, holding eating utensils in the left hand was impolite, unreligious: the left hand was meant for cleaning oneself, while the right hand was reserved for the consumption of food and beverages.

Also, in the Gold Coast, pointing and gesturing with the left hand was considered rude or even a taboo. A person giving directions would put their left hand behind him/her and also physically strain to point with their right hand if necessary.

Thus, the incident in the market that morning brought all of this full circle for Sadjio.

"It's a pity that gender justice campaigners are only focusing their energies on what they consider significant forms of discrimination/abuse against women, leaving out these minor but grave offenses against the female gender. Why should a woman or girl be subjected to emotional or physical bullying, simply because she's left-handed?

Is there any justification for this? Was it her fault?

I believe it is time that our women's rights advocates began directing their time and energy towards these issues if we are interested in attaining total emancipation for the female gender," Makeeysha noted when Sadjio notified her of the market incident.

Overall, Sadjio's newfound role in her family helped her to learn more about herself as a person. As her family's sole income-earner, she learned to stand firm and be that solid rock on which others could lean. Her new task groomed her into becoming an independent woman and challenged her to defeat failure at all levels, by always aspiring for excellence in life. It helped to picture the challenges ahead of her (at that tender age) and mentally prepared her for them.

JUST AS SADJIO'S fishball business started booming, new-comers began sprouting everywhere. Almost every neighbor wanted her daughter to sell fish balls. Sadjio and her mom had inspired an entirely new snack industry that everyone couldn't wait to grab a share of. Soon, the market was saturated. In response, Hadjala launched an aggressive diversification strategy aimed to further sustain her brand, amidst fierce competition from emerging snack brands. She produced and sold parched peanuts (salted), powdered milk, popcorn, and milk candies.

This strategy paved the way for breakthrough opportunities into untapped markets—lovers of deliciously made parched peanuts and those of hard or soft milk candies. Hadjala never stopped exploring new and improved ways to strengthen the effectiveness of her products further. She was committed to adding value to her products for enhanced consumer experience. And her efforts paid off. Sadjio, her unrelenting sales agent, gradually began attracting and retaining new consumers, while exceeding the diverse tastes of existing ones.

Her new "rock your jaw" or "make your mouth sweet" business turned one-time or first-time buyers into returning, loyal customers who felt that that business existed just for them. They were glued to it. They were dependable and felt a sense of ownership. They took excellent care of what they perceived as theirs. These customers refused to buy from anyone else except Sadjio. They would wait for her to show up with her different jars of milk candies, powdered milk mixed gently with brown sugar, deliciously parched, salted peanuts, and popcorn.

Meanwhile, Sadjio had a silent goal—her eyes were affixed on a beautiful deep yellow flora dress sold at 15,000-francs (roughly $30 at the time). She always dreamt of herself wearing that dress and felt like a princess waiting to meet her prince.

At the very beginning of the Holy Month of Ramadan that year, Sadjio declared her intent about the dress to her mom. She proposed that a portion of the proceeds from her petty trade was saved toward the dress project. That dress meant everything to Sadjio. It was the only outfit she could picture herself wearing for Eid-Al-Fitr.

For a moment, Hadjala thought Sadjio's proposed deal would be an impossible one to honor, especially since the family's survival was hugely dependent on the snack sales – a lone source of income. The thought of splitting this meager income into two sounded a bit too scary. She knew even a splint from it would be felt so deeply. Yet, she refused to dash Sadjio's hope outrightly.

The end of Ramadan was usually a massive celebration in Fortesville. It was the time for everything new: clothes, hair, feet wear, jewelry, among many others. Everyone wore their best clothes for the congregational prayers held in the morning, marking the end of the 30-day fasting. It was a season of wild festivity. Dealers in clothing and textiles experienced sharp sales boom while tailors became overwhelmed by the number of clothes, lining their shelves, waiting to be doctored and ready to be worn on the day of Eid-Al-Fitr.

On the morning of Eid-al-Fitr that year (1996), Sadjio woke up earlier than usual. She had barely slept the night before, overwhelmed with excitement that she would finally be coming face-to-face with a dress she had longed and worked so hard for over the last few months.

Unfortunately, the harsh realities of the day starved Sadjio of the desire to look and feel like a fairy princess in that floral dress. Her family's survival rested on her shoulders; they survived on a meal (dinner) per day, courtesy of Sadjio's street vending. As such, her dream dress was stuck in her imagination for good.

Chapter TWENTY-THREE

A creative, uber-talented teenager with the weight of her family on her shoulders, Sadjio strategically complemented her street vending with backyard gardening. Surprised? Of course, not. She was the daughter of a farmer and a child born in the heart of rice and vegetable fields.

Baaba was obsessed with farming. So, farming was Sadjio's family's entire livelihood. It was, therefore, not a coincidence that agriculture ran through her veins.

She was 100 percent in love with the soil, a staunch believer in growing what you eat and eating what you grow. By default, she was a daughter of the dirt, effortlessly nurturing her backyard vegetable garden at the family's Quartiér Garman residence. She was 14 at the time and spent days preparing beds, ensuring that the soil was enriched and ready to plant. She made a mixture of both in-ground and raised garden beds to fit the shape of her garden plot.

Sadjio lingered the kitchen whenever Hadjala cooked eggplant stew, making sure the fresh tomatoes were carefully squeezed into a bowl filled with clean water fetched from nearby wells. She needed the seeds for her garden. She also took possession of the water in which Hadjala had washed diced eggplants, letting it sit for a while, then filtering it to gather the seeds. She would dry the seeds before dispersing them in the backyard.

She was incredibly invested in her backyard garden. She nurtured it, watering it nearly every other evening during the dry season. Neighbors were thrilled by the glows of dark purple and plummy eggplants; the hot reddish and greenish looks of peppers and tomatoes as they grew in Sadjio's garden were equally attention-grabbing. The peppers, tomatoes, eggplants, and bitter balls she grew enabled her family to enjoy a wealth of fresh vegetables up to a month. It made their meals more personal, enjoyable.

But Sadjio would develop even more profound affair with agriculture after meeting Annie, her childhood best friend, in the mid-90s.

ANNIE LIVED with her dad and two siblings in Quartiér Garman, Sadjio's neighborhood. The area was densely populated and famous for its polished marble stones. The pinkish granites were stunning and insanely enticing; nearly every aspiring homebuyer desired a home in Quartiér Garman, the town's luxurious settlement. The area, however, had a longstanding rule: cooking at night was strictly prohibited. Violators were cursed by the gods, leading to endless calamity, from generation to generation—this rule was targeted at breaking a proverbial link between the human world and that of the djinns.

In the beginning, Quartiér Garman was infested with notorious djinns, bent on making life unbearable for humans. Some would transform into beautiful humans to mingle with real humans, attracting and killing vulnerable folks. The story was told of a womanizer who fell in love with a pretty lady during the town's market day. He insisted on spending the night with her at his house. The next morning, relatives discovered his body, with parts extracted. A priest later revealed that the pretty lady was, in fact, an anaconda in the jinn world. While in the room that night, she transformed into her true self and stabbed her victim in the torso.

Another family was attacked by djinns after a little boy mistakenly kicked and poured the evening porridge of the baby of a jinni. Djinns, those days had a way of casting darkness between humans and themselves. Without supernatural or spiritual powers, humans could never see or hear djinns. So, this human child had no idea that his soccer field was, in fact, the dining room of a djinni family until this porridge incident. It was forbidden to speak while in the bathroom for fear that this might claim the attention of a promiscuous female or male jinni in search of a human with whom to have sex.

"If you speak while taking a shower and there is an evil jinni around, they get to see your nudity and will wait around until you go to bed to have sex with you. It might appear to you like a dream. But in reality it's a jinni, disguised as a human, with a familiar face, having sexual intercourse with you," parents would say, warning their sons and daughters against speaking or singing while using the restroom or in the shower.

However, cooking at night was outlawed after a jinni nearly wiped out an entire family. The story was told of Massa, a longtime resident of Quartiér Garman, who was well known for her late-night cooking. The heavy sound of Massa's wooden mortal and pestle pierced through the night as she pounded ingredients for her peanut soup that the family ate with the traditional *töo* made with powdered cassava and cornmeal. The powered cassava was evenly blended with cornmeal in a large pot of boiled water to produce a thick paste that was chased down with the peanut soup.

Each night, before Massa began mixing and blending her *töo*, her pot of boiled water served a separate purpose—it was used by an old jinni woman to clean her age-old foot ulcer. The late cooking encouraged the jinni to religiously visit Massa's outdoor kitchen. Once there, she made herself comfortable on a wooden stool she brought along, spread her leg across the pot while it boiled profusely, and began cleaning this terrible foot ulcer of hers. The filth from her sore went directly into the saucepan. Once done, she would make a special prayer for Massa before leaving:

> May you continue to be <u>*useful*</u> to none else, but me.
> Thanks to you, my sore is healing.
> May you continue to cook *only* at this time all day,
> every day
> May you *never*, ever forsake me
> Continue to be a great, late cook my child

Massa would then use the water to make *töo* for her family. This continued until one day when a stranger, who was also *karmor*, observed this bizarre occurrence. Karmor Daoud was an extremely powerful religious leader, with a vast knowledge of spiritual teachings. That night no one ate the food. He asked that Massa returned home sooner from the farm and be done with cooking no later than 4:30 PM the next day. She did as she was instructed. When the jinni came over, she found nothing. The usually hot fireplace was as cold as the North Pole. This angered her. So, she declared war on the family. Her first target was Massa.

"I will break your neck tonight. Your entire family will pay for this," she declared. But Karmor Daoud had sprayed enchanted powder on every member of the household, protecting them against any retaliatory attacks from the jinni.

On Karmor Daoud's advice, residents of Quartier Garma prayed and fasted for 21 days and 21 nights. On the twenty-first night, a rule was established against night cooking, every resident was warned against violating this rule in fear of the wrath of vengeful djinns.

SADJIO'S THREE-BEDROOM rough-and-ready home was situated in the heart of Quartiér Garman. It had no heating or cooling systems. They endured cold water baths throughout the harmattan season, squatted over a hole dug in the ground to pee and poop.

They also dealt with off-and-on electricity and endless mosquito bites throughout the year. Their home was bounded by those of four families of diverse backgrounds: to their east were the Baoulés; to their west were some Gola refugees from Pepper Coast; to their north were the Burkinabés and to their south were these Kpelles of Queens —Annie and her siblings. They were Sadjio's next-door neighbors and lived a life that revolved around subsistence farming, even at such tender ages— Annie, 15; Ouwah, 14 and Morry, 12.

Annie was a brown, slender girl with protruding eyes that were expertly layered with full brows and stuffed lashes. Her puffy orange hair was unkempt for the most part. Ouwah was short and chubby with a thick afro that she never allowed anyone to mess with. "It hurts like crazy," she would say whenever someone touched her seemingly irresistible hair. Morry was a chubby brown boy with a dark afro and golden edges. His golden eyebrows and corresponding lashes made him very attractive.

But Annie and her siblings were never lucky to grow up with a mother, leaving an indelible mark on their lives. "She abandoned us," Annie would tell Sadjio, whenever the question was raised. "Our mom eloped on a dark, windless night following an intense scuffle with our dad. We knew that our lives would never be the same without her presence," she would add, refusing to go any further.

Sadjio knew her friends' lives were impacted both emotionally and mentally. They lacked a natural protection and love from the person who brought them into this world – a bond so indispensable and an irreplaceable part of human existence. But this understanding never stopped Sadjio from probing further. She desired more than a scratch on the surface. Her quizzical look never spared Annie.

"Do you sometimes miss your mom?" Sadjio asked.

"Very much. After all, she is my mom. Isn't it natural?" Annie responded with a sad smile. "I blame those so-called gender equality campaigners. The very things this women's emancipation struggle sought to end are rather increasing sharply simply because some of the campaigners are preaching the message wrongly. In their advocacies, they outrightly placed the woman in the victim zone, painting the man as the oppressor."

With a crumpling forehead, she said, "Sadjio, I don't like thinking or talking about this thing. They were so wrong in their' knowing your rights as a woman' advocacies; they left out the other side of the coin, which is responsibility. "

"Because….," she paused took a deep breath before continuing "you know, rights and responsibilities go hand-in-hand—two sides of the same coin. But these so-called advocates, after securing a few dollars in donor funding, head for rural communities, like ours, with this message: 'gender equality is about us and our time to reverse all forms of discrimination against us.' And guess what? This only adds insult to injury."

"So, what happened to your mom?" Sadjio stepped in, redirecting the focus of the conversation.

"One day, our mom announced that she wasn't coming to the farm with our dad. She said she had a meeting to attend. The thing is, this was her first time to refuse our dad's order to go work the fields."

"He was shocked. Then, mom explained that the meeting she was attending was an all-women meeting. At the meeting, she and others were told everything about their rights, not their responsibilities. That night, she came home thinking a' 50-50' approach to life in the home was the deal, moving forward. But that birthed more violence in our home. Our parents no longer listened, dialogued, or even tried to understand each other. Our house was nothing less than a fierce battlefront," she explained.

"Our mom was given the impression that she had the right to speak when our dad did. And without educating women on how to exercise that particular right, they fell into trouble. Our mom got beatings all the time. For our dad, she was increasingly disrespectful as it relates to decision-making in the home. As soon as he talked, she would just get up and begin to shout, while displaying a rude behavior, provoking him into engaging her physically."

"What?" Sadjio screamed. "What these women's rights advocates are failing to acknowledge is that this is NEVER a gender war. Already, for die-hard Sub-Saharan men, such gender mentality among women is a gross disrespect for our customs, religious and traditional practices, because women are now challenging them in everything and at all levels."

Jumping right back in, Annie said, "Women have been catching hell. They are being flogged because none of these 'advisors' bothers to tell them that they cannot just start doing anything they want without realizing that there will be an equal reaction from the men. The men are just as determined to keep their power and control in the home—especially opposite their spouses. Do these women's right advocates bother to tell their female listeners that the process will take time; and that they might need to be taught how to go about doing whatever they hope to start doing in the home to become involved in decision-making? As a result of such one-sided advocacies about rights, rights, and rights, our mother felt it was her time to retaliate against all the deprivations and abuses she had suffered at the hands of our dad. She felt the time had come for her to express herself against any violation of her rights and dignity."

"And there's nothing wrong with that," Sadjio cut in.

"But remember, every right goes with a responsibility," Annie said, vehemently. "If you do it with its corresponding responsibilities, you will be on the positive side, but rudely, your action will constitute an insult to your partner who also deserves every degree of respect, honor, and above all, love. It becomes dangerous since today's women, as a result of rights advocates' 'advice,' step outside their boundaries with a deep-seated hatred for their husbands and other male counterparts in their communities by committing reciprocal acts of vengeance—an act that could set in motion a downward spiral of violence spurred on by the need to pay-back that often leads to more destruction."

Annie also noted that the coming of women's rights advocated in "our towns and villages to educate us about our rights are sending the wrong messages about how our rights should be protected, respected, upheld and adhered to. They told my mother and others that if a woman says 'No' to her husband [if she refuses to accept his overtures in bed for sex] and he subsequently makes her do it, that is 'tantamount' to rape. That, in itself, is creating serious problems for the women in this place! Most women are refusing to have anything to do with their husbands without providing compelling reasons for refusal, something that has the propensity of leading to severe violence. And this is mainly because these women's rights advocates come here and tell them that if their husbands violated their rights, they should report to the Government and Government would fight for them."

But the government never came to the aid of their mother. Eventually, she felt the need to abandon her young children. Annie and her siblings always longed for this most crucial figure of attachment in their lives. Although their father was present, he was hardly ever around. He did not spend enough quality time with his children; he was heavily invested in his farm work.

Annie and siblings inhabited a house made of orange bricks with thatch roofing. At such tender ages, they stayed in that house all by themselves, without a mother or father to watch over them, comfort them whenever they felt, soothe, calm and encourage them, chasing away their fears. Whenever they were nervous, scared, angry, or in pain, they had no one at home to look up to for unconditional support.

Their father, James, owned a large plot of farmland that was deeply buried within the thick rain forest bounding Fortesville and Ziagolo, a nearby town, also in western Ivory Coast. The farm was at least 3.7 miles (6 kilos) away from home and was only accessible by a tiny footpath. Annie and her siblings began their journey to their farm as early as 4:30 AM, and there, they spent the entire day doing all sorts of manual labor alongside their dad.

They would begin trekking back to town by 3:00 PM, heavily loaded with bundles of dry firewoods, freshly caught fish or bush meat hunted by their dad, bunches of golden yellow seed rice, fresh veggies and some leafy greens.

Once at home by 5:00 PM, the seed rice was briefly patched, poured into a mortar and pounded until transformed into plain rice, ready to be prepared for the evening meal. The bundles of firewood were sold to buy additional ingredients (cubes, salt, oil, etc.) and other provisions (bath soap, dish-washing soap, candles, kerosene, etc.).

Sadjio was a usual customer, ensuring that her friends didn't have to struggle or worry about finding a buyer as quickly as possible. Their dinner—which was their sole meal of the day—was *dependent* on funds raised from firewood sale. Sadjio assumed a personal responsibility of lifting this burden off their shoulders.

Being so passionate about farming, needless to say, she had it in her blood, Sadjio would accompany Annie and her siblings to their farm when she wasn't out selling fish balls. She actively participated in all sorts of manual works, including planting, weeding, hoeing. And she had fun doing so. She particularly adored the flat, rolling treeless and grassless land and the priceless time she spent there with her friends.

Her favorite part was the harvest season when colorful crops would compete for attention. Back home, Hadjala was becoming very worried; she couldn't bear the fact that Sadjio had voluntarily exposed herself to such energy-absorbing life. But, Sadjio enjoyed spending time with her new friends, no matter what.

Sadjio shouldered the weight of her family until 1996 when she had a chance to step foot in a classroom for the very first time. By then, Hadjala had sourced some seed money from a microfinance establishment to kick off a textile business, and this time, it worked.

Sadjio was finally ready to take on life and be the wondrous child she was destined to be.

Chapter TWENTY-FOUR

IN LIFE, when your experience of a specific past social injustice parallels those of others in similar vulnerable conditions, you feel obliged to amplify their voices and become an advocate for transformation in their lives. This was precisely the triggering force underlying Sadjio's insatiable interest in advancing the cause of women and children throughout her adult life.

The plain fact is that girls' education was not a priority in her family during her early upbringing. Girls in her family were labeled as domestic attendants, while the boys were the preferred gender for academic enlightenment.

Even after escaping Ida's wrath, Sadjio was still denied the opportunity of getting an education. Sidique, her stepdad, believed that education was only meant for boys and not for girls in the family. The most he did for his daughters was to send them to Arabic school to learn about Islam.

He was of the perception that girls were meant to be domestic attendants. It was a widely held notion among members of Sadjio's immediate and extended families, as well as scores of Dioula parents that exposing a girl child to education directly equated to giving her the green light to become a woman with easy virtue.

Such a deeply entrenched myth that education exposed girls to prostitution was very effective at keeping Sadjio away from school for nearly ten years. Scores of other Dioulas girls with promising futures were victims of this social myth. Such was the reality of hundreds of young African women and girls who, for decades, had been prescribed by society as a socially secondary and vulnerable group. Such branding stripped away their dignity and exposed them to all forms of gender disparities.

Fortunately, Hadjala was not ready to see her daughters' future dragged in the mud. Her parents had taken her from the 10th grade and given her hand in an arranged marriage to Baaba, a man she did not know.

She unrelentingly advocated evolution in her husband's gender perceptions to rebrand their daughters who had been labeled domestic attendants, not entitled to an education, and had no say in the formulation and implementation of decisions that directly affected their lives.

Hadjala's goal was to ensure a change of space wherein Sadjio and Saléma would be allowed to have a say and a role to play beyond the domesticated confines that had kept them controlled for nearly a decade.

Convinced that her advocacies were not yielding the desired results, Hadjala decided to approach the matter differently; she contested her husband's will by enrolling Sadjio at a local primary school in Fortesville. It was a stressful experience with this new development in the family, but Hadjala stood firm and fearlessly supported Sadjio's educational ambition.

Sadjio would go on to begin kindergarten at age 14. She was among the first batch of students that graced the opening of *School B*, a school operated exclusively for Pepper Coast refugees by the Adventist Development and Relief Agency (ADRA).

IT ALL KICKED off in late 1995 when two men showed up at their home. The night was cold and dark. After they had exchanged greetings, the men asked Hadjala if she would be interested in enrolling any of her children into a refugee school system that would be launched in the town.

She nodded in the affirmative and offered the names of her daughters as potential candidates for what she considered a golden opportunity to see her daughters become educated women. Hadjala purposely refused to provide the names of her sons because they were already enjoying this privilege. In fact, at the moment, Jamaal had been sent off to an out-of-state residential school for advanced studies.

A few months later, *School B* was opened. Sadjio was among the first batch of students; her class was "KG"—kindergarten—and her nickname was "ABC Grandma." Yes! That was, precisely, what she was among those young kids: the oldest, the tallest. It was her first time to ever step foot into a classroom.

School B was initially housed in a large warehouse situated within the Kéibli community. It was a rented venue. The school had no furniture. Sadjio and other students carried stools, on which they sat, to and from school every morning and every afternoon. Two years later, ADRA secured a piece of land on which a new school was built, entirely by the students.

Students were grouped into classes; each class was challenged to erect its classroom structure. Sadjio was in Grade II at the time. The classroom construction project had two phases. The first phase required each class to produce the following items: (a) sticks, (b) reeds (or bamboo reeds), (c) bamboos, (d) thatch, and (e) brown and white clay. A handful of families could afford to purchase these items for their children, making life a bit easier for their young, aspiring learners.

However, for those students, including Sadjio, whose parents could barely afford two-square meals daily, they had to report to nearby creek banks in search of clay and far away forests in search of reeds, bamboos, and thatches, often walking for miles. When found, they used little machetes to cut and tote the sticks, bamboos, and weeds on their heads back to town. They also mined and dug white and brown clay from creek banks, which they also carried on their heads back to town using large pans.

This daring adventure continued for days until the required quantity of each item was attained.

The next phase of the project was the actual erection of mud walls into classrooms. The sticks were first put into the ground; the fresh bamboos were cut and used as borders to hold the sticks together. At first, the structure seemed very fragile. However, after a couple of courses of mud walls erected, the frame was rigidly held in place.

A typical day of mud wall construction was divided into morning and afternoon sessions.

Once the walls had dried up, Sadjio and her friends began decorating with layers of white clay to give their classroom a beautiful look—all done with bare hands, defying the scorching sun and sometimes, raining torrents. Thatches were used for roofing purposes. The entire project had a completion deadline of three weeks, and the team did beat that deadline.

THOUGH SHE BARELY finished high school, Hadjala deemed it necessary to be fully invested in and incredibly supportive of Sadjio's search for education. She was committed to fighting gender disparity through education for girls, beginning with her own family.

"I need you to outdo yourself and outdo me," she would say to Sadjio. "I need you to be whosoever or whatsoever you wish to be. But, with the backing of a sound education to direct your path and your decisions."

Hadjala felt even compelled to focus more on seeing Sadjio succeed academically after Saléma heartbreakingly decided to stop going to school because she felt too old and considered it a waste of time.

"*Teeyah,* I don't think school is my calling. I prefer starting a business or helping you with what you are already doing. Besides, it all boils down to money," a blunt, determined Saléma had informed her mom.

No amount of encouragement from Hadjala could convince Saléma on the need to go to school. She had made up her mind, and it was final—something Hadjala considered a challenge and did everything possible to not see Sadjio fall along the way.

When the news of Sadjio being enrolled at a school finally broke, Sidique reacted with a very sharp look. Hadjala's action, in his view, was abominable. But Hadjala was prepared and ready for anything at this point.

Nothing made her happier than to see her daughter in her green and white jumpsuit uniform and black shoe with white lace socks each morning, leaving for school. It was one of her proudest moments. She felt pleased that her battle for evolution in the notion about gender roles in the home had yielded a much-desired result—Sadjio was finally a student.

During those days, girls' right to education often evoked emotionally charged discussions across communities, with many contending that education was bad for girls. Girls were denied the enjoyment of their right to school on this ground. It was regarded as a privilege designated only for the boy.

However, for Hadjala, it was about giving her girls a future. No wonder Sadjio was the only Dioula girl among the first batch of students that kicked off *School B*. The entire Dioula community of Fortesville reacted sharply with condemnation of all shapes and forms. They condemned Hadjala for disobeying her husband, the head of the home, the family's sole decision-maker. They also condemned her for "exposing her daughter to prostitution."

"If you send your daughter to school, she becomes a prostitute," they would say. "It's like giving your daughter the green light to become a prostitute."

In addition to the classroom, the dress code was also a significant benchmark used to judge a girl's modesty. The female body faced heavy policing by the community than their male counterparts. Pants were designated attire for men, while girls were compelled to wrap their bodies in pieces of cloth or *lappa*, thereby reinforcing disparities between both sexes.

This was another socially prescribed rule that Hadjala effectively kicked to the curb in addition to enrolling Sadjio, a girl child, in school.

"You are not only a girl; you are not just any girl. You are a girl and a student, someone seeking knowledge and wisdom," Hadjala would say to Sadjio. "Therefore, your dress code must reflect such. You need to be wearing jeans, not tying *lappa* around your waist. Students do things differently for others to follow. You need to be that student, one that leads change."

Seeing Sadjio wear pants sparked another round of emotionally charged debate, condemnation, and finger-pointing among Dioulas of Fortesville. As always, Hadjala remained unrelenting and weathered this storm by focusing less on what everyone had to say. She directed her energy at ensuring that Sadjio was doing great in school. She would throw a lavish party or buy the latest Uniwax Bloc fabric, printed exclusively in Ivory Coast, for Sadjio each time she came top of her class—sometimes as dux of the entire school.

Moreover, Hadjala was not solely reliant on classroom teachers. She continued to play an essential role in Sadjio's education. Sadjio learned to spell name at age 14, before having a full grasp on the entire alphabet, courtesy of Hadjala. The length of her first name, Sadjiolatou, was a bit of a problem for her, eleven letters. So, Hadjala put it into a song, and Sadjio was able to remember it within a few days. She recited her name at least twice each night before going to bed.

Hadjala would read to Sadjio or read side-by-side with her. She assisted with her homework, which helped Sadjio develop essential study skills. These study periods played a considerable role in helping Sadjio create a sense of responsibility and a disciplined work ethic that benefited her beyond the classroom.

Each day, Hadjala asked how Sadjio's school day was as a way of showing genuine interest in what Sadjio was learning at school. She often visited the school and knew its layout by heart: main office, recess area, soccer field, auditorium, and teachers' lounge. She was exceptionally versed in the school calendar, taking a specific interest in testing or exam dates to enable her to prepare Sadjio well in advance.

When Sadjio reached Grade II, Hadjala went a step further by ordering a custom-made wooden chalkboard made of reddish-brown mahogany timber, a rare and costly wood at the time. She transformed a portion of their home's front porch into a designated study area and installed the chalkboard there with necessary accessories and supplies.

Sadjio's study area was well-lit with a single fluorescent bulb, comfortable, and quiet workspace. She had a start time of 6:00 PM and an end time of 6:45 PM each school night during her elementary days. The creation of a productive study environment was Hadjala's way of helping Sadjio consider homework as a priority.

Hadjala made sure the study area was free of noise or any form of distractions. She would frown at anyone or anything attempting to steal Sadjio's focus. Sadjio learned by reciting and rewriting her notes—that was a secret weapon that had her shining throughout her academic journey.

To top it off, Hadjala joyfully and tirelessly played the role of after-school teacher for her daughter, while attending back-to-back PTA meetings to stay informed. Overall, Hadjala remained heavily and actively involved in every aspect of her daughter's academic life. And these efforts had a tremendous impact on Sadjio's achievement in school.

From the Second Grade, she received double promotions four years in a row. By the fourth double promotion, the school's credibility diminished drastically in Hadjala's eyes. She began entertaining the idea that the refugee school system which her daughter attended at the time was less challenging. Sadjio's grade point average hardly went below 98%. Hadjala was beyond proud but was equally concerned about the quality of education her daughter was receiving.

She would settle on sending Sadjio off to Ducor in search of a higher academic challenge or quality education. Though Ducor would be turn out to be emotionally and physically tormenting, Sadjio would beat all odds to excel. She remained steadfast, focused, and determined amid the odds. And like the sun, nothing could block sadjio's rays from extending across the horizon. It was impossible to stop her from shining. Those 11 years of no education were recovered at an incredible pace. She was uber-smart and made straight *As* in all of her courses.

Chapter TWENTY-FIVE

By 1996, Hadjala had two large stalls operating out of Fortesville's central market. She dealt in clothing and textiles, trading between the-then flourishing town of Guéguédou and Fortesville. She undertook at least two, five-day business trips between the two cities from Tuesday through Saturday when she would return with assorted goods. In less than a year, the family had a place to call home and could now afford to have three-square meals per day for the first time in three years.

Meanwhile, despite the raging war in Pepper Coast, Ida and family lived in Ducor – not at will, however. Chances of surviving an escape were just too slim at this point. Pepper Coast would later attain negative peace following the election of C.T. as president in 1997, paving the way for movement along the country's essential borders with neighboring states.

In mid-1997, a soft-hearted Hadjala invited Ida to Fortesville, intending to provide her with some financial assistance to help with her war recovery. Ida arrived in Fortesville with a toddler boy, making her children a total of four.

During her stay, she was fiscally empowered to begin her version of petty trading. The goal was that proceeds generated from that effort would be summed for her to take at the end of her stay. She was given 100,000 CFA (roughly $200 at the time) as seed money to kick off her business.

Ida would go on to become a wholesaler, dealing in brown beans. She traded between Fortesville and Bouaké, one of Ivory Coast's leading trade centers. It is the nation's second-largest city, with a population of 536,189. Bouaké, situated at 238 miles (383 km) of Simaya, is also the commercial and transportation hub of the country's interior.

After eight months of stay, Ida returned to her home in Ducor with enough finances to start a trade, and that worked out fine from the beginning but quickly vanished owing principally to fiscal indiscipline on the part Ida and her husband, Imran. This reintroduced their family to renewed hardship. The couple could barely afford to feed themselves and their four children.

In early 1998, thinking the dust had settled between her and her sister, Hadjala again decided to send Sadjio to Ida in Ducor in search of higher, challenging educational opportunities. She had become frustrated with the refugee school system, which Sadjio attended after receiving double promotions for the fourth time in a row.

After a brief telephone dialogue, Hadjala informed the rest of the family that Ida had promised to be caring and careful this time. A week later, Sadjio was dispatched to Ducor, accompanied by Jamaal.

Her school fees and tuition for the academic year 1998 - 1999 were $300, as advised by Ida. That money, together with 200,000 CFA meant for her upkeep, was given to Ida by Jamaal, who spent a week and had to return to school in the Gold Coast, setting in motion a second journey to hell for Sadjio.

SCHOOLS IN DUCOR, as well as elsewhere across Pepper Coast, were all scheduled to be back in session by September 20th that year. That date would, however, be rescheduled due to a firefight between rebels and government loyalists.

The fighting began on a bright, breezeless afternoon. While cleaning his shoes on the front porch of Ida's Jamaica Road home, Jamaal heard a huge blast. Though he could feel his heart punching against his chest, Jamaal still shrugged it off as a mere tire bursting. After a brief moment, a second horrifying sound, of a greater magnitude, came through, making it clear to everyone that a bullet storm had started.

Jamaal immediately abandoned his belongings on the porch and rushed back inside.

"Everybody down!" he ordered, instructing household members to take cover to avoid being hit by stray bullets.

"Take cover behind the concrete wall in the middle of the living room," Imran suggested.

"There is also a solid metal object to hide behind," Ida added.

As the shooting intensified, scores of mattress totting-civilians made their way into the suburbs, escaping the soaring gunfire, rocket and mortar battles in central Ducor.

The city was back in operation, which also meant that schools had reopened their doors for the academic year.

THE ENROLLMENT PERIOD for most schools elapsed with no actions taking to have Sadjio registered and prepared for the school year that was now rolling in full swing. The silence on this matter grew stronger each day.

Minutes turned into hours, hours into days, and days into weeks with nothing being said or done. Everything concerning this subject was swept under the carpet.

Three weeks into the school year, Sadjio was still out of school, and Ida showed no signs of remorse. Instead, she had Sadjio cooking, cleaning, babysitting, and fetching water all day. Once more, Sadjio had conveniently become the ideal maid Ida had always longed for. The only difference this time was that electric wires and belt knobs had been removed from the list of assault weapons. The new assault tools were high heel shoes, large metal cook spoons, and thick wooden combs.

As Sadjio strolled down Broad Street in Central Ducor on one sunny afternoon, she bumped into her maternal uncle, Yacoub, who, at the time, was beefing bitterly with Ida because she had been selfish with *his* children and had squandered funds earned from the sales of used vehicles he had sent to her while he resided in the United States.

"Sadjio, what are you doing here?" he inquired, looking very surprised.

"Hadjala sent me to Ida. She wants me to go to school here," she responded.

"But you don't look like you are in school. The school year has already begun," he furthered.

"Ida said there is no money to pay my fees."

"Wait..., so Hadjala sent her child to school without money? How is that possible?" he wondered.

"No. Jamaal gave the money that Hadjala had provided for my schooling to Ida. Jamaal had to return to school," Sadjio immediately clarified.

Yacoub assumed the responsibility of having Sadjio in school. He registered her at St. Mary's Catholic School in Duala, bought all the required accessories: uniforms, socks, shoes, books, and pencils. She was in the 9th grade and was due to sit the ninth grade West African Examination Council's (WAEC) O Levels exams that year.

THE DELAY IN GETTING her registered and ready for school, coupled with the daily doses of ruthlessness she endured at home, had a massive toll on Sadjio's performance during the First Marking Period of that school year's inaugural semester.

A typical Pepper Coast school's academic calendar comprised three semesters, with each having a series of major exams or assessments periods termed "marking periods." The First, Second, and Third marking periods made up the first semester and the second semester comprised the Fourth and Fifth marking periods. In contrast, the Sixth marking period and final examinations made up the last semester.

For the first time in her academic life, Sadjio's grade point average (for that period) was a point shy of 80%. This was a nerve-racking experience for her.

In addition to a disgraceful GPA that semester, Sadjio was further devastated by the school's intentional seating policy. A class' seating was done per students' accumulated average. Students were seated according to their accrued semester average.

Sadjio's class had seven vertical rows with six chairs per row. The student with the highest average or the class' dux sat on the first seat of the first row.

That seat was considered the "privileged" position because of its prime location. The student with the second-highest average sat next, and it flowed in that manner up to the student with the lowest semester average.

Visitors entering the class, immediately, knew that the person seated on the last chair, at the rear of the classroom, was the one with the lowest academic performance for that semester.

Sadjio's 79% average for that period placed her among the lowest-performing students. She sat on the 3rd chair in the fourth row. Though this arrangement was humiliating and psychologically tormenting for her, it challenged her into out-doing herself to make it to the top, a position she had been very familiar with through her academic sojourn.

Sadjio was famous for maintaining a GPA of 98%, often topping the entire school. This was her way of reminding her family, neighbors, and community of her very forceful rays—outshining the crowd. She would shine wherever she went—she was a star, *the* brightest of all-stars.

BY THE END OF THE SECOND marking period, Sadjio's average hit 95%. In line with the class' seating tradition, she claimed the third seat of the first row—straight to the third seat of the first row from the fourth row, making her the class' secretary by default.

Leadership positions in this class were earned through quality academic performance. The dux became the class' prefect, the second dux, deputy prefect and third dux, secretary—all positions were assigned by default.

Sadjio's duty as secretary was to note the names of noise-makers, among other administrative tasks. In addition, she was appointed as a teacher's aide for her French class. Her duty in this capacity was to teach, administer tests, and mark papers.

Both portfolios exposed Sadjio to the class' richest but ac-ademically lazy girls who often tried to bribe her with lunches, among other tokens. Little did they know that Sadjio had zero tolerance for ethical indiscipline.

Honesty, accountability, and self-transparency were among fundamental moral values that guided Sadjio's daily activities. She never succumbed to bribe and jealously protected her integrity. These values enabled her to implement her duty without fear or favor.

By the end of the Third Marking Period, Sadjio advanced to a seat further, becoming the only girl to come second in this male-dominated school that year. But this would be received with a not-so-pleasant reaction from the class dux, a male counterpart.

"This is your bus stop," was the verbal reaction of Charlayson to Sadjio's rapid advancement. He felt threatened and challenged, not by a fellow male competitor but a female.

But not a chauvinistic threat from Charlayson or Ida's inhumane treatments could dime Sadjio's raving glow. It was fierce; it was hungry; it was outrageous and exceptionally stubborn.

She emerged with a staggering 98.7% GPA by the end of the Fourth Marking Period, becoming the first female class prefect. As the school year progressed, Sadjio tightened her grip on *the* most prestigious seat of the class. She never intended to surrender it to anyone else—it was her eminent domain, and she was determined to keep it for the rest of that academic year.

Her uncle, Yacoub, would eventually return to the United States a few months later, leaving her at the mercy of Ida. She wrestled with hunger. She walked for 50 minutes each morning, navigating her way between swampy and bushy paths to get to Duala from Jamaica Road.

She walked a similar distance after school. The school was out by 2:00 PM, but Sadjio got home by 2:50 PM or later, and by the time she reached home, the kitchen sink was swamped with piles of dirty dishes awaiting her. The house had no running water system.

It was Sadjio's responsibility to fetch water at a 10-minute distance to fill up both barrels in the kitchen and bathroom for use by Ida and her family until she (Sadjio) got home from school the next day.

She was strictly prohibited from using the water she fetched for the barrels. She had to bring water whenever she needed to take a bath or needed water for other purposes. There would also be ingredients ready for her to prepare dinner—meals she was never allowed to taste.

Babé, a friend of Sadjio's, fed her throughout her stay. The well from which she fetched water was located in Babé's yard. She would sneak Sadjio into her room and have her eat something as quickly as possible before carrying on with her *water girl* duty. That would be the only food Sadjio would have and stay on until the next day, at the same time.

Chapter TWENTY-SIX

ONE DAY, UPON HER arrival from school, Sadjio was ordered to change into clean clothes and come along quickly. She climbed the split-level concrete staircase leading into the living room. As she entered the bedroom, she felt Ida's heavy breath through the door. Waiting outside for Sadjio seemed unbearable. She walked so closed behind Sadjio that she could feel Ida breathing down her neck.

Then Ida said, "don't waste my time. I have important things to do. Just take off those filthy clothes of yours, and let's get going. I hate to be late for appointments."

The word appointment clicked, leaving Sadjio to wonder what it was this time. Yet, she obliged, did as instructed and followed Ida outside. They both walked up the road, along the footpath Sadjio usually took to go to school. They arrived in a large compound belonging to a subsidiary of the Oriental Timber Company (OTC), a company used by "C.T. to fund the Pepper Coast war and Sierra Leone. During the heydays of the war, OTC had a virtual monopoly on all timber shipments from Pepper Coast and much of the country's internal transportation, which enables the transshipment of arms.

"What's this all about?" Sadjio thought to herself.

She dare not ask Ida their mission in that compound on that humid, cloudy afternoon in Rue de Jamais. She had no idea why they were there. She would steal a glance at Ida here and there in search of an answer, but there was none. She became extremely nervous and anxious.

Upon their arrival, they were directed to the waiting area and offered refreshments. Sadjio politely declined the offer. Her heart was in her mouth; she had no appetite and certainly wasn't going to accept drinks from some stranger. She sat quietly in one corner, hoping and praying to get out alive and in one piece.

"*Teeyah*, where are you? I am feeling faint. I think I'm going to die," she cried, but inwardly.

Then came another ruthless order from Ida, "go and wait in there," instructing Sadjio to enter one of the guestrooms of the compound.

As usual, Sadjio did as instructed. But the fear of *what if* was gradually consuming her. Sadjio had always owned her fear, conquered it, took charge of her worries, and grew stronger. But standing alone in this strange room didn't feel alright.

She panicked when she spotted a well-made king-size bed, entirely decorated with heart-shaped red roses. The beddings were plain white with tiny dashes of burgundy splashed across the four quilt patterned pillow shams that lined the bed.

There were limestone counters and glass basins in what looked like an eat-in kitchen. In one corner was a high table adorned with baskets of goodies: undies, bath soaps, lotions, exotic nighties, a wine-red lipstick with corresponding leggings, dark chocolate bars, and perfumes of all kinds.

She could hear her tummy eating itself up, not out of hunger but out of deep fear. Then she mouthed the words she hated the most – *I am finished* – aloud, sending shivers down her spine. Her feet were vibrating under her. At one point, it felt like they were melting away, her palms drenched in their sweat.

She felt immobilized, completely paralyzed by her pronounced fear of *what if*, and the *should-haves*. Her insecurities and the doubts crept up and began devouring her mind and soul.

Then there was a soft knock on the wooden door, and Sadjio felt her last drop of strength scurry right through the crack in the carefully crafted doorframe. She hurriedly retreated into a corner, but keenly watched the doorway.

An older man with brownish looking hair entered the room. On seeing Sadjio, he discharged a silly smile and pointed to a reddish-brown door, carefully hidden behind the hallway leading into the room's walk-in closet.

"Hello, Beautiful," he greeted. "Here, this is the in-room bathroom. I thought you would have made yourself comfortable by now," he said, scurrying off to the gift baskets that lined the lone table in the room. There, he lifted a set of hot red panties and bra from one the baskets.

"Here. Please go in there and get yourself in these. You will feel much more relaxed. There is also a jacuzzi tub with plenty of clean, warm water. Go and freshen up. And feel free to enjoy the hot tub. I will be right back," he instructed and left the room.

Through the peephole, Sadjio could see the man conversing with Ida in the living room. She was eating some mouthwatering baked chicken, fresh fruits, and soft drinks that she was already devouring.

"What's jacuzzi?" Sadjio wondered. She had never heard of that word and certainly had never seen such a tub in her life. It made no sense to her why she had to deal with a jacuzzi all of a sudden. "I see no logic in everything that's unfolding."

In an apparent quest to quench a soaring thirst she had fought so hard to suppress, she moved closer to the bathroom, pushed the door open, and right there was a jacuzzi overwhelmed by punches of bravado and a sea of rose petals. There was also a magnifying makeup mirror.

"So, what am I doing here? What do all of these have to do with me?" she kept asking, rhetorically.

But just when she was about to embark on another deep mind journey, she heard the door open slowly but surely. The elderly reappeared from behind the door. The man was shocked to see Sadjio still rocking her tight blue jeans and long sleeve t-shirt.

"You don't want to enjoy the luxury in here, right?" he asked her, but she said nothing.

Then, he began touching Sadjio. Without any idea of what those touches signified, Sadjio became uncomfortable. As the touches intensified, she began to cry. Gradually, she started screaming at the top of her lungs for help, claiming the attention of other residents of the compound. A crowd of four gathered and was thirsty to be in the know of what was going on.

"Is someone beating his girlfriend in there?" asked a member of the curious crowd.

"But this is very unusual. We've never heard such noise coming from this apartment," another stated.

Feeling very uncomfortable, the older man let go of Sadjio. She instantly dashed out and headed for the main gate.

Ida followed closely, obviously pissed off. "What's wrong with you?" she yelled.

"This is, exactly, what your friends do to get money to buy food, clothes, perfumes, underwear. What's your point? What's wrong with you? Do you think it will kill you? How do you expect to eat? You are such an idiot! What a stupid and spoiled child you are. But wait and see what I will do to you today," Ida continued ranting as the duo walked home.

As Ida vented, Sadjio paid her no mind. She was deeply engrossed in fear and couldn't grasp the fact that she merely escaped being raped. She felt her lips moving side-to-side, back and forth involuntarily. Her arms and legs were shaking uncontrollably, and suddenly her body temperature soared.

For the rest of that sleepless, restless night, Sadjio ran a fever of 105 °F. But that didn't deter Ida from fulfilling her promise to Sadjio. Ida instructed her to lie flat on her belly in submission to a cruel flogging.

This punishment was, however, a much more preferable alternative to being raped and used as a sex slave. Had Sadjio given in, this would have been her introduction to sexual exploitation. She was only 17 years old at the time and had never had a close or intimate relationship with the opposite sex.

She was a shy, clueless girl whose innocence was nearly robbed, in a brutal manner as well. She had no idea what the deal between Ida and this older man was. She also had no idea what Ida meant by "this is what" other girls did to earn money for their personal needs. All she knew was that at her age, she had no business worrying about clothes, perfumes, undies, and so forth. Her mom, Hadjala, was consistently providing those items. Her sole concern at the time was doing a great job academically and nothing else.

Saléma came to Ducor with loads of personal effects for Sadjio: dresses, skirt suits, and pants made of top-quality African fabrics (Vlisco Dutch Wax Hollandais) —each fabric with its eye-popping design, pattern, and color.

The bubbly colors, bold patterns, and popped texture of the fabrics brought Sadjio's beauty-full circle. Each suit cost

50,000 francs CFA (roughly $100). Saléma had also brought along some shower gel, body lotion, undies, feet wear, hair pomade, and $200 in cash. But upon her return, Ida took effective control of all the supplies and physical cash. She remodeled each attire to fit her slender body.

AS THE WEAC EXAMS DREW closer that year, Sadjio stayed up late each night to review her notes in preparation for those national and regional exams. Upon concluding her daily chores that lasted four hours per session, 5:00 PM to 8:00 PM, she would stay up until to 1:00 AM to study. But even those study periods were often disrupted by Ida blowing off the candlelight upon which Sadjio depended to review her notes.

The house had no electricity and no running water.

"It is mine. Go and buy yours," Ida would say, reminding Sadjio of her authority and ownership of everything in the house, including the candlelight.

This incident caused Sadjio much headache, especially since she needed the light to study ahead of her exams. She would eventually bring her friend, Babé, up to speed with this development. Babé, a chubby, dark-skinned girl, responded with dozens of candles for Sadjio to use.

But Ida had a counter plan.

Whenever Sadjio began to study, Ida would incite her young sons to drum on the table where Sadjio sat to study. When she tried to change seats, Ida would either hit her with a shoe heel or a cooking spoon for attempting to "restrict her kids in their own home."

Sadjio would go on take the annually administered West African Examinations Council's 9th Grade exam, marking the official end of her mission to Ducor that year and was more than ready to return to her mom, Hadjala.

One day, she confronted Ida on this subject: "The school year is over. I want to go to Hadjala."

For a moment, Ida acted as though she never heard Sadjio speak.

"….and who do you think will pay your bus fare? You will have to walk from here to your mom," she eventually responded, still looking away while humming aloud.

She was right. There was no money to pay Sadjio's bus fare from Ducor to Fortesville. But was that enough reason to deter her from going home? Not with the level of ruthlessness being meted out to her.

"I will go to Stacieya. She's familiar with frequent travelers between here and Fortesville.

She might be able to help me get to Hadjala. I will like to move in with her," Sadjio insisted. She was determined to call it a quit.

Stacieya was one of Hadjala's loyal friends. During Sadjio's stay with Ida that year, she spent most weekends at Stacieya's *Maison des Gens Heureux* residence, where she had unfiltered access to food, clean water, and a decent bed on which to sleep. Stacieya also gave per diems to Sadjio whenever she stayed over. Sadjio was positive that Stacieya was her lone savior at this point.

"Start going now. I am not holding you," Ida responded, somewhat reluctantly.

By then, the sun had started its descend across the horizon. It was 6:30 PM, the skies were clear. The city was gearing up for the weekend—commuters where making rush hour rounds to their final destinations.

Sadjio immediately went in and grabbed her bag. She walked to the bus stop, waited there for a moment for a bus to *Maison des Gens Heureux.* When a bus eventually showed up, Sadjio negotiated an 'arrive-and-pay' deal with the driver— meaning Stacieya would pay upon Sadjio's arrival; this is how Sadjio traveled whenever she went over to see Stacieya. She always never had money to pay her way to and from *maison des gens heureux*, from Rue de Jamais.

The driver agreed to Sadjio's deal, and they sped off. She would spend an additional two weeks in Ducor in the comfort of Stacieya's home with absolutely no harassment whatsoever. When she finally found suitable adult guidance for Sadjio's journey to Fortesville, Stacieya paid Sadjio's way and gave her an additional 10,000 CFA (roughly $20) as miscellaneous funds for the trip back to Hadjala.

It was an endless journey from Ducor to Loguatuo, Pepper Coast's border with Ivory Coast in the far north. After completing immigration and customs formalities, Sadjio continued her trip to Danané. There, she boarded a bus to Fortesville, arriving at dawn.

Once off the bus, she loaded her bag on her head and made her way to Quartiér Garman.

AT HOME, NO ONE expected her arrival. Suddenly, the yard came to life. There was jubilation everywhere: *Sadjio is back! Sadjio is back!* This rhythm rocked the yard for the very first hours of that day.

Amidst the celebration, Hadjala had a weird feeling about Sadjio's appearance. She pulled her in a corner and began a probing session.

"Why are you looking so skinny? You look unhealthy. What's the matter?"

"You should be thankful. I spent two weeks with Stacieya, eating, and sleeping well. Otherwise, you would have fainted on seeing me," Sadjio began, recounting her ordeals, one scenario after the other, including the attempted first degree or statutory rape that was instigated by Ida.

Hadjala dreaded hearing Sadjio's tribulations during this second trip. It sounded more like a roundtrip to hell. She had previously dismissed rumors of possible maltreatment of Sadjio by Ida, assuming that gossips were a major divider when given credence. But seeing her daughter looking all malnourished, famished with a body inundated with scars, Hadjala was filled with an indescribable sense of terror.

Chapter TWENTY-SEVEN

By late 1999 to early 2000, the refugee school system was fading out. The international and donor communities had trimmed their support to most schools due principally to low attendance, a sudden change in philanthropic focus to support other causes, and so forth.

At first, they tried to encourage attendance by introducing nutrient-rich high energy biscuits, storybooks, and toys. Fridays, the last school day of the week, was distribution day. Quantities were measured against students' daily attendance: if you showed up for two days, you had two biscuits to take home; if you came for the five days, you got an entire pack of five-piece cookies and other goodies. Sadjio always got her full packet of biscuits.

The supplies were a way of improving the school retention rate while strengthening students' attention and learning. But not even the Beauty and the Beast, Cinderella, Snow White, Puss in Boots books and toys could keep the students returning for the same experience.

Eventually, by the early 2000s, only a few cities still had ADRA-operated schools. One of them was St. Jeans based in Danané, a bustling town in western Ivory Coast. Though very hesitant to see her daughter off to a completely different world,

Hadjala was determined to hop on a passenger bus headed for Danané at the slightest chance. The distance between Danané and Fortesville was conveniently short.

Moreover, Jamaal had moved to Danané, chasing after his bearings in life. He was now a high school graduate in search of a part-time job while trying to figure a direction for his life. The agreement was that Sadjio would share Jamaal's one-bedroom studio apartment while going to school. She would stay in the living room.

With this idea forged in fire, Sadjio was dispatched with Saléma accompanying her to make sure things were under control and in place.

On a wet Thursday afternoon, they boarded the last minivan leaving Fortesville for Toulepléu, where they would board another van for Danané. It had started to drizzle, making the yellow dirt road muddy and slippery. Halfway through the journey, their 22-seater bus plunged into a gutter on the side of the highway. The accident, though bloodless, had everything to do with spillage due to the bad weather. The road was hazardous.

Once everyone was confirmed unhurt, and the minivan had no signs of damage, they boarded and went on, arriving in Toulepléu at 6:00 PM. Saléma swiftly made the necessary arrangement to get them on their connecting minivan.

The 2hr 16 min journey ended at 8:00 PM that night when the pair arrived at Jamaal's nearly vacant apartment. There was a mattress resting on the floor of the bedroom; there was a medium-size metal bucket used to fetch water for household use. There was no furniture whatsoever, no cooking utensils, no drinking or eating apparels. The apartment lacked a cooling system; you had to squat over a hole in the ground to pee.

The next morning, Saléma dashed off to the *grand marché* and bought a brand-new mattress for Sadjio and nice beddings before returning to Fortesville.

But Jamaal would travel to Simaya for weeks, leaving Sadjio all by herself in the apartment at age 17, going on to 18. This live-in situation was considered unacceptable by *N'Bor*, a paternal aunt of Sadjio's, who had been visiting them. *N'Bor* rounded up Sadjio's belongings and took her to a friend's house where Sadjio stayed for the remainder of the academic year.

Her new host, Allida, was a very nice, patient woman who treated Sadjio like her very own. But Allida's daughter Sadia insisted on being hostile with Sadjio. She subjected her to intensive cooking daily.

Sadjio cooked every morning before leaving for school in the afternoon. She was also required to do manual laundry every weekend. Besides, Sadia demanded that Sadjio slept on the floor only covered with a thin floor mat. Occasionally, she restricted Sadjio's access to food.

After two weeks of sleeping on the floor, she wrote a letter to Hadjala:

> *"Dear Teeyah,*
>
> *I hope this letter finds you doing well. This letter is to inform you know that I am starving and sleeping on the floor. At night, I can barely sleep because I feel too cold. I am also always hungry. Please do something or come and get me.*
>
> *I love you,*
> *Sadjio"*

Hadjala responded with a brand-new king-size mattress, backed up with bags of yams, plantains, among many other supplies. There was a new consignment of supplies coming in during the last week of each month, eventually ending Sadjio's hunger. This move also made a strong statement to Sadia, who later relaxed her attitude and redirected her energy toward more important matters.

Following the completion of the school year 2000 – 2001, Sadjio would go for further studies, in the Gold Coast.

Chapter TWENTY-EIGHT

THE FIRST word that came out of Hadjala's mouth whenever Ida's name was mentioned was, "I was such a fool to have trusted her all those years." It was clear; she had had enough.

Her newly crafted motto was: *never trust your child with anyone*. Ida's behavior was disruptive, arrogant, and confrontation. Her pronounced lack of empathy and humility had had damaging impacts on their relationship as siblings. Hadjala's once impeccable trust was missing, and this bred uncertainty and doubt over their entire lifetime of interactions.

Further, developments in Danané had Hadjala avoiding any thought of sending Sadjio away to school. But she had no choice. Ssdjio's thirst for education was insatiable, and Hadjala shouldered the responsibility of quenching this soaring desire.

"Jamaal, I am told that the Gold Coast has some of the best schools in the region. I am considering the idea of sending your sister there for school. What are your thoughts on this since you studied there?"

Jamaal's eyes popped out. "You know how expensive it is to sponsor a student in the Gold Coast. I mean…. you know this from experience."

"Jamaal, my son, in this life, never be afraid to take a risk. If it doesn't kill you, it makes you even stronger. I supported you from beginning to end, though it was a tough call. That has prepared me for this," Hadjala responded, cracking up more fresh peanuts harvested in their backyard garden.

"Think of life as a pool of water: if you don't test it, you will never know its true temperature. But if you daringly plunge into it, you are privileged to know whether it is cold, hot, lukewarm, or warm."

Bouncing his soccer ball against the wall, Jamaal asked, "why don't you tell me more about this plan? I believe you have a plan in mind. Let me hear it."

"I am just tired of her being mistreated by others simply because she's staying with them while pursuing her dreams. She should NOT suffer while searching for education. No-body should suffer because they are deeply in love with edu-cation."

"Can you please speak a bit clearer for me?" Jamaal cut in.

"Everyone is exploiting her loneliness, her vulnerability. She wants an education, which is why she was in Ducor re-cently, and now, Danané-but was abused in both places. There was much cruelty meted out to her, and I am sick of it."

"In the Gold Coast, she will be at a dorm, and I am pre-pared to foot the bills. I cannot afford to put her in harm's way again. I will need you to accompany and enroll Sadjio at a good school in the Gold Coast, preferably Cape Coast. Make sure it's a decent one," Hadjala instructed.

Then Jamaal asked, "staying on the dorm sounds great. But what happens in the event of an emergency?"

"On that, you are so right. But you have been there. You have lived and went to school there. Why don't you recom-mend someone, you know?" Hadjala quickly interjected.

"I know a lady in Cape Coast. Her daughters are at a boarding school. I will reach out to her to see if she will be interested in serving as Sadjio's primary guardian," Jamaal assured Hadjala.

In September 2000, Jamaal and Sadjio embarked on a two-day trip to Cape Coast from Fortesville. It was a long drive down stretches of roads adorned with potholes. At the time, the 499KM or 6 hours 36 minutes trip from Fortesville to Simaya happened at night—departure was at 4:00 PM, and arrival in Simaya was at dawn the following day.

Entering Simaya after 10:00 PM was strictly discouraged for safety reasons—the city was teeming with marauding bandits than it could contain. Travelers arriving at night were harassed, robbed, and, or killed for their belongings by heavily armed thugs.

On the day of their departure, a mini crowd gathered at Fortesville's dust-covered parking station. Some had the explicit goal to bid Sadjio farewell and wish her well with her studies.

Prominent members of this group were: Annie, Ouwah, and Mayongbeh – Sadjio's childhood friends.

Others, too, came around to convene small talking circles on how Sadjio was free to explore the world of prostitution beyond the borders of Pepper Coast and Ivory Coast, as she headed for the Gold Coast.

"Why will any mother send her daughter to an unknown land in the name of education?" they asked among themselves.

Those with guts put the question to Hadjala, who shrugged it off as mere fear of the unknown and paid them no attention. She was resolute.

On that bright, humid afternoon, Jamaal and Sadjio boarded the first STiF bus, and off they went.

Bus brands, such as STiF, UTB, ST, among many others, were thriving at the time. Generally big, modern, and comfortable, these buses transported people to Simaya, Ivory Coast's central city, from everywhere across the country, daily. They were one of the country's most accessible and affordable means of transport. Each bus business owned its uniquely branded station.

The best part of the overnight travels was the chance to get a fulfilling view of Yamoussoukro. The multi-million-dollar Basilica stood tall in that city. The 300-million-dollar structure was a must-see, absolutely stunning. The size, scale, and symmetry of the Basilica were breathtaking. It was a jaw-dropping Cathedral sporting an enormous gilded cross that adorned its top.

Upon arriving in Simaya, the pair boarded a minivan that was headed for Aboisso, where they boarded a shared taxi to Noé.

The road to Noé from Simaya was paved and in good condition. Scenes on this road were practically the same: remote villages comprising no more than ten homes owned by a few dozen farmers living in these thatched-roof huts and quietly tending to their crops and livestock.

This road also had a few police checkpoints at which travelers were stopped and were asked for their *carte d'identité*. There were a few checkpoints that required commuters to get down and walk in a single file for ID card inspection. Unfortunately, some passengers were harassed and extorted along this highway. Noé was a border town in Ivory Coast, and its corresponding city was Elubo, in Gold Coast.

Jamaal and Sadjio were at the border by 10:00 AM. Before crossing the bridge by foot to enter Elubo, they adhered to immigration formalities, though no visa was required for sub-regional citizens at this intercountry crossing point. They had to pay 4,500 CFA per luggage. They went through a passport check, then a health check before proceeding to the Gold Coast side of the border.

There, they had to present their yellow or vaccination cards, which they didn't have. They also had to pay 35,000 cedis each to get vaccinated. Authorities claimed that it was a legal requirement per Gold Coast laws to have the meningitis vaccination before entering the country. To avoid getting into a dispute at the border, Jamaal paid the money.

The towns of Noé and Elubo were supper bubbly with commercial transactions happening on either side of the main street that split both cities into two even halves. After clearing immigration and customs, the pair boarded a bus for Accra, dropping off at the Buduburam refugee camp where Jamaal left Sadjio and drove back to Cape Coast to meet with Mya.

A MOTHER OF five young girls, Mya was a light-skinned middle-aged woman with puffy golden hair. She was soft-spoken and had large round eyes. She was extremely kind-hearted—always willing and ready to serve humanity. All of Mya's girls were Sadjio's age group and were attending top boarding schools in Cape Coast.

She almost immediately agreed to being Sadjio's guardian without question, which was a bit weird considering how Dioulaes, a socially stratified group, were famous for diving into one's background before mingling with or associating with you. It all boiled down to credibility; for the most part, your parents were used to define your moral, social classification. If one of your parents was a descendent of a well-off family, a friend, or an affiliate of a societal heavyweight, you were off the hook. If not, you were tossed into the no-nobody basket and treated as such.

It all started with this powerful probing question: *Whose child, are you?* Never take this question for granted. It had very little to do with the mere name of your mom or dad, but everything to do with their background, their upbringing, the area or location in which they grew up, their marital status, and so forth. It was a fundamental background check question that defined your relationship with the other side.

But Mya had no time for such idleness. She was more focused on things that mattered the most in life than rolling out a robust social background check. The weirdest part was that this woman just didn't care; she saw no point in running a word-of-mouth background investigation before taking in a girl in need, especially one that was focused on chasing her dreams through education. Though unlettered, Mya valued girls' education and did everything to support such a worthy cause.

While in Cape Coast, Jamaal proceeded to the the Varsity School, per Mya's suggestion. Her daughters attended there. As a parent that was very involved with the education of her girls, Mya was happy with every aspect of this school.

The Varsity School was a mixed high school with strictly separated hostels along gender lines: the girls' hostels were miles away from those of the boys – Open Arms. Both sexes only met and interacted during school hours, and that was it, at least that's how it was supposed to be until disgruntled members on either side began jumping the high walls fencing them in.

During his visit, Jamaal made a quick stop by the Roses Hostel, the girls' dwelling place, to obtain relevant information about life in there: fees, policies, daily routine, study periods, etc. After successfully fulfilling his mission, he set out for Buduburam that evening, boarding a raggedy bus that was en route to Accra from Takoradi. The main interstate highway connecting Cape Coast to Accra ran through Buduburam.

Back in Buduburam, Sadjio was nursing soaring anxiety. The ETA – estimated time of arrival – provided by Jamaal had come and was long gone. Before leaving that morning, he promised to be back before nightfall since the distance between both cities wasn't that of a big deal. Sadjio would spend half the night awake, eager to hear Jamaal announce himself.

The next morning, she got up earlier than usual, checked around to see if he showed up while she was asleep. She ran outside to make a 360° visual check, but the result yielded was not what she expected. She ran back inside, took a haphazard bath, running a toothbrush up and down her teeth, and dashing right back in the room to get dressed.

She then scurried up the central expressway leading to Cape Coast. There, she made herself comfortable on an abandoned concrete brick by the sidewalk and kept a keen eye on the road in hopes that Jamaal might be getting off one of the buses at some point. Little did she know that this would have been her routine for the next four days: a longing for her brother.

ON THE 4th DAY, while sitting in her spot by the sidewalk, she observed a light-skinned young man get off one of the buses. From a distance, he looked everything like Jamaal, but one thing was off about this young man—his right arm rested in stacks of bandages.

"Is that him?" she wondered, struggling to stay still.

But once the bus sped off, Sadjio got a more unobstructed view of the bus stop and could make up the person she had been examining from a distance.

"Jamaal! Jamaal! Jamaal!"

She rushed to hug him but came to an abrupt stop, not wanting to aggravate his pain.

With eyes filled with tears, Sadjio asked, "what happened to you? Who or what hurt you?"

Jamaal looked at his sister and flashed a brief smile. "It's ok," he said. "We should be thankful. It could have been worse. The vehicle I boarded was involved in an accident. But ...let's be grateful. I'm here."

He reached out for Sadjio's right hand. Placing her palm facedown into his, he further narrated: "As we approached Salt Pond, a small, peasant town along the beltway, I heard a loud sound emanating from the front of the car: one its front tires had busted while the driver was doing 130mph in a 65mph zone."

"The vehicle suddenly shot across the street, hitting a tree and somersaulting end over end. The car hit two more trees before coming to a full stop. Several passengers were injured and taken to a clinic in the town. Two persons died on scene from their injuries; it took fire-rescue longer than expected to arrive. I received 28 stitches to my right underarm and was kept at the clinic where I spent the last four days," he explained.

But his words of compassion did little to suppress Sadjio fear, guilt, and pain. She was afraid of losing her brother. She blamed herself for his sufferings, and that compounded her own grief. It was a moment of deep emotions for both. But like always, they wither this storm and got on with fulfilling their mission to Gold Coast.

They spend another week at Buduburam, nursing Jamaal's wound, before heading to Accra to buy needed provisions for Sadjio ahead of her grand entrance in school.

WITH THE HELP OF MYA, Sadjio was enrolled at the Varsity School. By then, she was in the 11th grade but was demoted to the 10th grade or Form One by authorities at the Varsity School. This academic adjustment, they said, was meant for her to smoothly integrate into Gold Coast's educational system, which was considered robust compared to the Pepper Coast system.

Two days to the official start of school, Sadjio came face-to-face with a cultural shock: unlike the Pepper Coast, where hair had nothing to do with education, in the Gold Coast, girls had to crop their hair to be in school. Jamaal took her to a neighborhood barber who did the honor. When he announced that it was all done, Sadjio looked down and saw the floor covered with her thick, brownish afro hair.

She felt naked without it; her hair made her feel free and feminine. She loved her unaltered hair with all her heart. She styled it in numerous ways: braids, ponytails, buns, you name it. Her dense, bouncy coarse-textured hair defined her beauty. She maintained proper grooming and hygiene.

But now, it was all cropped so low in compliance with school regulation. At first, she couldn't understand why. Why are female students forced to cut off their beautiful hair? It seemed so unfair.

Sadjio mourned for herself and other bald head girls. Without their hair, one could barely identify girls in the crowd. Their freedom to fearlessly express their beauty had been snatched and would stay that way until they were done with their secondary education.

"This policy is implemented across the Gold Coast. Keeping hair short helps students to focus less on their social class," Jamaal explained as the pair sat in the barbershop.

Sadjio would eventually fall in love with various lengths of hair and enjoyed all for the unique styles and advantages they brought. She no longer believed her hair defined her beauty, femininity.

BEING A FRESHMAN or a form one student in a senior secondary school in the Gold Coast was a totally different, extremely shocking experience by itself. First-year students were subjected to abuse of all forms: bullies, harassment, sexual abuse (touching of genitals), physical assault, and mental injury. The most painful part was that perpetrators got away with their nasty offenses, some of which took the form of torture. Basically, seniors were bent on brutally snatching a freshmen student's happiness at every opportunity. Whatever you did was equivalent to punishment.

From day one, through to the end of the academic year, you were a direct target of mockery, unnecessary punishments at the hands of seniors, and you dare not complain.

Besides, seniors consistently fished through your chop box for provisions at your displeasure. Again, you dare not refuse or question their acts. If you did, it would rain punishment for you. They used you as an entertainment machine.

As a Form One student, you dared not report a senior's inhumane acts to school authorities no matter what you went through. If you did, you were doomed. They would make your stay as hot as hell.

Once enrolled, Sadjio was lodged at The Roses Hostel. On her inaugural night at The Roses, her chop box was ransacked by seniors, hungrily fishing through and taking possession of nearly every provision there were. But that was only the beginning of an entire night of terror.

That night, after dinner, Sadjio scurried to her bed, hoping for a sound sleep. And as sleep crept in, she heard a loud knock on the door. A bunch of seniors kicked in the door and commanded her to meet them in the main lobby area. Rubbing her eyes with one hand, with the other side throwing on a sleeping jacket, Sadjio made her way to that night's meeting area, as directed.

There, she met many Form Ones or first-year students waiting to be served with a list of weird punishments. Some had been ordered to kneel; others were lying face down on the bare, concrete floor. Others, too, were standing with both hands wrapped around their heads, face tucked in dark corners. A few girls had been ordered to take off their undies to be examined to verify their claim of being virgins.

Sadjio's feet could no longer support her. A severe quaking feeling consumed her in a flash.

Then the order came, "We need you to perform a song."

"I can't sing," Sadjio replied.

This instantly aggravated the seniors, who then complained that she was embarrassing them and was made to kneel for hours.

When she finally succumbed and decided to sing *Notre Histoire* by Pierriette Adams, they said her performance was too awful. They accused her of wanting to burst their eardrums and curse their day. So, her punishment doubled.

She was later asked to fan two seniors who were ready for bed. Her task was to fan these ladies until they slept. Whenever she stopped fanning, thinking the seniors were asleep, they woke up and added to her punishment.

On that first night, she barely had two hours of sleep, was up by 5:00 AM to get ready for class.

Three months into the academic year 2001-2002, Sadjio suffered fragile health.

Residents of The Roses Hostel in Kakumdu were given a rude awakening one morning when Sadjio began yelling for help. With both hands tightly cuddling her head, she cried from a merciless headache that attacked her at 2:00M that morning.

Her school mother, Ruby Lawson, and other friends rushed to get a bucket of cold water with some ice wrapped in a white sheet or towel to make an ice pack to aid her pain. But none helped. She was eventually transported to a major hospital in the city for immediate medical attention.

After spending three nights in the emergency room, she was discharged to go home and rest. No diagnosis was made. Her vital signs were all in good condition. Results from her blood works came back with no signs of illness. She was subjected to further testing and lab works, yet, there was no diagnosis.

Sadjio would spend the next six consecutive years of her life battling a silent illness that doctors in Gold Coast, Pepper Coast, and Ivory Coast would never diagnose.

DOCTORS IN CAPE COAST first claimed she had pneumonia and treated her for that for three weeks but realized she really didn't have anything close to that illness. They then came back with a diagnosis for asthma and started her on asthma treatment, but soon aborted that because she never had that either.

After several other wrong diagnoses, Sadjio was left at the mercy of this mysterious illness. She would eventually come face-to-face with a dagger after a wrong diagnosis pointed in the direction of uterine fibroids.

She was confused—never experienced heavy bleeding or prolonged menstrual bleeding. Her monthly periods, for the most part, were regular. She felt no unusual heaviness or pressure of any sort in her lower abdomen. Yet, doctors told her that she was nursing this silent conqueror.

By then, when fibroids assailed a woman, she was compelled to face the dagger of one surgeon or the other. Sadjio was scheduled to undergo surgery but was advised against the procedure by a friend who felt Sadjio's symptoms were pointed in a completely different direction.

Sadjio defied all odds and left the Varsity School with resounding success, completing the A-Levels and a West African Examinations Council (WAEC) certificate in August of 2003.

She studied General Arts – electives: Literature-in-English, Economics, French & Geography (both Human and Physical Geo), graduating with credits for academic excellence.

As always, Sadjio was usually counted among students achieving the highest academic distinctions at the end of each Term. She won numerous academic prizes for either topping her class or the entire school during a given Term.

She was a winner, a conqueror extraordinaire. There was nothing the various opposing forces could do to stop her from thriving. The more they tried to frustrate and distract her, the more she soared. She was a star, one with an unforgiving, uncompromising brightness.

AS SADJIO chased her dreams across the Sub-Sahara, Hadjala and the rest of the family were anchored in Fortesville. Life in this western Ivorian town was relatively peaceful until September 2002 when Ivory Coast was exposed to a civil war, rooted in electoral violence.

As the conflict raged throughout the country, Fortesville remained relatively untouched until December 2002 when it was attacked by mercenaries from Pepper Coast, recruited along ethnic lines to avenge killings of their Guéré kin across the border—in Ivory Coast.

These mercenaries were predominantly ex-combatants of C.T.'s *Jarsar*, who knew no other trade but warfare. They preyed on the Ivorians' internal conflict to maximize their financial gains by looting towns and villages along Pepper Coast's multiple borders or entry points with Ivory Coast in the west. These bloodthirsty thugs only thrived during warfare.

Before the arrival of Pepper Coast ex-fighters on the scene, the Ivorian war seemed primarily targeted at then-President Laurent and his loyalists. The Ivorian rebels appeared sensitive and disciplined. Their mission, according to them, was to unseat the then government of Laurent. They, therefore, targeted their rebellion at political heavyweights, doing everything possible to avoid aiming their arms at unarmed civilians. They branded themselves as protectors of lives and properties, warriors of, by, and for the people – *les guerriers*.

This was a huge contrast from what happened in neighboring Pepper Coast. There, the rebels were exclusively focused on killing civilians and destroying the country's infrastructure. Such was the kind of guerilla warfare they knew and understood. They were remarkably scruffy and undisciplined.

As the Ivorian war raged on, Pepper Coast mercenaries began regrouping and launching fresh attacks on towns and villages across the border. Fortesville and surrounding towns and villages were the first to fall prey to these marauding beasts who looted, raped, tortured, and killed unarmed civilians.

Reports of brutal attacks on Toulépleu hit residents of Fortesville one morning. It then became apparent that nowhere was safe. The thought of Toulépleu, the nearest town to

Fortesville, resting in the hands of ruthless thugs, was enough warning that Fortesville was next in line. But at this point, the city had been encircled. Every entry point had been locked down.

December 6, 2002, marked the end of the Holy Month of Ramadan. It was a cold and cloudy morning. Under normal circumstances, the day would be greeted with various festivities in commemoration of Eid-Al-Fitr. But this Eid was an extremely bitter one.

With their safety and survival in jeopardy, Eid was as dead as the town. The least residents did, was to gather for the required congressional prayer that characterized the observance of Eid feasts, per Islamic teachings. That prayer was, in fact, brutally aborted by a disturbing rocket sound. Fortesville was officially under fire. There were shooting, killing, burning of houses and huts, and looting going on across town.

Like many others, Hadjala and her family remained caved in their Quartier Garman residence for three weeks until their survival was counter-threatened by the lack of food and water. By then, many of their relatives and neighbors had been shot dead or mutilated. They had no choice but to leave, taking cover in nearby bushes and forests.

They walked for several days, eventually ending up in Guiglo, a major city situated at approximately 60KM from Fortesville. There, they board a passenger bus for the Queens.

Like the war in Pepper Coast, the Ivoirian war stole everything Hadjala had worked hard to earn for her family during their stay in Fortesville. The relatively decent life they lived there was cruelly aborted.

Life in Queens as refugees was another rough experience. They could barely afford a two-square meal per day; the entire family was boxed in a single bedroom. The family was taken back to zero by the war.

FRIDAY, AUGUST 23, 2003, marked the official conclusion of Sadjio's secondary school days in the coastal city of Cape Coast. This came after nine years of intense struggle for education, and now it was time to say goodbye to grade school. She drove to Simaya, in Ivory Coast, on Saturday. Unfortunately, that Sub-Saharan state had plunged into a brutal civil conflict that went full-blown in September 2002, forcing Hadjala and others to seek refuge in Queens. They stayed in Queens as dual refugees, uprooted from their community of origin in Pepper Coast and now, by a raging conflict in their newfound safe haven, Ivory Coast.

After spending a week in Simaya, Sadjio drove west, to Man, Ivory Coast's western capital. The city of Man was picturesquely nestled in a ring of 18 steep green mountains with waterfalls. Saléma had been waiting in Man to receive Sadjio.

Road travels across the country at the time, were very risky. A failed coup attempt in September 2002 had birthed a significant division in the country. Rebel forces claimed the northern part of the country and parts of the country's central region, leaving the government only a minute southern half. Simaya was reasonably calm.

Before the civil war broke out, the journey from Simaya to Man took eight or nine hours. This time, it took Sadjio two full days, because she had to pass through at least seventy roadblocks. In some places, there was a roadblock every half hour. They were makeshift checkpoints made of tree limbs, pieces of junked machinery, tires, and concrete blocks.

The men on guard, especially those in Logoualé (the last major town before entering the city of Man), roused themselves from the shade of Mango or coconut trees, grabbed their AK-47s, and glowering behind sunglasses, they walked over to the minivan conveying Sadjio and others, fingers on triggers.

They wore leather thongs with polished wooden or stone amulets, leather clubs, or sheathed knives around their necks, with tones of rings on their fingers. Wearing these, they believed, made them bulletproof. Also, carved fetish collectibles stood guard alongside the roadblock.

The boys ordered everyone in the minivan to identify themselves and bring their luggage into a tiny warehouse for inspection. They searched inside each, demanded to see travel documents/identifications, and collected roughly $20 from everyone onboard.

Sadjio made it through to Saléma, who then found another shared bus to convey Sadjio to Simaya, where Hadjala had been residing since the Ivoirian war. Saléma stayed in Man to make arrangements for the family's return.

MEANWHILE, life was booming for Ida and her family back in Ducor. She was now trading between Simaya and Ducor, dealing in assorted goods. On one of her business trips to Simaya, she located Hadjala and her family. As strategic as she was, she managed to convince Hadjala again to send Sadjio to her in Ducor, where she (Sadjio) would begin a career, having completed high school successfully. The idea sounded very pleasing to Hadjala's ears, especially considering the family's economic status at the time.

"Upon hearing that Sadjio had completed her studies in the Gold Coast, I contacted her school in Ducor," Ida said. She was very conny and knew when to kick off a conversation with her sister. Both women were seated outside. Hadjala was cooking that day's dinner in the front of Hadjala's rented, un-coated bricks room.

"For what?" Hadjala inquired.

"To see if she made it through the 9th Grade WAEC successfully," Ida responded.

"And what did you find?" Hadjala instantly retorted, knowing that Sadjio had taken those exams under compounding stress.

"Well, as you know......Sadjio is the type that leaves her mark wherever she goes," Ida added, with a very sinister smile. "I have her certificate here with me. She passed the exams."

For a moment, Hadjala looked dumfounded but soon snapped out of that mood, knowing that Sadjio was her *gifted* child, a *fighter*. Though her education was delayed, once presented with the opportunity to explore, Sadjio never ceased to flourish academically. Her unapologetic academic brilliance had neighbors accusing Hadjala of furnishing Sadjio with supernatural concoctions, in addition to labeling her as a jinni.

"You should send her to me once she gets her high school certificate from Gold Coast," Ida added, searching Hadjala's face for forgiveness. "Pepper Coast is recovering from war, and things are picking up. She can come there and start doing something with the knowledge she has gained. That way, she can help you all."

"But first thing first: let me apologize for all that happened between Sadjio and me. I promise to be good moving forward. Please forgive me," she said, kneeling and bowing down, with both hands resting at the bottom of Hadjala's feet.

Traditionally, Ida's gesture was considered the highest form of repentance. Such display of remorse, genuine or not, came off as an awareness of her unacceptable behaviors. She had taken ownership, had sought forgiveness, and proposed a new strategy to make amends.

"You are forgiven," Hadjala said.

That again sealed another deal, except that this deal would be the *final deal* ever struck between the sisters.

Chapter TWENTY-NINE

DAILY LIFE in Queens was exceptionally grueling for Hadjala and her family. They barely could afford food, surviving on hand-to-mouth with minimal access to pipe-borne water, and proper sanitation facilities. The family of five was bundled up in a single bedroom studio, and for the most part, they slept with empty stomachs, skipped meals, or relied on limited food handouts from friends to fill in the gap.

A combination of sharp economic decline, chronic poverty, widespread malnutrition, backed by limited access to essential social services like health, water, and sanitation, made living in this town an unyielding nightmare.

Despite its unusual economic hardship, Queens had generously offered to house thousands of refugees from neighboring countries – Ivory Coast, Pepper Coast – during the peak of regional civil wars in the Sub-Sahara. It shared borders with both countries. A bulk of the refugees lived in camps dispersed across the country, struggling to put food on the table. Though some had access to limited food rations made possible by the UN, hundreds of families, including that of Hadjala's, remained food insecure; they lacked consistent access to adequate food.

Sidique, Sadjio's stepdad, was the family's sole breadwinner at the time. To make ends meet, he spent most of his days hauling fresh produce from one remote village to the other with the help of a four-wheeler. Whenever he could afford it, he would send some money down to Hadjala for food and rent.

But after spending four hunger-stricken months in Queens, the family returned and settled in Man, western Ivory Coast, where they began a new life. They stayed in a rented two-bedroom mud house in Man's Blocôs community.

Even here, Sidique continued to perform his sole income-earner role to sustain the family diligently, a duty he performed with impeccable dedication and courage. This time, he worked as a vendor for wholesalers based in Man's inner-city – *Grand Marché*. He took assorted goods on credit, traveled by bicycle to surrounding villages and towns to sell his wares. He was usually given a one-week turnaround period as loan repayments were due on Friday of each week. Meager profits generated from this undertaking fed and clothed the family, as well as paid the rent.

The city of Man was ridiculously loveable, home to eighteen mighty mountains dubbed *Les Dix-Huit Montagnes*. A set of twin mountains overlooked the city – *Mt. Tonkoui and Mt. Les Dent de Man*. With a population of nearly 200,000, Man was also home to a breathtakingly scenic beauty – *Les Cascades de Man*. This eyepopping waterfall was one of Ivory Coast's loveliest. The town's designated market day was Friday.

On this day, seas of vendors and traders traveled to Man from far away villages, walking or riding on bicycles or driving in crowded pickup trucks. Many were women, carrying their wares on their heads. In addition to wares on stalls, wheels, or displayed on store shelves, some sellers displayed their wares in temporary shelters made of banana leaves or grass thatch. Sellers traded everything from fresh farm produce to non-perishable products such as contemporary textiles either by cash, on loan, or by barter.

Save Sunday, this open-air market operated throughout the week but was exceptionally crowded on Friday. Merchants – tailors, barbers, carpenters – made their way to the market to sell their services.

Life in Man was a new experience. Here, the family enjoyed consistent access to three-square meals. Residents were primarily farmers; the city was always awash with freshly harvested produce: lettuce, tomatoes, peppers, yams, cassava tuber, plantains – all grown locally and were super affordable.

On a typical day, Hadjala would take 1000 francs (roughly $2 at the time) to the market and would get fresh cow meat, oil, cubes, seasonings, fresh potato leaves, rice, among other dietary staples, for a two-day meal. A stew or gravy prepared today was split into two with a portion consume on the day of preparation and the other reserved for the following day.

Few months into this new life, Sadjio received her A-Levels certificate. She passed the exams, gaining distinctions in French, Physical and Human Geography, as well as Literature-in-English.

Leaving her family behind, she returned to her home country, Pepper Coast, with the mission of seeking personal and professional advancement to aid with the family's upkeep. Accompanied by Hadjala, Sadjio began her homecoming trip on a warm Monday morning in late August 2004.

"You are the leader of this family, our sole hope. Go out there and use your education to help us. I am confident that you will do wondrous things. Go, child," Sidique said to Sadjio as she boarded a Noorah Transport bus headed for Danané. He then proceeded to make a sensitive disclosure to her, "There have been multiple suitors for your hand in marriage, but I declined every one of them. You know why?"

Sadjio shook her head in disbelieve, staring directly into his eyes.

"Because I want you to advance your education, pursue your dreams."

"Wow!" Sadjio said, jumping onto her feet.

"Completing high school is a new beginning to an end. I want you to go to university and learn *plenty* books," Sidique noted, patting her on the shoulder as though to reawaken her spirit and her confidence to make a difference.

Sadjio tried smiling but was overwhelmed with emotions. She couldn't believe her ears. For a moment, she thought she misunderstood his points. Here's a man who fervently opposed her schooling because of her gender. Now, he was a true believer in the power of girls' education, a frontline warrior for girls' right to education. All of his sons, his once preferred gender for education, had abandoned school. They were either driving taxi cabs across the city or being a fulltime live-in burden on the family.

"Baba, I will make you proud," Sadjio said, tears racing down her cheeks.

Then Sidique issued a call-to-action, "All of my friends have cellphones. And you know that I cannot afford one. But I know that one day, I will be a phone owner, thanks to you. So, go on. You have my blessing."

To Hadjala, he said, "don't mind what happened in the past. Take her to Ida and Imran and ask them to take care of our little girl as she finds her bearings in life."

As both women made themselves comfortable in the window seats aboard the bus, Sidique hopped on and gave his final farewell blessing. Touching Sadjio's head, he said, "always remember that you are not alone. There are millions of good people out there. There are good people everywhere. And with our blessings, you shall succeed. Be fearless and take on the world. You shall stand before kings and queens, not mere men."

In Ducor, Sadjio was again lodged at Ida's, beginning a new Chapter of her life, aged 22.

HER INITIAL PROJECT in Ducor was to focus on sharping and sharpening her computer skills. She took computer training courses at a local IT school, during the first three months of her arrival. Through it all, Ida fought to stay true to her promise.

Four months after her arrival, Sadjio interviewed and was offered the post of columnist at a biweekly newspaper, owned and operated by James Jackson, a renowned Pepper Coast fictional storyteller. At the time, *Le Quotidian* newspaper was on Crown Hill, central Ducor. Her employer gave her a cellphone for work-related communications. The new job and cell phone quickly birthed a nasty twist in her relationship with Ida.

Fueled by a fit of innate jealousy—a trait shared by many women – Ida began treating Sadjio with much aggression. She attacked her over material things, a 3310-navy blue Nokia phone that Sadjio herself disliked due to its massiveness and brief battery lifespan. Outpowered by her soaring ego, however, Ida remorselessly ruined her pseudo-well-intension goal. However, well-intentioned, she must have been this time around; her display of jealousy overshadowed all else.

Before Sadjio's probationary period ended, she had no access to food in the house. But she seemed to handle this well.

After all, she was 22 years old now and knew how to deal with these types of crises. She religiously visited Stacieya's home, Hadjala's friend. There, she ate and was showered with love. But Ida had a Plan B in store.

A few weeks later, everyone in the home was instructed not to speak to Sadjio. She handled this. Then, Ida's children became verbally and emotionally abusive toward Sadjio, with Ida's backing. Knowing who Ida was, Sadjio dealt with that well until 10:00 PM one night when she returned from work and found her belongings dispersed on the front porch of the home.

For Sadjio, this was a deal sealer; she had had it and was more than ready to explore and take on the world, all by herself. She moved out that night and never returned to Ida's dent of hate, pain, and joyless life. As the survival she was, Sadjio did not suffer from depression later in her life from her horrible experiences with Ida. She wasn't emotionally destroyed, either. She was, however, much traumatized by her war experience.

WHEN SHE finally broke up with Ida, Sadjio moved in with Ursula, her best friend, who would later become her sister from another mother. Ursula was a dark-skinned girl with thick, bouncy black hair that she always had in an up bun. She was soft-spoken and always willing to listen as opposed to vying for the last word.

Sadjio's goal at the time was to briefly stay at Ursula's while waiting to be granted permission to move in with some members of her external paternal family that lived in Clara Town. After three weeks of back and forth, she was finally told that she wasn't welcome because "there was not enough food."

Sadjio, an extra mouth, would not be added to an already struggling family.

But the food was of no issue for Sadjio at the time. She was more concerned about her family's honor—doing everything to protect its integrity and image jealously. At the time, the Dioula tradition strictly frowned on single girls living on their own. It was a taboo for unmarried girls to rent a flat, an apartment or a house all by themselves. A girl staying at a rented apartment, all by herself, was labeled a prostitute, uncultured. And that could be traced to her parents. They were blamed for her poor upbringing.

Girls were under pressure to keep their family's honor intact by staying at *home*. Living on your own meant you were living on the *street*, which was an abominable act. No wonder Sadjio felt extremely hopeless when her extended paternal family rejected her. It was a slap in the face. She desperately needed that family attachment; she wanted to be under the roof of a family member, not on her own.

But when her attempt at blending in with this paternal family failed, Sadjio returned to Ursula with a new proposal: "Can I stay with you for an additional two weeks? I promise it will be two-weeks only," she said, looking directly in Ursula's eyes, in search of sympathy and empathy. "I am expecting some money from Hadjala to enable me to pay my bus fare to Man. Ursula, I am returning to my family. I think that's the best thing for me to do," Sadjio added, still searching Ursula's eyes.

But Ursula didn't seem interested at all. When Sadjio was done speaking, she looked around her, making sure nothing was distracting Ursula's attention. And of course, there was none. It was just the two friends sitting at the foot of the ninety-nine stairs leading into one of the two-level buildings of Dama Yard, located on Crown Hill, central Ducor.

Turning to Ursula, she asked, "did you hear what I just said?" For a moment, there was no response, and this made Sadjio very uncomfortable. She began to wonder what was going on in Ursula's mind. "Is she just ignoring me?" she thought. "But that will be an extremely insensitive thing to do. Right now, I need all the support that I can get, and that includes emotional support."

Then she looked up and said, "hey Ursula, I am sorry if I'm bothering you. I just wanted to know if you heard me and what your thoughts were on this matter."

"I did .... but only the first part of what you said, since that's the only part that I have interest in," Ursula answered.

"What do you mean? Did you hear the part about my anticipated return to Man?"

"I didn't. And that's because I hate the idea of you returning to Man. That whole idea is an acceptance of defeat. You must stand up and fight for yourself and your family," Ursula said, bluntly adding that "first of all, you are in the middle of a skills training program...you are currently taking advanced computer classes. Leaving now will mean forfeiting the money invested in that program. It will also mean that you are leaving without completing your program, which is a shameful thing to do. Wow! Are you this weak?"

Ursula looked tense as she spoke: "Also, with you being *the* only person with at least a high school education in your family, you *are* your family's sole hope. I wonder if you understand what that means, Sadjio. Returning to Man now will mean dashing everyone else's hope. You will be running away from this all-important responsibility."

"Remember, it is no longer about you now. An entire family's survival rests on your shoulders; an entire family looks up to you for a better tomorrow. That's leadership! You are their future, Sadjio; you are their HOPE. And you can't afford to disappoint your mother either. She has sacrificed so much to see you navigate your way on the educational ladder."

Sadjio was baffled. She readjusted her sitting position, leaning forward with chin resting in both palms. She was ready to be schooled constructively.

"Lastly, there's no future for you in Man. I am being candid with you. You won't be able to use your education there. You will probably end up becoming a roadside vendor, dealing in *attiéké* and grilled fish, or a roadside mobile phone booth operator. And guess what? That will be such a failure. It will be a disgrace, considering your level of brilliance. It will also be a slap in the face of those who sacrificed everything to see you through your schooling. You owe it to them," Ursula completed her speech and waited for Sadjio's reaction.

There was total silence. As though Sadjio needed some time to digest what her candid friend had just told her. Then tears began gathering in both eyes; her face became red, cheeks suddenly appeared shaky.

"Just snap out of the self-pity and use this as a challenge to prove everyone wrong; don't worry about food and shelter. You can stay with me, here", Ursula added, pointing at her warehouse-size one-bedroom with a cute queen-size bed. "That bed is enough for us," she said with a split smile.

"Thank you" was all Sadjio had, her eyes drenched, voice trembling.

As expected, 35,000 francs (roughly $70) was painfully raised by Sidique from his struggling trade and sent to Ducor to facilitate Sadjio's return home. He had had it and was not going to play the family game with anyone, not even Ida, or the folks in Clara Town. Enough was more than *enough*. Man was always a place Sadjio could call home. He felt compelled to double his hustle to raise funds, taking him nearly a month to reach his goal, because he didn't want her to wander around Ducor without a home. The lesser of both evils was her returning to Man, where she had a family, a home and unconditional love.

When Sadjio received the funds, Ursula encouraged her to double it up from her meager salary and send it back. "They need it more. Their main worry is accommodation. Send them a letter stating that you now have a new family here. I am and will forever remain your family. I promise." And Sadjio did just that.

URSULA LIVED with her older sister at the time, and this sister paid all the bills. Ursula was still in high school. One month later, Hadjala arrived in Ducor, on a mission to make sure Sadjio was in good hands. She made a stop at Ida's and requested a meeting with Ida and Imran and other neighbors as witnesses.

At that meeting, Hadjala demanded that Ida returns to her what she (Hadjala) had placed in Ida's care—her daughter, Sadjio. Per tradition, if you were handed something (in this case, someone) for safekeeping, it was your duty to safeguard and return it to its owner in one piece upon request.

"I specifically accompanied my daughter here and placed hands in yours for safekeeping. She was your responsibility. No matter the circumstances, you should have exercised patience, contacted me, or asked me to come and get my child. Throwing her out was wrong. And in all honesty, I am very disturbed by this action of yours. What you did is called abandonment. You neglected her," Hadjala explained. "I am here to take back what I had entrusted you with. Where's my child?"

"I don't know. But I know a friend of hers who might help us."

"Ida, I gave my child to you, not a friend."

The meeting became a heated debate over Sadjio's whereabouts. Eventually, it was agreed that Nadi, a good friend of Sadjio's, would be contacted, to lead Hadjala to her daughter. When contacted, Nadi initially refused to help, out of anger for Ida. But seeing the face of a distressed mother in search of her daughter melted Nadi's heart.

"I will take you to her," she said to Hadjala. "Let me make it clear that I am doing this because of you, not this evil witch," she added, casting a demonic look at Ida.

After verifying Sadjio's living condition and making sure that everything was in place, Hadjala returned to Man, leaving Sadjio to explore the world.

For four months, Sadjio enjoyed the comfort of Ursula's studio apartment until her sister began to raise issues with Sadjio's presence. She confronted Sadjio on this subject one morning, "With your presence in this house, our bag of rice no longer lasts us a month, which had always been the norm. In short, your presence here is having a direct toll on our food. Here's what needs to be done: I need you to leave."

SADJIO'S DAYS at the biweekly newspaper were short-lived. The paper eventually merged with a leading digital media agency. There, Sadjio started as a *Mousso* columnist. She researched and produced this weekly column. *Mousso* covered social issues, produced analytical lifestyle articles, touched on political and economic issues affecting the ordinary women of Pepper Coast and elsewhere across the sub-region.

Of course, Sadjio didn't forget to extend her journalistic lenses to those female political heavyweights, those shakers and movers of the society. She was concurrently started as a cub reporter in the newsroom—officially launching her into the journalism field. At the beginning of her career, Sadjio struggled with lead paragraphs and headlines. However, with the right coaching and mentoring, she began producing coherent, accurate, balanced, and engaging articles. Her narrative or storytelling style, analytic, and descriptive writing style added much value to her reports.

She eventually navigated her way to the upper echelon of the newsroom, becoming a junior report, then a senior political reporter covering the country's presidency, its Ministry of Foreign Affairs, as well as state-visits by foreign heads of state. A year later, she became an associate editor, then senior content editor.

Through it all, she was paid a meager income of $135 per month. And whenever she got paid, she dashed off to Ducor's Red Light commercial district to dispatch 90% of the funds to the family in Man. She would eventually manage to buy a flip-top, very cheap phone for Hadjala at one point.

WHILE PROGRESSING professionally, Sadjio was still being troubled by her mysterious illness. It attacked her now and then, with the worse episodes happening at work. Whenever she entered the office, she would faint or suddenly pass out and would spend days in the hospital.

Like Gold Coast, doctors in Ducor could not detect the root cause of Sadjio's illness. They first claimed that her white blood cell count was low, then moved to low red blood cell count and anemia. In late 2005, she lost her stepdad, Sidique, to tetanus booster overdose. For years, he nursed a large pus-filled boil on his right temple. While doing his roadside business across remote villages in western Ivory Coast, he was convinced by a quack doctor to get multiple tetanus booster shots, which are typically recommended every ten years. According to this unlettered doctor, the shots would have shrunk the lump on his ear. By the time he was rushed to Man's central hospital, it was too late.

Upon his death, Sadjio traveled to Man to mourn with her family. The family went to an ancestral village to perform rituals for the departed in observance of his forty-day feast, in line with tradition. There, they were informed about two herbalists whom locals believed had the spiritual prowess needed to relieve Sadjio's pain. The herbalists had an established policy: before they treated or healed a person, they had to research and reveal the cause of sickness.

In Sadjio's case, they had a series of questions to ask. After a brief spiritual ritual, they began:

"Did you fight while at school in the Gold Coast?"

"No. Fighting on campus or at the dorm was prohibited," Sadjio responded.

"Ok. But do you remember anyone slapping your forehead, whether jokingly or not?"

"No. I don't," she answered.

"Well, someway or somehow, you were slapped on your forehead on campus."

"If it wasn't done in broad day, it must have been done spiritually."

"Why would anyone want to hurt my daughter? She's only a child. Her mission to Gold Coast was to study and return with knowledge, not to fight," Hadjala interjected, feeling very uncomfortable with what was unfolding. But the herbalists paid her no mind. They responded with SHSHSHSH sound, telling her to keep it down or cut it off and let them do their job.

"The intent was to stall your professional, academic, and personal progress in life," both men said, almost at the same time. "The doer(s) wanted to mess up your life for good."

"This is why your sickness only bothers you when you are at work or in school. Other than those, you are just fine. The doer(s) meant to stall your growth in these areas."

Hadjala and Sadjio sat quietly, looking all confused. The herbalists then asked if the family wished to know who the doer of the act was.

Both women shook their heads. Then Hadjala said, "my child's health is what matters at this point. The doe(s) can wait for the day of judgment when all of humanity shall be answerable of the Almighty."

That didn't deter the herbalists, however. They proceeded with their probing session.

"Do you remember the first time your name was called for a prize during an honoring ceremony for seniors at your school in Gold Coast?"

Before responding to their question, Sadjio looked at her mom in search of answers. The look in her eyes was screaming, *who are these two? Are they normal humans or …?*

Responding, she said, "Yes. It was at the end of my First Term. I was still new on campus, in Form One. It was my first year. It was a shocking experience for me. I had never been recognized in such a manner."

Peeping through what appeared to be a white microscope feeding on a calabash of clear water, the men said, "that event was meant EXCLUSIVELY for seniors. But your GPA was a record-breaker. School authorities were wowed and couldn't ignore your performance. Honoring you on this day was an exception to the rule. You topped the entire school for that Term. It was a record-breaking GPA."

As though there was a replay or playback of Sadjio's life on campus going on, the men continued, "After that ceremony, you went home with your prize, feeling very excited to share with your mom who was a staunch supporter of your education at the time. But that night, your headache began, right?"

This statement sent chills down Sadjio's spine. *"Why are they explaining it as if they were there?"* she wondered.

"Yeah. It was that night. I started feeling cold that evening before going to bed," she managed to say.

"That's not important right now. Please, heal my daughter," a confused Hadjala again interjected.

"Hey woman, would be kind to use your inside voice? This is how we function, mama", they said to Hadjala. "We are obligated to trace the source of the problem, expose it, before taking it on. So, please be patient and let us do our job the way we know it."

Hadjala retreated to the bench they had initially provided to her. Sitting there, she starred at Sadjio, who was lying helplessly on a traditional handwoven mat before the herbalists.

"To be honest, mama, the main goal of the doe(s) was to kill your daughter. But the energy and power of her star were too strong to let that happen. Each attempt at killing her failed. Convinced that her star was uncompromisingly powerful, they resorted to messing up with her life, and that worked."

Turning to Sadjio, they said, "everything about you from birth to now has been a mystery. Too many people want to know the secrete behind your power, your conquering spirit. From the day you were born, they relentlessly watched every step of your life. They have never ceased to conjure your spirit, study it to know what the future held for you."

"You were destined for greatest in the Gold Coast. It was your land of limitless opportunities. On your 18th birthday, you were destined to claim your full power and excel beyond mere man's imagination. So, all was set for that moment. This explains why you were attacked on the eve of your 18th birthday—disrupting the course of your life from then on."

Unable to sit still, Hadjala crawled back to the mat and held Sadjio's hands in hers very tightly. The look on her face was that of *can we get past this stage already?*

Turning to Hadjala, the men said, "the good news is that we can heal your daughter. She won't ever complain of this sickness."

The herbalists then provided a bunch of three neatly cut roots and instructed Hadjala on how to implement the herbs:

"Go home. Place these in the sun for them to get dry. Then, peel the bark of each root, place those into a mortar and pound into powder. Pour the powder in raw shea butter and rub her entire body, including her hair. Repeat this for three nights, and that will be it."

And as they said, that was it for Sadjio's six-year-old mysterious illness. Shear butter and dry plant roots were the answer to her sickness.

She returned to Ducor, feeling healed and refreshed, ready to pick up from where she left off. And things were going her way. In 2009, she landed a job at the United Nations as research support and monitoring officer. In June 2010, she returned to mainstream journalism, following the completion of the research project at the UN. For a period of one-year-six-months, she researched and wrote news and features, conducted high-level exclusive interviews, directed the operations of the newsroom, and wrote articles for publication on the web in her capacity as associate editor. She also commissioned and edited stories; liaised with newsroom staff (reporters, freelancers, photographers), printers, and layout staff.

As a senior political reporter, Sadjio provided complete, accurate, and compelling coverage of the activities of Pepper Coast President Ellen Johnson Sirleaf, state visits by foreign heads of state, and the Pepper Coast Ministry of Foreign Affairs. She wrote, edited, and produced news articles for multiple platforms, including print and online. She also researched and wrote news articles while covering the Oval Office and working the breaking news beats. This position exposed her to lots of foreign travels, often accompanying President Ellen Johnson Sirleaf on international state visits, including Copenhagen, Dakar, Brussels, Niamey, Conakry, and London.

Chapter THIRTY

SADJIO LEFT London and arrived in Freetown on August 14, 2007, after spending two weeks in the British capital on vacation. She was dressed in a long, deep yellow blazer suit that looked perfectly polished, thanks to a pair of black flamingo heels, a pair of Michael Khols glasses, dark-purple lipstick, and full lashed. She looked fashionably edgy. Her hair knotted in a bun with the help of a half-piece bubbly wax prints that smoothly aligned with her outfit, bringing her beauty full circle.

It was a cold, very windy and dark Monday night. The Meridian airliner, Astraeus Airlines, touched down at about 8:00 PM local time at the Lahai International Airport. There was thick darkness everywhere, covering the lights that lined the main entrance from the runway. It was apparent; the clouds were heavily pregnant and soon began emptying their bellies.

A family friend, Momoh, was on the standby to receive Sadjio. After successfully concluding border security formalities, the pair boarded a rusty blue cab that drove them to the ferry station. There, they waited for roughly an hour before boarding to cross the Antiques River separating the Airport and Freedomville.

Waiting felt uncomfortable, adding to her anxiety. She longed for her mom, her siblings. But waiting an hour to board a ferry, upon its return from the other side of the mighty ocean, was worth every second. The boats were the cheapest option – costing less than $2, unlike the $40 fare charged by the Coach Express and Eco-Water taxi or the hovercraft, which charged $50 for adults and $25 for kids. Unfortunately, the ferries were, however, indeed not the quickest option neither the most convenient.

As they disembarked the ferry, a cab driver rushed over to help Momoh carry Sadjio's two heavily stuffed suitcases over to the vehicle, and off they went. Throughout that night, she kept thinking and hoping that she would get going the next morning to Man, Ivory Coast, where Hadjala and the rest of the family had been residing.

Initially, she considered traveling along the Bo - Genden Highway and onward to Nileville then to Man, western Ivory Coast. On second thought, that felt like a hugely tiring and stressful journey to undertake.

"Why not connect through Queens and then, Man, Ivory Coast?" she wondered.

Eventually, she reached a decision: route through Nongowa, Guéguédou, Macènta, Nzérekoré and then, Man.

First thing Tuesday morning, Momoh stopped by to accompany her to a parking station in central Freetown. There, they searched for a bus headed for Kailahun, the largest town before getting to the border town of Koindou, on the Sierra Leonean side–everywhere was muddy. The torrential rain of the previous night left most parts of the city flooded. The traffic from Crossworks to central Freedomville that morning was hefty, getting jammed throughout, almost every single time the traffic jam happened, Sadjio saw long lines of brake lights ahead. Finally, they were there. But the parking was empty, a scene that instantly dropped her jaws.

She became very nervous, anxious about losing a day without getting started on her long journey to see Hadjala and the rest of the family. She felt her blood boiling, rushing through her veins, her heart pounded the loudest.

"What an ugly way to begin! Getting started this way is NOT a good sign; not all ALL," she said quietly to herself, fighting to stay calm. She remained calm; fought back the sudden frantic state she had been launched in. She was brought back to reality when Momoh exchanged greetings with authorities at the station.

"Good morning, Sir."

"Hello," responded a feeble looking man who occupied the ticketing booth.

"Has the first bus left already?"

"First bus? Not even the last bus is leaving today. Haven't you heard the news?"

Momoh cast a hard look at Sadjio; her forehead had rumpled. He turned to further to probe the ticket dishing man: "No, Sir. What's going on?"

"We, officials of the Mandiana road transport authority, have issued a press release informing the general public that there will be no vehicles plying the Freedomville-Sikidou highway until after a week."

Sadjio received this breaking news with a stiff punch in her chest. She had been standing all along, but now, she felt a sudden urge to sit. Her tummy felt hot as though she had just finished consuming a very hot veggie soup, spiced up with powdered habanero peppers.

"What?" Momoh managed to say.

"Young man, what about this that you don't understand?" the man fired back. "Drivers and car owners are *striking*!! We are striking against soaring fuel prices!! What else don't you understand?"

Seeing how nervous she had become, Momoh quickly suggested that they wait, patiently. In her heart, she prayed for a truce in the standstill between the government and drivers. "But when will that happen?" she thought.

"He said a week. Can you afford to wait here for a week? You barely have enough money to sustain yourself till then. And if you did, that will be the end of your journey: you will be financially drained to continue with this project." Sadjio would endure endless mental torture with her mind wandering and pouring in everything but positive thoughts.

After several hours of fruitless wait, Momoh succumbed, and a decision was reached: "Sadjio, I am very sorry this is happening. You have two options: stay here until the strike is over or take a cab to Kenmou. Should you choose Option 2, I will make arrangements for you to spend the night with my aunt, who's a police commissioner there. You can then continue from there the next morning."

Of course, in her hyper state of franticness, the second option sounded very pleasing to Sadjio's ears. All she longed for at that very moment was to be reunited with her family.

"Option 2 means my trip will have to be a pick-and-drop pattern, instead of the straight shot that we all hoped for, right?"

He nodded.

"I will dare to do that." And she meant that to the letter.

IT WAS 10:00 PM. The cab conveying Sadjio drove noiselessly through the city. Kenmou's main streets were all de-peopled by heavy rain. The taxi driver drove from one police station to the other; no one knew the Commissioner's residence.

They later came across an officer who knew the Commissioner's residence but charged Sadjio a US$25 service fee. The Commissioner lived in a large compound situated within a sparsely populated neighborhood of Kenema. It looked reasonably modern and formidable.

"Good evening, Madame," greeted the officer leading this search and rescue crew.

"Hello, Beao. What brings you here tonight?"

"Oh, Madam. I come bearing a sister here that says your nephew, Momoh, had sent her to you," responded the officer.

"Hi, my daughter. Is everything ok?" the Commissioner, a heavy-built, dark-skinned woman, addressed Sadjio.

"Hello, Madame Commissioner. I am a friend of Momoh's," she responded, with an outstretched right hand holding a piece of white paper. It was a letter from Momoh to his aunty.

After reading the note, she ushered Sadjio in, ordered her servants to attend to Sadjio's needs.

"Make sure she's comfortable. It's a rainy night, get some hot water ready for her to take a bath, and feel refreshed. It's a long journey from Freetown to here. Treat her with all respect; she's my special guest," she ordered and left for work.

The house was vast, lavishly beautiful. It was fully glitzed up in white paint that was carefully complemented with burgundy in the baths: clean, modern marbles, floor to ceiling glass windows, plenty of ventilation, an expansive pool in the heart of the compound, and a beautiful landscape. This cozy feeling of the house was a perfect distraction for a moment. Sadjio took a self-guided tour of the modern villa. She explored the house's luxurious bangalore and pool before returning for a warm, therapeutic bath and snuggled for a restful, peaceful night.

The next morning, as though everything was happening from the wrong side, Sadjio could not get a vehicle. She spent the entire morning sitting in the Commissioner's office, munching on crunchy fruits and vegetables while praying silently for a positive turn of events.

It was mid-day, still no car. The only option that stood out was to join a police vehicle that was due to transport a notorious murder convict to the Sikidou Central Correctional Facility.

Save a pair of ruffled blown shorts; the convicted felon had nothing to cover his body. He was heavily chained at the back of a police-marked pickup. Along with him were Sadjio's luggage. She was then squeezed at the end of the pickup's front seat.

They drove for endless hours before arriving in Sikidou at about 11:00 PM on Wednesday. The town was as quiet as a graveyard. Sadjio could hardly see a street lamp, except for a few candle lights in the various huts across the city.

SHE WAS DRIVEN to the police chief's house to spend the night, per directives of her host in Kenmou, a police commissioner. Unfortunately, the wife of this police chief was not the kindest person on earth. She kept Sadjio standing outside, in the dark for the longest.

Sadjio was famished, but in the middle of fear, any desire for food or water was quickly swallowed down. Her skin was sticky and itchy because her regular bath hours had come and gone. She grew tired of standing and sat on one of her suitcases. She wasn't allowed in the house until 1:45 AM when the police chief himself arrived home.

"Holy goodness! Samantha! Samantha, when will you treat your fellow humans like humans? When will you stop humiliating me as your husband? A fellow officer asked me to host a guest, and you refuse to usher her in?"

"Well, how sure am I that she's who she claims to be? She could well be one of those disgusting acquaintances of yours," the wife responded. "I have little to no patience for ungodly girls, and you know it."

With that, she turned off the TV she had been watching while Sadjio stood outside, and sped off to bed. Turning to Sadjio, the police chief said, "please pretend this didn't happen. I am very sorry for embarrassing you."

Inwardly, Sadjio had no time to process Samantha's rants. Whatever the issue was between the two, it was bigger than her. "They have bigger issues, and I am not one of those," she thought.

The police chief ushered her inside what looked like an abandoned warehouse, partitioned into segments to make for a bedroom, dining room, living room. There were no inside-baths. A pile of dirty dishes sat comfortably in one corner, while a tiny black and white TV screamed local news in the other corner. Outside was a red dirt house. Inside of this dirty house was a round hole dug in the ground for use as a toilet. Squatting over this hole was a necessary struggle.

At the main entrance of the house were three bricks stuffed with firewood for cooking. There, he made hot water for her to take a shower. There was no bathroom or bathhouse. Bathing was done outside, under a couple of banana trees. But Sadjio was too jumpy, too afraid to take a shower in a bushy area.

She took the water, stood near the house, and washed her feet, face, and arms. As she returned to the living room, the police chief had made a tiny space among his wife's dirty dishes and saucepans she had dashed all over the place. The area was enough for Sadjio to sit, place her head on her luggage, and call it a night.

Chapter THIRTY-ONE

AGAIN, there was no vehicle to convey Sadjio to her destination the next morning. The one way out was to hire two bikers to transport her, along with her suitcases. At first, she was hesitant, but soon gave in and was charged an arm and a leg by the bikers before transporting her to the Katiola - Sinfra crossing point.

Katiola had been shattered as a result of the Mandiana civil war. Sadjio hardly saw people in the town. The town was noiseless as they drove through to the crossing point.

As the only available passenger, Sadjio had to wait and pray for three additional passengers to join her before boarding the canoe that would ferry them across the river. It was 11:00 AM on Thursday.

The canoe operator charged huge crossing fees. His canoe held about four people, and the crossing took 20 minutes. It moved from side-to-side as he directed it across the furiously flowing River Mao. He barely said a word; his clients included anyone who showed up at the riverside. He drove his canoe with a raggedy wooden paddle. The alternative to this river ride was to walk about 6 miles in either direction before reaching a motor road.

At about 1:00 PM, two young men showed up at the crossing point. Still, the canoe operator won't leave; they needed one more person. Time was flying by fast, and so was Sadjio's patience. Unable to suppress her brewing nerves, Sadjio opted to pay for the extra seat. They then sailed across the river into Sinfra, Queens side of the border.

Sinfra was a small town surrounded by palm plantations and virgin forests. Like Katiola, it was sparsely populated. In the center of the city was a small market of stalls and wheels. Sadjio observed no more than 60 persons engaged in various transactions, and the primary commodities being traded were palm products: nuts and oil.

There was also a makeshift booth-like structure where ticketing for cars leaving for Ténéndou was being carried out. From a distance, it appeared as though the booth had not been in operation for over six months. Its white and blue paints had been layered with thick brown dust.

Cars heading to Ténéndou only came to Sinfra on Tuesdays. It was 2:00 PM on Thursday. Sadjio fought hard to hold back her tears from racing down her cheeks. She slammed her suitcases against the brown earth and sat on them, hungry and thirsty. Then a Kia-motor, heavily loaded with multiple gallons of fresh palm oil, arrived in the town. Sadjio walked up to the driver and asked him to please take her to Ténéndou.

The old, bearded man asked if she could manage at the back of the Kia-motor, atop the gallons. Sadjio responded in the affirmative and made her way up there. She sat and held firmly onto the rails at the back of the vehicle.

"Give me your fare upon arrival," the man said to Sadjio.

Sadjio obliged without a word. As they departed, Sinfra, pregnant clouds began gathering; accompanying winds combed through leaves of palm and banana trees, carrying with them thick dust, which clogged her nose, ears, and eyes.

Arrival in Ténéndou was around 7:00 PM. The Kia driver dashed her at a roundabout in the heart of the town. There, another round of vehicle search began. She needed a vehicle to take her to Macènta.

After roughly an hour of fruitless search, she had to deal with bikers once more.

This time, it wasn't so easy; every motorbike rider she tried talking to, declined; they didn't want to deal with her, plus her two loaded suitcases.

It had started to drizzle. This marked Sadjio's third day en route to Man, a journey that would typically take a day or two to complete. At this point, she could no longer contain the tears; they were screaming down endlessly. She had had very little to eat, no proper bath taken. She would later console herself with thoughts of resilience.

"I can do this," she thought. "I will see Hadjala, Saléma, Babadéni, and Jamaal.....no matter what."

Then she heard a voice advancing towards her.

"I can take you to Macénta. Just pay me plenty money," came a voice from a distance.

"Let's go before it starts to rain. Buy some plastic bags to wrap around you and your luggage. It will protect you and your clothes from getting drenched. You will pay me 125, 000 Francs," added the skinny, fair-skinned young man of the Fulani (Péule) ethnic group.

That amount was outrageously high; it was nearly three times the standard fare of 50,000 Francs. Sadjio knew she was being exploited and would have been more than happy to protest such blatant extortion, but she was helpless.

She pleaded to pay him 70,000 Francs because all she was left with was 125, 000 francs. He settled for 75,000 francs, she paid him and off they went.

THE ROAD WAS IN a terrible state; even motorbikes wouldn't dare. For every 30 minutes they drove, Sadjio was dropped off and asked to walk for 10 minutes, to cross a cake of sticky mud, piled up in the heart of the road.

During one of her mini treks, she almost got swallowed up by thick mud. The outer layer of the caked mud appeared to very crispy. But it was a death trap—it was wet underneath, ready to suck anyone or thing into its deadly belly. As Sadjio placed her right foot on it, she began to sink. She felt herself descending up to her knees.

The more she struggled to save her life, the faster she descended. She yelled for help, but the biker was very far off to hear her cries. It would take an inhabitant of a nearby village to come to her rescue.

He found a slab of concrete debris to stabilize himself, then had to dig Sadjio out by hand. The biker later joined him. She was scared but unharmed. She would later develop skin rashes from the mud.

Throughout the trip with this biker, Sadjio felt very uncomfortable and insecure. Her gut feelings were telling her that her life was in danger. The driver stopped for smoking breaks every sixty minutes. He would park the bike, walk behind a tree, and smoke his weed. This further aggravated Sadjio's fear.

"What if he gets intoxicated, pulls out a knife and chops me up into pieces?" she wondered, as her thoughts went wild. "My mom, my sister, and brothers won't even see my corpse."

This went on until they arrived in Macénta at about 3:00 AM on Friday. The town was buried in sleep; the only place with a handful of folks was the parking station. They drove right up there. There were no motels to book for the rest of the night. The only place available for rent was a large warehouse shared by merchandises, humans, and insects. There were sheets of brown paper spread across the bare floor for use as mattresses. Passengers from everywhere converged there. The man operating the warehouse charged 5,000 francs per head. Services there were prepaid before gaining access. Sadjio paid her 5,000 francs, entered and sat on her suitcase.

Inside was as hot as an oven set to preheat at a 350°F. There were thousands of mosquitoes scrambling for a victim to prey on. Luckily for them, they had Sadjio's face to feast on all night. There were also ants making the rounds and randomly stinging guests. Sadjio sat up until 6:00 AM, was picked up by the biker, and taken to a place where she would board a vehicle to go to Simaya.

FOR ONCE, finding a bus was a no issue. From Queens, onward to Man, there were no more vehicle problems. She traveled throughout Friday and arrived in Man at about 5:00 AM on Saturday.

All the while, her mom and siblings had been worried. They had contacted Sajio's hosts in London and were informed of her departure from there. They approached her hosts in Freedomville, only to be told of her departure from there as well.

The hosts in London remained on the phone with those in Freedomville, Ducor, and so forth. But no one could confirm her whereabouts as she struggled in the middle of nowhere to see Hadjala and her siblings.

The vehicle conveying her from Queens drove to the central parking station of Grand Marché, downtown Man. She got off, looking all muddy with scores of dark spots all over her face from those thousand mosquito bites. She waved down a taxi, got in, and headed to their Blocos residence.

The gates were still locked. Hadjala, Saléma, Jamaal, and Babadéni had gone for the congregational prayer at the mosque; a neighbor told Sadjio. It was Eid-Al_Fitr. She sat outside and waited.

"What's that at the gate?" asked Saléma on seeing Sadjio's luggage.

Suddenly, the trio turned and found her sitting on the opposite side of the fence. They were dumbfounded for few seconds before rushing over to give her *that* warm embrace she had longed for throughout her journey of reconnection. Such was her dilemma as she journeyed through Mandiana and Queens to enter Ivory Coast.

SADJIO SPENT TWO WEEKS with her family before re-turning to Ducor, into an apartment. She was fed up with un-warranted bullies from Ursula's sister. She was never prepared for another Ida-styled life.

Ursula would eventually be kicked out by her sister, leaving her with no choice but to join Sadjio. The pair lived together for eight years, in rented apartments at multiple lo-cations in Ducor. They spent nearly two years living in a sin-gle-family home on 16th Street. They did practically everything together: eating, sleeping, and so forth.

Meanwhile, Sadjio continued to work at her digital media company. From January 2012 to August 2013, she ran the editorial department of as Editorial Director. That position re-quired her to formulate editorial guidelines/policies, edit daily editions of the various channels or platforms, and direct the development of content, including social media campaigns, e-blasts, blog posts.

She also prepared written content to daily deadlines, wrote news, exclusive features and editorials, directed and managed operations of the newsroom, pitched story ideas to reporters, correspondents and freelancers, and made final decisions regarding the placement of stories for submission to the layout department.

Sadjio knew that slow and steady won the race. She refused to use anything or anyone in her life, not even Ida, as an excuse for not achieving her dreams. She kept her eyes fixed on the prize and continued to push her boundaries.

In it all, she was very meticulous about having a relationship. She always shrugged off the idea of dating whenever that subject popped up. But little did she know that her action was hurting lots of people around her. It was an excruciating experience for those who admired her secretly. But for Sadjio, her clueless life was the perfect life she wanted to live, at that very moment.

Chapter THIRTY-TWO

STORMY CLOUDS BEGAN gathering earlier in the morning, casting impenetrable darkness over the city. Wild winds blew provocatively across the mysterious, endless ocean that overlooked the city of Ducor. One thing was for sure: the clouds were pregnant.

Sadjio was scheduled to attend a significant press briefing at the Oval Office that Wednesday. The media briefing was planned for 10:00 AM in the Press Briefing Room (PBR). As a tradition, the Oval Office held weekly presentations on every Wednesday to update the press on topical national issues. Senior political reporters assigned to this high-level Newsbeat were duly accredited to provide comprehensive coverage of Pepper's Coast's presidency and its *Ministère des Affaires Étrangères*.

Though it promised to be a very wet day, Sadjio would do everything to be at her assignment at least fifteen minutes ahead to time. One of the things she admired the most about her job was that it did not only train her mind to write thought-provoking articles; it sharpened her time management skills. Personally, Sadjio had a thing for promptness, and being a digital journalist brought that to the forefront.

The media agency was solely dependent on her for originality of events happening at the Oval Office, as opposed to being reliant on a diluted, bias-angled press release. Moreover, Sadjio knew just how to produce stories with stimulating headlines, well-researched, highly descriptive, and analytic. She specialized in stories about gender, women's empowerment, and involvement in the social, political, and economic life. She also focused her reportage on peace, security, and development. Sadjio was a formidable person and a results-driven journalist.

It began to drizzle at dawn, and Sadjio enjoyed the soul-soothing rhythm of falling rains. She snuggled under her warm wax-printed blanket and slumbered, but was awaken by a naughty roster croaking in her backyard. She hopped out of her queen-size bed, scurried through the tiny door leading to the bathroom of her apartment, showering as quickly as she could. In less than twenty minutes, Sadjio was attired in a two-piece Ankara suit. She sped off to the main road to catch a cab to her assigned news beat.

The daily scuffle for a cab, minibus, or any commercial transport services in Ducor was relentless. After a few failed attempts, Sadjio retreated to the front of a fula shop to escape an ensuing downpour. The city was pounded merciless, triggering flooding in some parts. That day's torrential rain also caused the inner city's skimpy waterways and appalling drainages to burst their banks, causing flash floods that carried with them loads of human wastes, coupled with tons of trash littered in the streets. Most slum neighborhoods were knee-deep in floodwaters with scores of residents lingering the streets in search of a place to call home.

As Sadjio waited for the rain to cease, she was joined by a light-skinned young man. She tried avoiding direct eye contact with him, but it seemed like his eyes were fiercely searching hers the entire time. And when their eyes met, he flashed a sweet smile, his teeth as neat as those of a girl who spends heavily on whitening products to nail that bright, hypnotizing smile. His exotic brown eyes were invasive and aggressively enticing. For a moment, she felt lost in their brownness, their beauty, and the mysteries of their stuffed lashes and perfectly shaped brows.

"A guy with a girl's face!" screamed a voice in Sadjio's head. She blushed, feeling very ticklish by the competing voices in her head.

"And that smile is contagious. Where on earth is his origin? He certainly doesn't look like one of the usual types." This prompted her to steal another glance at this magical being that stood so close to her.

He was smartly attired, with absolutely zero embarrassing gaps in his clothing. His light-blue and greyish mud cloth shirt blended perfectly with his sky-blue cloth pants that were complemented with a neatly polished pair of black Versace shoes. He looked sophisticated, fashionably, bold, and classy.

"He is a flawless symbol of next level fierce," went the voices in Sadjio's head.

Just then she heard his greeting: "Good morning." It was the young man, finally breaking his silence.

"Good morning," responded Sadjio.

"Goodness! Why so much rain? I mean…it's raining cats and dogs," he added, hoping to kick off a conversation with her. Instead, she turned her face in the opposite direction.

"I knew it was going to be like this today. That's why I came out with my umbrella. This rain is so heavy, not sure if my umbrella can help me, though," added the young man.

Suddenly, it became very windy, spraying freezing drizzles across the area, leaving Sadjio with a chilly feel.

"Hey, are you heading to town? I'm on my way to *Le Ministère des Affaires Étrangères*. I can drop you off on Capitol Hill if you want."

This caught her attention, especially since she had started to feel so cold. But, was still held back by her competing inner voices.

"He's headed in your direction. But how sure are you that he's not bad news personified?" went Sadjio's thoughts. "He could be the perfect trouble monger, and you better not fall for his charisma." Then a very wild voice intoned, "Girl, why not milk this opportunity? This rain is relentless, and the clock is ticking. You've got just 25 minutes to be at your assignment. Just take the offer and let the rest handle itself. Don't overthink it."

Eventually, she said to him, "that's very nice of you. I'm headed to *Le Ministère des Affaires Étrangères*."

"Great, let me call my driver," he said, one hand holding a dark-blue Nokia phone to his right ear.

In less than five minutes, a grass-green Jeep Grand Cherokee Highlander pulled up in front of them. He opened and held a door to a passenger seat in the back. She got in, looking all timid. He sat in the front, and the vehicle sped off.

"I am Michael. I live in the building immediately across from the Fula shop."

"I am Sadjio."

"Wow. That's a unique name".

"Well, it might be a unique one around here, in Pepper Coast. It's trendy in Mali."

"Ah. I see. Are you from that area? On second thought, you look more Senegalese to me."

Sadjio said, "No.... not all. Not even close. I was born here, in Pepper Coast, but grew up in the Ivory Coast due to the civil war."

"Just like me…" he said, with an index finger nailed in the middle of his chest. "I was born in Burkeville, to Pepper Coast parents. My parents spent several years in that country as ex-pats. I also grew up in exile due to the war. Right after their return to Pepper Coast, the civil war began. My family fled and settled in Germantown, MD (USA)."

"Oh, so you are a southerner by birth," she said, smiling.

"Yes, I am."

"Have you been there since your childhood?"

"No. But I am planning on taking a mini-vacation there soon."

Then Sadjio said to him, "I was there recently, but had an awful experience that has stained my perspective of that country."

"Really? What happened? I've always been told that southerners are peaceful and kind."

A timid Sadjio tried changing the subject but was encouraged to proceed by Michael's persistence.

"Unfortunately, my experience was the opposite," she began. "I flew into Burkeville in transit to Benkadee, the City of Love. I was lodged by my airline at The Stanley Hotel, a breathtakingly beautiful and luxurious, five-star hotel in the heart of the city. The deal was that I would spend the nine-hour wait time there and head to the airport at 8:00 PM to catch my connecting flight that was scheduled to leave by midnight."

As Sadjio talked, Michael maintained direct eye contact. "I was informed that a reminder call would be placed to my 9th-floor room by concierge whenever the airline's designated shuttle bus showed up to get me, along with two other travelers."

"So, I made myself comfortable, had a lavish dinner of grilled salmon and charcoal-roasted veggies, and enjoyed cozy bath time. By 7:00 PM, I stood guard, kept a close watch on the phone. Then, 8:00 PM came and went with no calls. I held myself for another 30 minutes before heading downstairs to figure out what was happening." She paused for a breather, searched Michael's face for reaction. But he seemed too focused and eager to learn more about this story.

"I was told by concierge that my airline had canceled the shuttle service for the rest of that evening, advising that I wait while they got clarity from the airline's customer service. After a while, I was advised to rather take a taxi to the airport."

At this point, Michael looked very concerned. "Were they trying to trick you into something or what?" he asked.

"Wait for it.....," she responded, and they all laughed heartily.

"By 9:00 PM, I started to get very scared. The 12.98KM (8.07 miles) distance from *Centre Ville* to *l'aéroport International du Sud* was nerve-racking, especially considering my fast approaching boarding time. After a few minutes without an update, I walked to the counter and sought updates. The concierge then informed me that my flight had been canceled. Disturbed by this, I asked to be allowed to contact the airline directly but was denied access to the hotel's phones. I asked to speak with a manager. A tall, skinny man dressed in all-black was called forth, only to reiterate the concierge's message."

"As I sat in the lobby, I regretted the very second I stepped foot at The Stanley. I hated myself for getting drowned in its luxury, only to be held hostage in the end. I buried my face in both palms and sobbed quietly, yet profusely. By 10:00 PM, I saw a van pull up in the compound. A flight had just landed, and there were transiting passengers being lodged by the airline. I walked up to the driver's window and begged him to take me to the airport. A huge verbal exchange would suddenly ensue between the driver and the hotel staff."

"Over what?" an impatient Michael screamed.

"Well, their conversation was in Swahili, which I don't understand. Eventually, the driver, an older man, asked me to get in, and off we went. He would later explain to me that the verbal altercation was all about me: concierge ordered him not to take me to the airport. They wanted me to board a taxi, which would have given them 30% of the fare as commission. It was a deal between the hotel and cab drivers."

"What? That's human trafficking!" again screamed Michael.

Ignoring him, Sadjio continued: "He said I did great by refusing the cab ride because taxi drivers operating on this dark, very distant highway, were notorious of robbing, raping, and killing female travelers. They also told the older man that because I refused to take a cab, they wanted me to miss my flight. The driver eventually told them to allow him to drop me off at a local communications center to get in touch with my family. Why risk everything for me, a stranger? I asked the older man. He said he had a young and felt obliged to protect me, just as he would for his daughter. Long story short, I made it to the airport just in time for the final boarding call."

The ride that morning birthed a protracted, casual friendship between Sadjio and Michael. She would later learn that Michael was a PR and Marketing communications enthusiast and a true lover of pop music. His innate musical talents were indescribable. He worked in the media department of a leading PR agency – *La Starz*.

As their friendship progressed, so was Michael's admiration for Sadjio. He grew fonder of her with every day that went by but was very afraid to voice it out. The fear of *what if she doesn't like the idea? Things would go downhill, and our beautiful friendship would be stained*, had him trashing the concept, and doing his best at suppressing his rapidly advancing feelings.

One day, he proposed a lunch date, but Sadjio politely turned it down. After several fruitless attempts, Michael concluded that she was an emotional bully.

"I wonder who you think you are. Your friends are succeeding in this field, not because they are exceptional. They are not smarter than you either. You are a far better writer than most of them. But do you understand why they are leaving you behind?" a very frustrated Michael began clearing his chest.

"It's because they are *free-handed*. You are too *tight-handed*, and that's why you are always hustling in the field, under the scorching sun, when others are sitting in cool air offices and collecting fat checks at the end of each month."

"I am me and they who they are," Sadjio responded.

"So much for you, 'Ms. Holly," he mocked her and drove off.

Michael was among several other men who made fruitless advances at Sadjio during the early days of her career as a digital journalist. But the fear of *what if* was too powerful to let her experiment anything.

"What if I am deeply in love and get dashed off at the same time? What if he's a fan of polygamy? What if he's only interested in a one-night stand, not love? What if he cheats? What if I get too distracted by him?" went her thoughts.

Her first ever encounter with the opposite sex was nothing near love. It was the case of an older, uncultured, unscrupulous guy attempting to steal the innocence of a 17-year-old girl. He drugged and nearly raped her. He was Jamaal's best friend, a sex predator who believed he could get away with anything, including rape.

It happened when Sadjio had been transferred to Danané to further her studies. This friend of Jamaal's also shared the same compound in which Sadjio lived. One night, he offered to take her to the movies. Sadjio had never been to a cinema before. The offer sounded very exciting to her. Besides, she trusted him; he was her brother's closest friend. Jamaal had traveled to Simaya on a business trip, and being a close friend of Jamaal's, Sadjio felt safe in his company.

That night, she hurriedly threw on a ruffled blouse complemented by a wrapper, and off they went. After the movie, he asked her to come with him to a mutual friend's house. On arrival, this mutual friend offered them sour milk. Sadjio took a few sips and was knocked out shortly after that. Only to wake up the next morning in Mayongbéh's bed.

"What happened? How did I get here?"

"You nearly got raped last night."

"How? By whom?"

"By Jamaal's friend, Erique. You should thank your stars, your guardian angels, and me for saving you from sexual abuse and a lasting emotional trauma after that," Mayongbéh intoned. "I overheard him as he disclosed his evil plans in a phone conversation. He was going to rape you. He's obsessed with you and thinks rape is his best bet at quenching his lust for you. I don't care if I eavesdropped on his private conversation. Lord knows I did so to protect my friend from sexual exploitation."

As she explained, Sadjio sat speechless, tears dripping from both eyes.

"As you both walked to Cinéma Moyé last night, I tiptoed behind and stood guard until the movie was over. I quickly bashed in, just in time, when he tried to touch you. You were fast asleep, and just then, I knew he had drugged you. I wailed for help, and soon the entire compound was overwhelmed with people. He tried escaping but was caught and flogged for attempted rape. He nearly got mobbed to death. You know how it is with mob violence in our society. If you don't want to be subjected to jungle justice, do the right thing."

When Sadjio informed her mother and brother about the incident, this friend of Jamaal's denied ever attempting to hurt Sadjio. It became a bitter family feud that ended nowhere. This experience made her wary of the opposite sex. She never trusted men.

Also, the possibility of unfaithfulness kept Sadjio on the fence when it came to the issue of relationship. A cousin of hers had committed suicide, having discovered the dubious acts of her husband. One day, Sadjio went to visit this cousin. Instead of her cousin, she met her 46-year-old in-law sitting on the third layer of their brick stairs, weeping, head bowed.

Everyone in the yard wept quietly, yet profusely; even the neighbors couldn't hold back their tears. They were mourning the death of Aminata, who had taken her own life. Hakeem, Aminata's husband, claimed he had no idea what must have moved his wife into doing what "she did to herself." But neighbors hinted to Sadjio that Hakeem "likes the girls." Thus, "Aminata murdered herself" because she could no longer bear Hakeem's soaring spousal betrayal.

Aminata had spent a little over fifteen years of her life with Hakeem. Throughout their marriage, Aminata had had to bear Hakeem's infidelity. Ami, as she was affectionately called, was often introduced to new babies fathered by her man with different women. She took it all, and not once did she allow her disdain for her husband's external affairs to harm her relationship with his outside children who were increasing each year.

It was when Hakeem began abusing the little respect left for his wife—by introducing his babies' mothers to Aaminata whenever he wanted, that she began to take offense. Aminata buried her pain in her heart. She never allowed it to take control, something she struggled with, though. As time progressed, Ami found herself being pushed to her grave, and that was precisely where she finally landed when she took her own life. The bus had reached its final stop.

"It is unfortunate that Aaminata's case ended up the way it did. Like Aminata, hundreds of wives with cheating husbands suffer in silence or tolerate their husband's infidelity. They feel compelled to do so because they have no alternatives," Sadjio would say to herself; though friends encouraged Sadjio to see the bigger picture, her fear of *what if* never ceased.

"You can't sit back and be a helpless victim, do so, and be swept along with the tide. You must do everything to make the best of a bad situation. All you have to do is protect yourself emotionally, sexually, legally, and financially," Ursula would say to her.

Besides, Sadjio had a clearly defined mission to Ducor. Her eyes were fixed on a unique prize—work hard, earn honest income and take care of Hadjala, her struggling stepdad, and the rest of the family, just as she did as a teenager when she assumed the family's sole breadwinner role. A hefty portion of her monthly income was sent for her family's upkeep in Man.

She always reminded herself of what her stepdad had told her: "Sadjio is the one who will make me a phone owner and a proud dad." This revelation stuck with her and challenged her throughout her journey. The only thing she ever wanted to was to buy a phone for her stepdad who had later understood the importance of girls' education and had thrown his weight behind Hadjala in supporting Sadjio through her educational sojourn.

Unfortunately, he would be dead and gone even before Sadjio began to get her feet wet in her career. Also, Hadjala would be diagnosed with Type 2 diabetes with Sadjio taking full responsibility for ensuring that Hadjala received the best medical care.

With these in mind, Sadjio was very less interested in flirting with the men of the media in the name of favor or whatsoever. She believed in hard work, honesty, and account-ability. She always adhered to and upheld her values.

Yet, Michael's rant was a clear revelation of how the men of the media thought or felt about her. They tried luring her with money, and goodies but Sadjio was fully aware that in this life, nothing was free.

"Take the money and be prepared to pay back with your body," she thought.

Top government officials, ministers had a crush on her, and she knew it but preferred to ignore it all. She simply hated the thought of commodifying her body. Through hard work, dedication, and honesty, she moved through the ranks of the media agency from Digital Content Writer and Strategist to Editorial Director.

It was then that real love happened to her, for the first time, in nearly ten years. It was such a strange feeling falling in love and experiencing love after all these years.

"CAN YOU BE my girlfriend?" Jake proposed.

He was light-skinned, medium built and medium height with wild lashes and eyebrows. He had been a casual friend of Sadjio's for nearly ten months. He was friendly and funny, always saying something to get her cracking up.

"But I am already your Girl...friend," Sadjio responded with a confused look.

"I mean.....I know we are friends," he continued. "I just want us to be closer."

"What are you trying to say? Or, where are you going with this?" she retorted.

"I want us to be lovers," he quickly cleared the air.

Sadjio would later burst into loud laughter. She laughed so hard.

But Jake meant every word he had authored during that meeting. He loved her and needed her to complete his life. It would, however, take Sadjio another ten months to connect with him emotionally, romantically, and affectionally.

It was a bizarre, extraordinary feeling, especially considering the fact that Jake's dad had previously engaged Sadjio for a younger son. "You are Ben's wife....my youngest son," Mr. Kirk had said at his very first meeting with Sadjio. "But I don't know how his older brother, my first son who's currently on vacation in South Africa, will feel about this," Mr. Kirk continued.

As he spoke, Sadjio sat and stared him in the eyes, wondering why will anyone try to matchmake in this day and age. "What if I don't even like his son? What if *he* doesn't like me? And who told this man that I came all the way here looking for a husband?" she was lost in deep thoughts while Mr. Kirk went on.

At home that night, she informed Ursula about her encounter with Mr. Kirk, and they laughed it off. But Mr. Kirk meant what he said. He announced it at events, family meetings, or gatherings, making everyone believe that Sadjio was his prospective daughter-in-law. "Pepperbush," she was nicknamed by the men who had a crush on her but couldn't come forth because she was now a person of interest to Mr. Kirk, a renowned CEO of the country's leading marketing and advertising company. *MirriorIt* was a fortune 500 digital marketing company with offices in nearly 50 countries across the Sub-Sahara.

A year later, Mr. Kirk's elder son, Jake, made his grand entrance in Ducor. After a few months of stay, he fell in love with Sadjio, and despite warnings that his dad had already handpicked Sadjio for his little brother, Jake would not let go of the girl, he considered the *love of his life.*

The duo would spend the next eight years of their lives as an inseparable pair. They got secretly engaged, lived together for two years, took regular road trips across the country and the Sub-Sahara. They simply enjoyed their moments together.

Sadjio would later decide to move on. She felt Jake was not ready to settle with her. She was obsessed with babies but never wanted to have any out of wedlock. But each time she confronted Jake, he seemed cold about the subject. More importantly, Sadjio's religion, Islam, was an issue of great concern for Jake's parents, especially his mother. She was exceedingly intolerable of the idea.

"What would the kids become? Christians? Muslims?" she would ask.

And that was a question to which Jake never provided an answer. He would instead let his parents have their way. He preferred to let them dictate the course of his life.

So, in 2012, convinced that this was a significant roadblock preventing their relationship from advancing to the next level, Sadjio walked out. It would take the pair another five years to heal emotionally and accept the fact that it wasn't meant to be. That's how deeply-connected they were emotionally, spiritually, morally, and everything else in between.

Letting go was extremely painful; it was a subtle poison that lingered the longest. It was hard, but Sadjio knew she could do it, and so she did; there was no turning back. She cherished her memories of him but erased her ability to reach out.

She faced her pain, didn't run from it, never attempted to bottle her feelings either. To heal, she forgave, pursued a passion, expanded her networks. She did everything to create new experiences, memories, and connections to replace her old memories with Jake.

But as she began to dig deep to rediscover happiness, Hadjala's dwindling health took center stage. Sadjio's pain of lost love was now compounded by grave concerns about her mom's life.

HADJALA WAS diagnosed with Type 2 diabetes in the mid-1990s after experiencing frequent urination, among critical symptoms.

Jamaal accompanied her to a referral hospital in Guiglo, where doctors delivered the bitter news. She shrugged it off, kept it to herself, never tested her blood in public, and refused to manage her symptoms appropriately. Hadjala also paid no attention to her symptoms. Her effort to hide her diabetes was reinforced by unwavering stigma attached to diabetes back then.

Diabetes was grouped with few chronic diseases, such as HIV/AIDS, cancer, heart, or kidney diseases, that carried more stigma. She was afraid that instead of being showered with sympathy, her Type 2 diabetes would expose her to mounting criticism for being too fat, junk food junky, and lazy.

Everyone who knew her at the time knew that she was a lover of 'good food': stewed yam with grilled cow meat freshly bought from the slaughterhouse. Hadjala was also obsessed with fufu, chased down with palm butter stew that was exceptionally flavored by a conglomerate of crab meat, shrimps, cow meat, dry and fresh pike fish, among many others. She was a heavy coffee drinker and never took her love for white rice porridge lightly.

Put bluntly, Hadjala was obsessed with sweet and starchy foods. So, when she was diagnosed with diabetes, her blame-the-victim feeling kicked in.

"I will be bullied. Our people will say that I am paying the price of my unhealthy eating habit," she would say.

It was later discovered that an uncontrollable risk factor, family history, was a significant contributor in Hadjala's case. Her dad, Papa Moh, had died of diabetes. Her older brother, Yacoub, had nursed diabetes for over 30 years. However, shame plus denial was a dangerous combination as it concerned managing Hadjala's diabetes.

By hiding her condition, she was not as careful about monitoring her blood sugar level, and eating healthy was totally out of the question. As such, her Type 2 diabetes was poorly managed.

Chapter THIRTY-THREE

In 2004, when the family moved back and settled in Man, Hadjala barely checked her blood sugar level. To add insult to injury, Man's central government-funded hospital was not in full operation as a result of the war. Its infrastructure had been totally damaged with little to no qualified medical staff available and willing to render much needed medical care to the public.

All of the doctors, physician assistants, and nurses had emigrated to Simaya, the nation's capital, in search of safety and greener pastures. Man was under rebel rule for nearly eight years after a failed coup d' état resulted in full-fledged warfare. Guerilla warfare broke up in September 2000, eventually splitting the country in two. The southern part, including Simaya, remained under government control, while the rebels controlled the northern, western, and some parts of the eastern regions.

During this period, nearly every professional sought refuge in Simaya. The rebels had declared every social service—pipe-borne water, electricity, landline phone, healthcare, education – FREE. It was their way of attracting the population's attention and affection. AND it worked, though it was never a win-win with regards to healthcare. Professional service providers moved to Simaya, which was then under government rule and functioning relatively well.

As such, in addition to shame and denial, inadequate healthcare, late diagnosis, poor education, insufficient access to insulin played a massive role in worsening Hadjala's condition. Also, the lack of glycemia self-monitoring devices and the absence of a controlled diet further aggravated her condition.

She would undergo a life-threatening crisis in 2012 that will change her life, and that of Sadjio's, forever.

AT ABOUT 8:30 AM on Tuesday, May 22, 2012, Sadjio arrived at the Tuo border post from Man, en route to Ducor.

With her was Hadaja undergoing a life-threatening health crisis. Hadjala was in need of critical medical attention. The physician's assistant in the city of Man had advised Hadjala that she had a sore/ulcer in her chest. The entire family was terrified.

Sadjio was informed about this development by 6:00 PM on Monday. She instantly dashed out of the office and went home. She bashed in, grabbed a bag with only a blouse and a pair of jeans, and headed for the RedLight commercial district, where all sorts of vehicles were boarded for rural Pepper Coast. RedLight also happened to be the area where cars were boarded for the town, Tuo, bordering Pepper Coast and Ivory Coast, through Nileville, northern Pepper Coast.

Unfortunately, it was late. So, Sadjio had to spend the night and got going the next morning as early as 6:00 AM. Thankfully, she arrived in Man by 11:00 PM. She immediately went into Hadjala's room and met her mother lying prostrate on her bed. Hadjala looked helpless; she was unable to move any part of her body. Pools of sweat beats oozed out of her body. She endured continuous rounds to profuse coughing–a single round of coughing lasted not less than an hour. Sadjio became even more terrified by that sight.

She began fishing into Hadjala's closet, grabbed a few clothes, took her to the bathroom, and managed to give her a refreshing bath to calm the fever. She then changed her clothes and the beddings and put her back in bed. She couldn't wait to see the daylight for them to begin their journey back to Ducor, where, for some reason, Sadjio believed they would access some amount of advanced medical care. Due to the hasty nature of her parking of clothes, she mistakenly took a piece of paper she thought was Hadjala's refugee attestation card.

Hadjala and the rest of Sadjio's siblings had been residing in Ivory Coast. They fled into that neighboring state in search of peace, security, and safety – to escape the turmoil in their homeland, Pepper Coast, in 1990. After 22 years of residing in that country, and having lost everything to Pepper Coast civil war, Hadjala had been hesitant about returning home, to Pepper Coast. However, she had no choice this time; she desperately needed medical care to save her life.

They began their journey the next morning as early as 6:00 AM in a chartered private car. They traveled the 102km distance, passing through Danané and Gbinta, with exceeding ease. No custom, immigration, or police officer on the Ivoirian side of the journey bothered them. They were sympathetic and empathetic of a dying woman in desperate need of urgent medical attention. They were allowed to cross through to Pepper Coast's side of the border with their chartered ride by the Ivoirian officials without a word. They only prayed for Sadjio and Hadjala.

The main bridge connecting Pepper Coast with Ivory Coast was destroyed during the heat of the civil war. To access

Pepper Coast from Gbinta one had to cross the narrow River
Gao over a shaky log. Pepper Coast's official point of entry was
a small town. Tuo was previously a booming city before the
onset of the country's civil war. Most of the town's buildings
were typical mud-brick huts.

The leading immigration inspection point at Tuo was a
large hall demarcated into sections to include the customs, lais-
sez-passer, and health posts. Immediately adjacent, this central
hall was a newly erected structure that now housed the office
of the immigration commander.

Once in Tuo, the trouble began. Officials insisted that
Hadjala came out of the car to explain her mission to Pepper
Coast. First of all, Hadjala could barely author her words; she
couldn't walk; she couldn't sit. She stayed in a reclining position throughout the entire journey.

Sadjio tried explaining to the officers that Hadjala had
been residing in Ivory Coast as a refugee. Due to the critical
nature of her condition, she took the wrong documentation
about Hadjala's residency status in the Ivory Coast, instead of
the attestation issued to her by the UNHCR.

All they did was slammed her explanation, terming it a
fairytale. They termed it a scam put together by Sadjio and
Hadjala. They added that Sadjio's mission was to "import" an
illegal immigrant in the country. They got into an intense ar-
gument with Sadjio regarding her relationship with the woman
in question. They argued that the woman was never Sdjio's
mother but had no scientific means to back up that allegation.

Shortly after that, one of the men rushed to the car and
asked Hadjala to get out and see him in his office.

Sadjio immediately intervened and said, "you can't do
this. This woman can't walk. Don't you see for yourself?"

He turned and yelled at Sadjio, "keep out of this."

"If she can't walk, then I will have to interview her here," he added, with a demonic look in his eyes.

He began probing Hadjala. She managed to respond to his first question. However, by the time she responded to his second question, she lost her breath. Hadjala began rolling from end-to-end, on the ground, fighting to regain her breath. The sight of Hadjala in such a condition got a pool of tears streaming down Sadjio's cheeks. She came in and told Hadjala to never respond to any of his questions. She turned to him and asked him to direct all of his questions to her. He refused, noting that the pair were being dramatic.

The driver of the chartered vehicle had gone above and beyond his call of duty to convey Hadjala to the Pepper Coast side of the border, which was pretty usual. Drivers like him weren't that caring; they typically dumped their passengers at the Ivorian checkpoint. It was the responsibility of voyagers to walk across the bridge to the Pepper Coast border. However, as gracious as this driver was, he, too, was becoming impatient and needed to return, deeply frustrated about the attitude of these Pepper Coast officers.

At this point, Sadjio became too hopeless, because that meant Hadjals would be placed on the bare floor because they were still a few meters away from the parking lot, where they could board a cab for Ducor. When Hadjala finally regained her breath and calmed down, Sadjio tried getting her out of the car so that they could both sit on the floor with her head resting on Sadjio's laps. These officers, Sadjio thought, were only bent on killing her mother – her only source of hope, psychological and emotional support.

The unfolding event outraged every other traveler and by-stander who began raining insults at the officers. They insisted Hadjala remained in the chartered car while arrangements were made for another vehicle to transfer her in; she was becoming very very fragile. Some residents of the town got deeply involved in the matter. They attacked the officers and threatened to strike if Hadjala wasn't released. Sadjio was then referred to their commander, who simply asked her the full name, date of birth, and age of her mom. She provided him with Hadjala's biodata in a split second.

Overwhelmed by the compounding crowd demanding that the pair be let go, they were allowed to continue with their journey. By then, Hadjala's condition had further deteriorated to the extent that she wouldn't eat anything. All she did was stare at Sadjio.

What struck Sadjio the most about the technicality employed by these immigration officers was that these were the very people who sat at the border and saw illegal actions, such drugs, and human trafficking, happening across this porous border without lifting a finger.

"What did they want to prove by attempting to murder an innocent woman in the name of the law? What were they up to?" she wondered throughout her journey.

Sadjio and her mother arrived at the Kennedy Medical center in Ducor by 8:30: PM that night. Hadjala was admitted and treated for diabetes. She was also treated for chronic blood anemia - spending 15 days in bed at the hospital. She was finally discharged, feeling much better and ready to proceed with her life. However, from this moment on, Hadjala was headed on a downward spiral of health crises, with one appearing to be more life-threatening than the other. Having spent a month in Ducor, Hadjala was ready to return to her home in Man. But would almost immediately be rushed to the Simaya barely a week after her return due to chronic anemia.

From that moment onwards, Hadjala would be prone to blood transfusion more than ever. Each time she had a health crisis, she needed to be transfused almost instantly. Poor empowerment, knowledge, and poor self-care were prominent contributing factors to Hadjala's ever-declining health.

IN SEPTEMBER 2013, Sadjio settled in Sun City. She was in graduate school, doing everything to get herself moving along with life. It was never going to be easy, but she was prepared for the task at hand.

By mid-2014, Hadjala began losing the battle to cataract. She was nearing blindness, but doctors refused to touch her eyes due to the aggressive nature of her diabetes. Sadjio was hit with the news one morning during a brief phone call.

"Sadjio, *Teeyah* has gone completely blind," came Jamaal's voice.

"What?!" screamed Sadjio, dropping and cracking her iPhone 6. She was shocked, in total despair.

Before that call, Hadjala had been complaining of her sight. "My sight is always foggy," she had informed Sadjio during a phone conversation. "I can barely see clearly. Everything appears so smoky."

Sadjio, though practically not employed at the time, had still managed to use her contacts to have Hadjala seen by the best ophthalmologists in Simaya. However, there would be pretty much nothing done.

Practitioners in Simaya finally recommended a pair of prescription glasses with super high-resolution lenses costing a total of $800. The model of lenses prescribed was unavailable in Simaya. So, an order was placed with a provider in Paris,

France. They arrived two weeks later and were used by Hadjala for three years. However, the more the cataract surgery was being put off due to her fluctuating blood sugar and pressure levels, the more aggressively cataracts conquered and subsequently consumed her sight.

In early 2016, Hadjala was exposed to severe foot trauma. She could no longer see by then. A somewhat careless live-in care provider at a time had placed a pot filled with hot water in Hadjala's path upon with she stumbled and sustained deep burns on her right foot. This resulted in a foot ulcer that impaired Hadjala's movement, launching her in and out of coma. After spending nearly a week at Man's central hospital, doctors there concluded that they could no longer revive Hadjala's condition.

This was mainly due to the hospital's lack of essential medical equipment to provide the kind of care that was needed. The Ivoirian war had ravaged Man's hospital, leaving this major referral hospital that once served the entire western region of the Ivory Coast in a vulnerable state. It lacked incubators for premature babies, no oxygen supplies for ailing patients, no resuscitation or surgical equipment – and no qualified care provider or specialist.

At that critical moment, Hadjala was in dire need of instant blood transfusion and advanced care for her fast deteriorating foot ulcer. She was eventually transported by ambulance from Man directly to CHU medical center.

Four of her toes were amputated at the CHU, where she spent three solid months, going in and out of diabetic coma while being transfused multiple times daily. Without any regard for the exceptional financial toll that lingered at the time, Sadjio ensured that Hadjala accessed the best of care. She owed it to her mother and refused to allow emotions to stand in her way.

Saléma stayed with her all the time, providing much-needed backup support, spending most of her days at the hospital's blood bank, where she invested 12-16 hours in line nearly every other day.

At CHU, like any other general or referral hospitals in Simaya, getting a blood prescription processed was *the* most horrific experience of all-time. As a patient relative, that responsibility fell squarely on you. It was your duty to make available every prescribed drug. All doctors did was to write you prescriptions; the provision of the medication was up to you. This is because in this part of the Sub-Sahara— availability, accessibility, and affordability of healthcare was a complete battle of its own.

Healthcare was disbursed on a pay-as-you-go basis or prepaid; you were only treated or seen by a doctor upon full payment of all medical bills. If you were unable to pay, you were left to die. It was that simple.

The only services that were narrowly exempted were the cases of delivering pregnant women; these could be done on a postpaid arrangement, but a mother and her newborn would be held if the bills were not cleared. It was never a surprise to see women nursing their newborns in hospital hallways while waiting for weeks or months for their husbands to borrow money from relatives to pay hospital fees.

Besides, there was very little known of health insurance since this was perceived to be better suited to the wealthy – social, political, and economic heavyweights. A bulk of the population survived on subsistent farming, living on hand-to-mouth with barely anything to save, talk least of investing in health insurance. And with substantial *prepaid* user fees being charged by hospitals, the majority of citizens took solace in the herbs.

Chapter THIRTY-FOUR

SALÉMA played an invaluable role at CHU during Hadja-la's time there. Again, this was extremely important because when you are first told the amount charged per night to get a semi-private room within the walls of the private ward of this medical center, you might be inclined to assume that that money would also be worth the services provided.

Sadly, that wouldn't be the case. It was up to you to get ready to deal with unbecoming behaviors from the nurses on duty. And the sad thing was that those nurses and nurses' aides got away with such weak, unprofessional actions and the level of moral among them, unfortunately, found itself right there in the dump.

CHU was one of the primary referral infirmaries in Si-maya and the region's finest. Patients traveled from all parts of the country, walking miles before boarding minivans to access the hospital in search of desired medical attention. CHU also treated patients from across the Sub-Sahara. It was notable for its fast and efficient diagnoses and subsequent treatment of some of the region's stubborn diseases.

At the time, most hospitals across the Sub-Sahara lacked required medical equipment. Generally, the region's healthcare system was awful. Save CHU, nearly every medical facility lacked necessary diagnostic and treatment equipment. Years of tribal wars had left the region with a defenseless health system; it was incapable of meeting the competing health needs of the people. Besides, residents of the countryside, where more than half of the region's population resided, turned to bush medicines for an answer to their growing health needs.

Diseases such as asthma, stroke, erectile dysfunction, pneumonia, and typhoid were immediately referred to traditional healers for quick results. Locals strongly believed in the mental and spiritual prowess of local healers. Moreover, the accessibility and affordability of herbs, coupled with an ingrained faith in traditional healers, made traditional medicines the first and last line of defense against diseases. However, city dwellers were heavily reliant on raggedy health facilities for help. The majority of these facilities were lacked essential cleanliness, as well as necessary medications.

CHU, a government-operated health center, was primely situated, fully staffed and equipped. Unfortunately, it was one of the poorest in terms of service delivery or patient care and respect for human dignity. The 2,500 Francs (roughly US$50) charged per each night spent in the private ward only went toward the bed. The rest was left with you if you deemed it necessary to enjoy the comfort that *should* have come with the amount charged.

In the first place, there was no assigned or on-call nurse to assess and triage cases in that ward. However, patients were in direct eye-view of nurses in the general ward, watching over them all night. In most instances, if the nurses didn't get their way, they became very condescending to patients.

Some of them committed a multitude of professional errors with no excuse but arrogantly defended their actions saying, "But I didn't know that something would have happened to the patient after I served those pills. But in any case, why didn't you inform me directly, instead of letting the doctor know about the error?" Patients were subjected to constant harassment, extortion, emotional and physical abuse in addition to the illnesses they were helplessly nursing.

So, as a patient's relative and a care-taker, you would do well to be prepared to play the role of a nurse-aid or assistant nurse, once you were within the walls of the private ward; otherwise, your patient's condition would be played like a deck of cards.

You didn't have to be surprised whenever you were asked by the nurse or nurse-aide on duty to clean-up your patient, change the beddings, and ensure that your private room was kept tidy to impress the doctors who began their rounds by 8:00 AM each morning. You needed not to be surprised if asked to stay up all night, while the nurse on duty snored at the nurses' station. Your task was to watch over your patient. And, in case of any development, you were to dash out to the nurses' station, report it to the nurse in charge. Then, return to your "private room" and wait there for at least half an hour or more for the nurse to finally clear the sleep from her eyes.

Mind you, everything you had been doing so far, besides taking care of the bill and keeping the patient company, was the nurse's job. But Simaya being a third-world medical environment, there was a visible level of a grey area between the responsibilities of the nurse and you, the patient's guardian.

So now you were the nurse's assistant, and if you truly loved your patient, you would do what the nurse said, above and beyond your responsibility as "guardian."

Sure, for you, it would be a labor of love.

For the nurse, however, she got to relax in your apparent willingness to help. And you better adjust yourself to doing independent research of your patient's condition, because that would turn out to be the best way to understand the status of your patient.

After all, she was (the nurse) there when the doctor wasn't; and was the next best source if you wanted answers and help at those ungodly hours when your patient was in pain and could hardly sleep. With the nurse, you were on a total information block or a "need-to-know" basis at best.

If you were lucky, she would show up, looking all worked up and frowning. But be careful, because in that mood she would be increasingly aggressive. If you were unlucky, she would just not show up, waiting for you to get fed-up, return to her and ask what was taking her so long to come and see your patient's condition.

At that point, she would look you directly in the eyes and say, "I'm waiting for the doctor to come." Don't try to panic over what might be the next thing to happen to your patient while you all waited indefinitely for the doctor; because if you did, it would be at your own risk. For the nurse, she was comfortable with her unprofessional attitude on the job.

And just in case you were new to Simaya, these would be enough snapshot of health care delivery in action at the level of emerging practitioners, especially the nurses and new doctors in the field. But could the public just sit by supinely and swallow the pains it endured at the hands of clueless, unscrupulous agents? It was everybody's duty to unearth those ills by sharing their stories about happenings within the walls of any ward at hospitals and clinics across the country.

Simaya's health care delivery system was rife with stories of nurses' maltreatment of patients up to and including death, at hospitals and clinics throughout the country. And with the unavailability of credible autopsy facilities in the country to validate the actual cause of death, many healthcare practitioners got away with murder daily. Such was Simaya, where standards in nearly every profession, including health care, went ignored to the peril of innocent persons and well-meaning institutions.

The personal experiences of patients needed to speak well of both doctors and nurses, thus converting first-time patients to retained, loyal customers. And for this to happen, hospital and clinics staffers needed to emulate the diligence and professionalism of their call to duty, or risk ignoring these standards to the peril of themselves, their patients and their practice as a whole.

Hadjala would recover from this crisis and return home. This time, not to Man, where she had a 4-bedroom villa, fenced-in with a car garage and a boys' quarter, to her name. Her deteriorating health was of great concern. And the fact that doctors in Man could do so little about her condition was a solid justifiable reason to rent a studio apartment, located at a 15-minute distance from CHU, for her to stay. Her new home was now Marché Bagnon.

WHEN JAMAAL finally broke the most bitter news ever during that phone call, Sadjio was left to wonder why her mom should have to go through this.

"Each time I come over to visit, she won't know that I am in the house until I speak. Sometimes, I will join her for an afternoon nap without her noticing. I will then hear her saying, 'Jamaala hasn't come over or call to check on me today. I wonder why.' At that point, I will speak for her to know that I am there with her," Jamaal explained.

This information bothered Sadjio so much. The thing is, she hated to hear of or see Hadjala in pain. It was such a cruel pain to endure. Nothing made her happy the most than seeing or hearing Hadjala smile, looking all cheerful.

Though worried, Sadjio wasn't going to allow her sorrow to consume and distract her from following through with her promise to ensure that Hadjala was doing fine, health-wise.

"Do you know of anywhere she can be taken for evaluation? She needs to be seeing by a medical practitioner as soon as possible," Sadjio inquired, sounding very worried.

Hadjala was only 56 years old at the time.

"There are some surgeons in Bonoua. I will take her there," Jamaal assured Sadjio.

"Just let me know the cost," she added.

It would take another two months to finally get Hadjala's blood sugar level under control and get her ready for the surgery. The surgery would go well, restoring her sight after nearly a year of total blindness.

While this victory was being celebrated, Hadjala had another episode of chronic anemia that would be reversed with another dose of transfusion, setting in motion multiple blood transfusion, occurring at a rather short interval. While doctors debated the root cause of these latest developments, Hadjala made numerous roundtrips in diabetic coma.

Eventually, she was diagnosed with an advanced stage of chronic kidney disease—both organs had failed. Hadjala would be placed on dialysis for the rest of her life, a new challenge Sadjio had to brace herself for: financially, emotionally, and spiritually.

Through it all, she was determined to be that solid rock for her mom—her one-time, lone girls' education campaigner. She vowed to do everything to ensure that Hadjala's health was restored and remained true to that promise until the very end.

GLOSSARY
of Mandingo and French Words and Phrases

n'dorma: my namesake, someone bearing the same name as yours

amour: love

n'vatorma: daddy's namesake

n'matorma: mommy's namesake

djinna Saa: a jinni snake

nasijee: a rare concoction prepared solely by a religious authority—someone believed to have mastered the art of reading, digesting and translating or disseminating content and concepts of the Holy Qur'an. The potion was intensely fueled with outrageously strong-scented traditional fragrances as a cover up for the foul smell it oozed just days after its invention. *Nasijee* were believed to make any dream, wish or desire—big or small—come true and were highly sorted by individuals in need of any kind of divine, supernatural intervention in their lives.

n'den: my child

attiéké: is a prominent national meal in Ivory Coast

car loaders: self-impose vehicle apprentice

juju: traditional concoction; voodoo

lappa: a piece of cloth, preferable African wax prints

nitélé: Mandingo word for "Hello"

tanamatélé: said in response to "Hello"

yanaboys: street hawkers, seasonal sellers

ngôrô: signifies seniority

m'boreen: the Mandingo word for uncle. It was considered a wife's way to exhibiting love and respect to her husband.

moan: used for daughter-in-law or mother-in-law

ma'aa: means "*mommy*"

susu clubs: traditional system of banking widely used by ordinary market women and other petty traders across Pepper Coast

fleurs de Marriage: wedding flowers

les yeux de ma rivale: the evil eyes of my cowife, my rival

hommes Ingrats: Ungrateful men

mousso dendan: a childless or childfree woman.

töo: a traditional meal made of powdered cassava and cornmeal

karmor: a religious leader/teacher

maison des gens heureux: home of happy people

grand marché: big market

carte d'identité: id card

les guerriers: the warriors

mousso: women

le ministère des affaires étrangères: The Ministry of Foreign Affairs

l'aéroport international du Sud: The South's International Airport

hatai- a locally brewed drink

aucune dose – no dosage

najee: a traditionally prepared veggie soup

ville libre: Free city/town

kan'eh loumaa: Kan'eh's Residence

djinnadou: Home of the djinns

dumboy: a traditional meal made of cassava dough

lanaya: Trust

simaya: Longevity

jhöns: slaves

Hôrô: elites

Fasso: fatherland

Jarsar: regardless

Sida: HIV/IDS

About the Author

Fatoumata Nabie Fofana, MSM, BA, is a seasoned journalist and results-driven nonprofit professional who has served as consultant with several international non-governmental organizations including UNICEF and Save The Children. Her media work has featured on the UN Peace Women; NGO News Africa; the International Press Institute; among many others. She is also a former Research Support and Monitoring Officer of the UN Office for Project Services. Fatoumata has more than 10 years of professional journalism experience, with a strong visual sense, impeccable writing and editing skills, backed by exceptional storytelling skills.

As a child, she was denied access to education because of her gender. Girls in her family were labelled as domestic attendants, while the boys were the preferred gender for education. With the help of her mother, who unrelentingly advocated evolution in such gender perceptions, Fatoumata first stepped foot into a classroom at age nine. She went on to defy all odds and is now an award-winning digital and print media journalist working on political, developmental, peace and conflict issues. In 2018, Fatoumata graduated with a Master of Science degree in Nonprofit and Associations Management from the University of Maryland Global Campus with a 3.9 GPA. She also has a Bachelor degree in Political Science—GPA of 3.7. During her graduate studies, Fatoumata was honored with the Presidential Award for Academic Excellence for two consecutive semesters and recognized by the Honor Society for academic excellence. She is a 2009 recipient of Rotary International's World Peace Fellowship. She also holds an Advanced Certificate in Digital Journalism from the International Academy of Journalism in Hamburg, Germany and has studied Good Governance and Leadership with Integrity at Marquette University's Les Aspin Center for Government based in Washington, D.C.

As senior political reporter of Liberia's first independent daily newspaper, *Daily Observer*, Fatoumata provided complete, accurate and compelling coverage of the activities of former Liberian President Ellen Johnson Sirleaf, state visits by foreign heads of state, and the Liberian Ministry of Foreign Affairs. In 2010, she became the *first* female editor of the country's *first* independent daily— the *Observer*. Fatoumata believes when girls are given the opportunity and tools that they need to climb the education ladder, there is no limit to how high they can fly and what trails they can blaze.

Made in the USA
Middletown, DE
04 May 2021

38362195R00187